Praise For Dreda Say Mitchell

'As good as it gets.' **Lee Child**

'A truly original voice.' **Peter James**

'Zippy, twisty plot…and a bevy of memorable supporting goodies and baddies.' **The Sunday Times**

'Thrilling.' **Sunday Express Books of the Year**

'Awesome tale from a talented writer.' **Sun**

'Fast paced and full of twists and turns.' **Crime Scene Magazine**

'Nothing is but what is not.'
Macbeth, William Shakespeare

Prologue

He really meant it this time.

On the bedside table was an unopened bottle of brandy and a tumbler. But he didn't need the chemical numbness from them or the tranquilisers that he'd taken on all those other occasions when he'd really meant it. In his hands was the letter he'd written explaining his decision. Over the years, he'd written lots of those as well. Some were short and others were long. Some were blunt and curt, getting straight to the point. Others rambled and pleaded for understanding and sympathy from the person who may or may not have been concerned. Many of them were left unfinished when he realised that he didn't really mean it after all.

But this time, he did. He really did.

He didn't want to look up, but he made himself look at the length of rope tied above. Below that, the chair. It was all so simple. Climb on the chair. Pull the noose tight around your neck. Step off. A few minutes of pain and panic while the rope did its work, squeezing the life out of you. Most people would be grateful for only a few minutes of pain before they died. And he'd seen plenty of death in his younger days. A few minutes of agony were nothing. And in those final few moments, as you hanged, when the brain was starved of oxygen, he'd read that the pain went and you floated, carefree, drifting away into nothingness. And that's what he craved most of all.

Nothingness.

In the bowels of the house, the voices raised up again, fiercely arguing. He could hear her screaming and him shouting back. He wished they would stop. Why couldn't they give him the precious minutes of peace he deserved before leaving this world?

Silence enfolded the house again.

He sat back down on the bed and reached for the bottle of brandy. A couple of swigs wouldn't do any harm. He didn't need any Dutch courage this time – the drink was to warm his cold insides. He poured a tumbler full and then stared up at the noose while downing the blazing booze. He poured another. Only on the third glass did he realise what he was doing. Just like all the other times. Drinking himself into a stupor. Anything to avoid actually doing the deed. He slammed the bottle and tumbler down, carefully rested his note against them and stood up.

Swaying slightly under the influence, he strode the few steps to the chair and climbed unsteadily onto it. He gripped the noose firmly in his hands and pulled it over his head. Tightened the knot as if it were a tie. He closed his eyes, taking deep breaths. Concentrated, trying to clear his head of any doubts and then made as if to step off his chair. He drew back. Then again, nearer the edge this time, one foot dangling in the air for a few moments before again he pulled his leg back.

He choked with despair. Why, when all he craved was nothingness, couldn't he do this simple thing?

The right thing. The only thing.

The voices downstairs were doing battle again. Why couldn't they shut up? Just shut the hell up.

He loosened the knot and climbed off his chair. Stumbling, he hurried back to his bed and poured another brandy. He took his note and, with a grim smile, carefully tore it to shreds and put it in the plastic bag that he used as a rubbish bin.

To whom it may concern? What a joke. Anyone who was concerned was long dead or long gone. No one was interested in his explanations or excuses, not even him. He threw the tumbler on the bed and picked up the bottle by the neck. Perhaps if he finished it off, he wouldn't hesitate when he was on the chair, the way a drunk driver doesn't hesitate when he gets behind the wheel. He gulped as much as he could take before his throat burned, and put the bottle down.

He took the few steps to the chair and climbed up again. Pulled the noose tight, closed his eyes and wrapped his arms around his body as if trying to embrace nothingness.

He stood there inert for a long time before he opened his eyes again. His body was drunk but he wasn't. He was clear and lucid and tugged at the noose around his neck.

It was all a lie. He didn't mean it this time and he wouldn't mean it next time either. He'd rather be among the living dead than do the right thing. Weak, weak, weak. That's what he was. Weak and pathetic. And it was that weakness that had led to disaster in the first place.

He pulled at the noose that was trapped tight under his jaw. He struggled with the knot, his drunken body swaying. In drunken frustration he tipped over. The noose tightened, cutting into his neck. In a blind panic, he tried to regain his footing but his shoes slipped and slid on the chair. The chair crashed to its side. Oh God. He was suspended in the air, arms and legs wheeling, crying out. No more air going into or out of his lungs. No cries, only desperate choking gurgles. He grabbed the noose in his hands and fought with it. The instrument of his own death tightened around his neck.

In shock, he struggled to grasp the length of rope above his head with his weakened fingers as he tried to haul himself up to safety. For a brief moment he succeeded. His lungs sucked on the precious air. Then the air was no more. His tired hands slipped through the rope, burning the palms and fingers as it went. He fell and the noose jerked his head backwards as the slack gave out. His arms and legs twitched as what remained of his life ebbed away.

Then there was only nothingness.

Advert

Room For Rent
Gorgeous double room to let to single person
NEW TODAY!
Beautiful room in wonderful large house in North London.
Spacious and cosy, light and bright.
Perfect blend of modern living and historic London.
Newly decorated and furnished.
Inclusive of bills.
A minute's walk from underground station.
Amazing access to the city.
Free wifi.
Current occupants are the owners who are looking for someone to love their home too! ☺

One

My breath catches as I stare up at the house. It's grand, stately even. Three storeys, probably a basement too. In the late summer afternoon sun its stone walls are biscuit-coloured with a warm cheerfulness. Welcoming. Ivy creeps up its front walls towards solid chimney stacks where a cluster of birds perch, peering at the world. None of them sing. It's easy to imagine it in a bygone age as the home of a respected Victorian gentleman needing space for his growing family with plenty of room for the serving classes upstairs.

Detached obviously; no Victorian father would want his daughter's piano lessons disturbing the neighbours or for them, in turn, to hear him dressing down a maid who'd had the audacity to serve him burned kippers.

The avenue is lined with plump green trees that serve as a screen for the homes behind. This clearly wasn't a showy area back in the day and, even now with its prosperity plain to see, it remains cosy and snug even if some of these houses are now subdivided into flats and bedsits. Spare rooms.

The one thing that distorts my snapshot-perfect picture sits on the drive. A white van. 'Jack the Lad' in large print on one side, 'All household work taken on, no job too small' written on the other. There's a mobile number too. Lashed to the roof rack with ropes is a ladder with coloured fabric tied to either end. When the first Victorians owned the house, no doubt 'Jack' would've been told to park his modern-day horse and carriage at the rear.

Clutching the online letting agency details in my hand with the intensity of holding my last will and testament, I walk across the drive, the gravel pinching and digging through the thin soles of my low-heeled black shoes. My palm is sweating, making the paper damp, some of the ink blurring. As I go, my eyes are drawn to the unusual mark high on the wall above the porch. It's a large circle engraved in the stone with the impression of a key inside. There's a date – 1878.

The front door is solid, glossy black with a no-thrills knocker. The blood thrums through me as I knock. I can't hear any footsteps but after a while I get that unnerving sixth sense that someone is watching me. My nerves calm when I find the tiny, round, plastic twinkle of a spyhole in the door. Whoever is observing decides I am no threat and the door is pulled wide.

'You must be Lisa? From the letting agency?'

The man is about my age, mid-twenties, but that's where the comparison stops. He's dressed casually in faded jeans and T-shirt, his hair loosely pulled back in a man bun. This is a modern man who likes to be noticed, from the pirate-style looped gold earring to the tattoos competing for attention on both arms. Why do people insist on marking their skin? Skin should remain flawless and smooth, only the inevitable passing of time allowed to leave its stamp behind. He's actually not bad on the eye; the only blip in his square-jawed maleness is the yellowing on his teeth from one too many cigarettes.

'That's right,' I finally answer, keeping my tone hopeful and friendly. I really need that room.

He looks at his watch. Pulls a face. 'Well, you're a bit early.'

Would he twist his face some more if he knew I'd been pacing the avenue for the last twenty minutes?

'Is that a problem? Shall I come back?'

He pulls a face again, this time a bright, nicotine-stained smile, and waves me inside. 'Of course not! I don't stand on ceremony here.'

I can't step inside quick enough. It's as if I'm coming home. And that's what this imposing house would become if I secured the room: home.

'Come into my parlour as the spider said to the fly. I'm Jack by the way.'

He leads me into the hallway, which sucks me in. I can't stop my eyes widening in wonder. The house seems even larger than it does on the outside. The hall, floored in original black and white tiles, leads down towards what looks like a dining room and beyond that a glimpse of a kitchen. Other doors are shut tight. Rooms that Jack isn't interested in showing me. Instead, he heads straight for the stairs, which has an ornate wooden bannister and a fussy patterned runner.

A large rug sits on the hallway floor. It is striking, black and red with borders of flowers and what looks like Arabic writing in the middle. It reminds me of the rugs and dust-blown carpets in the Moroccan market I saw when I went on holiday with Mum and Dad in my late teens. I make myself stand on it. Inhale in the heart of the house. That's what the hallway is – the heart of a house. Don't believe any of that modern estate agent chatter about it being the kitchen. The heart beats in the space between the front door and the stairs where the house is usually motionless. Still.

'Are you coming?' Jack asks, already part way up the stairs.

I step off the rug and follow.

How odd that a young guy like this would be the owner of such a magnificent house. It must be worth millions and then I wonder if it is his. The letting agency didn't say who the landlord was, just provided a direct messaging box to book a mutually convenient time to view.

'So what do you do for a living, Lisa?'

'I work in software for a bank.'

Jack seems surprised at my choice of profession. 'Software? Bit geeky for a girl, isn't it?'

Do guys really say lines like that still? I wonder if Jack has heard of the #MeToo movement. I don't dignify his comment with a response. Alex never would've uttered crap like that.

It occurs to me that I'm putting myself at risk being on my own in this house with this man. A stranger. Then I wonder if

I'm being a snob. Private education can do that to you. I've got no reason to think he's dangerous. He could be 'charmless but harmless' as my mum would say. I try to reassure myself with the thought that the city is crowded with people who have no alternative but to find lodging in strangers' homes. Besides, the letting agency has a record of my visit.

We reach the first-floor landing. All the doors are closed except one, giving me a peep into what looks like a large bathroom. I'm led along to another flight of stairs, more crooked and narrow this time, no runner or any type of carpet to lead the way to the top of the house.

The stairs creak and groan as we climb.

'Have you been to view any other rooms?' he asks.

I shake my head even though I know he won't be able to see. 'No. This is the first one that's caught my eye. Have you had other people viewing it?'

'A few,' he answers. 'Had an actress last week. Seemed nice enough, but let's face it, acting sounds all fun and glam but it isn't steady work. No work means no rent being paid.' He glances back at me. 'We aren't a charity.'

I quickly reassured him: 'My job is permanent and I've been there for the last four years. I've got references and a police check.'

He halts at the top of the stairs and turns to me. He seems very pleased indeed. 'A police check? You are keen. I like that.'

I pant lightly as I reach the top of the stairs.

'There she is.' Jack points to a door facing us at the end of a very short corridor. It's painted bog-standard matt white, facing me full on like it has been silently waiting for me all our lives.

My breath holds awkwardly in my throat as Jack turns the old-fashioned handle. He pushes the door wide. Steps inside.

I remain rooted to the spot, an outsider looking in.

'Are you OK there? You look like you're freezing.' He points at the large dormer window on the far side of the room. 'Do you want me to shut it?'

'No, I'm fine. I'm shaking off the tail end of a cold.' I walk inside.

'I was going to say it's not like you haven't got on enough clothes there.' He smiles good-naturedly at his pointed observation.

No one needs to tell me I look like this year's latest fashion trend is Frosty the Snowman with my long-sleeved knit dress that stretches from under my chin to just below my knees where it meets a pair of thick leggings. The only skin on display is the top of my feet, hands and face. I should be sweating, but I'm not. I know what else he sees: a woman with short, feathered, layered hair, a long face dominated by large eyes. Zero make-up. Slaps of artificial colour and shades aren't really my thing. And that's it really; nothing more than that to see. A plain Jane is what I consider myself. That suits me fine.

'So, this could be your new humble abode. Nice, isn't it?'

He's right, actually. The room is nice. Spacious and cosy was how the advert described it. It's in the eaves of the house and the ceiling bows from one side to another. It's awash with natural light; yellow beams of sunshine blaze through a skylight and a dormer window with commanding views down the avenue and over the suburbs of North London. There's a small ornate black fireplace with a metal plate to stop rubble from the chimney coming into the room. An oval-shaped free-standing mirror. The walls have been freshly decorated with white lining paper and the floorboards are newly painted white too. The furniture is sparse and functional: a double bed plainly clothed, a bedside cabinet, built-in wardrobe, desk and accompanying chair. But I like that. I don't need much.

This room was made for me.

The only slight problem is it reeks of air freshener. A cloying, sweet alcohol scent manufactured in a factory somewhere. No matter. If the room becomes mine it will be easy to chase away. Still, it clings to the walls of my nose and tastes bitter on the back of my tongue.

'Do you mind if I ask why the previous tenant left?'

'Previous tenant?' He cocks his head to the side as he peers at me, minus his smile. 'What makes you think someone else might've lived here?'

'I just wondered why anyone would leave such a gorgeous room.'

His smile jumps back. 'There hasn't been another tenant, Lisa. You're the first to sample! Do you want to see the kitchen and dining room?'

As we leave I can't help having one final long glance at the room.

***

The dining room is forgettable, its décor neglected, dominated by a 1990s clunky wooden table, chairs and cabinet. My mother would be scandalised. Her dining room is her pride and joy. A place where her family sits down to share, laugh and be together. An old-style notion to many, but for Mum, traditions are important.

The kitchen is a great size. Looks new but rather jerry-built. I guess that might be Jack's work; he doesn't look like the careful sort. Jack explains he'll allot me some space in the fridge. His voice goes on and on, but I'm not really listening. I'm staring out of the glass in the top half of the back door.

The garden seems to be never-ending. It's thickly coated with trees, tall bushes and patches of lawn interspersed with overgrown paths. Judging by the distance to the next house at the rear, the garden could be a hundred yards long, but with so much greenery, it's impossible to tell.

I try the back door.

Jack roughly pulls my hand off the handle. I flinch back in surprise.

'Woah, woah, woah,' rushes out of his mouth.

My heart beats wildly. Maybe Jack wasn't so charmless and harmless after all. Maybe he was a charmless serial killer.

He holds his hands up as a sign of peace. 'Didn't mean to startle you. The garden's our private space.' He eases off the acceleration in his voice, slowing way down. 'You know, you've got to have something just for yourself when you're renting a room out in your house, don't you think?'

Then he adds hopefully, 'If sunbathing is your thing, there's plenty of space out front. Although I see you've got a peaches and cream complexion anyway, so perhaps the sun's not your thing. Very wise; melanoma and all that.'

I rub my wrist where he'd grabbed me, although it doesn't really hurt. I swallow convulsively, my heart rate going crazy. All he had to say was that the garden is off-limits. No need for him to be so physically forceful. I know he's apologised, still…

'Lisa, isn't it?' A new voice distracts me from Jack.

An older woman of average height stands in the doorway. She's dressed in an elegant black trouser suit, sky-high heels and has the painful thinness of someone recovering from a long illness or an unhealthy commitment to diets. She's probably in her early fifties although it doesn't look as if she's going into middle age quietly. Her face is a study in fine bone structure but the skin has a stretched, immovable Botox-filler quality. Only those green eyes that flash at Jack, not me, suggest what a beautiful woman she once must have been. And still is, in a way.

I answer as I step back from Jack. I can still feel the urgent flesh of his hand on me. 'Yes, I've come to look at the room.' I give Jack a quick glance; I'm pleased to see he looks uncomfortable too. 'Your son has been showing me around your gorgeous house.'

Strangely she doesn't respond. Instead there's the click-click of her heels against the worn flagstone floor as she moves towards Jack. She leans up and kisses him – on the mouth.

Oops! Slap to the forehead moment! Mortification overheats my cheeks. I want the ground to swallow me. I should've remembered that the ad stated the house is owned by a couple, not a mother and son. For pity's sake, they don't even resemble each other. Anxiety creeps back; she's going to show me the door. I can't lose the room.

'I'm so sorry,' I sputter. *Shut up. Shut up, you're making a real dog's dinner of it.*

Jack's wife waves my words away as she approaches and sticks out her hand. 'I'm Martha.'

Her grip is firm, the skin smooth; not a woman who's had to work too hard in life. Expensive perfume settles delicately around me.

She gives her husband a beaming smile. 'Why don't you cut down some green beans for dinner tonight?'

With a simple nod in my direction, Jack is only too eager to escape into the garden I'm not permitted into.

'He didn't mean to grab you.' I switch my attention to Martha. 'He's a touch possessive of the garden. Grows all sorts out there.' Her voice lowers to a tone shared between close friends. 'Between you and me, he frowns at me sometimes when I go out there. Shall I make some tea and we can chat in the lounge?'

Tea sounds lovely but… 'Sorry, I'm on a tight schedule. Another time.'

She holds my gaze. 'And will there be a next time? Did Jack offer you the room?'

'We hadn't got to that part of the conversation.'

'If I say it's yours will you take it?'

I hesitate as I remember his hand on me. I shake the memory off.

'I'd be delighted to be the tenant in your spare room.'

***

I leave the house wearing an upbeat smile, feeling Martha's eyes on my back as I go. As soon as the door closes, I let out a huge puff of air and have the strong urge to sag against something.

'Had a good laugh at my expense, did you?'

I'm startled by the voice coming from my left. There's an old woman wearing a brown woolly hat with a mauve knit flower on the front peering hard at me from next door's front garden. She's pointing a pair of garden scissors with an attitude that screams she's ready to use them on me.

I step back. 'I beg your pardon?'

'Pointing and chuckling a bellyful at my garden. And it is *my bloody garden.*'

I'm completely bemused. 'Sorry… I don't…'

She doesn't let me finish, but sweeps back into her house, followed by two cats. The door slams behind her.

Two

After leaving Jack and Martha's house I sit in my car. I'm shaking and grip the wheel in an attempt to stop. But can't. I open the glove compartment, pull out my bottle of anti-depressants, dry-swallow two. I close my eyes as I wait for their magic to start. I lean back and gently place my fingertips to my temple. Rub. Inhale deeply. Use my internal breathing technique to quiet my mind.

One, two, buckle my shoe.

Three, four, knock at the door.

Five, six...

Slow and easy does it.

Once the tension within disappears I check my watch. Half past four and I've still got another visit to make today. My parents are expecting me to put in an appearance this evening at their home in Surrey. In normal circumstances, I'd cancel without hesitation, but these aren't normal circumstances. If I don't go or don't appear, they'll panic, alert the relatives. Worse still, the police. The last thing I need is a posse of my nearest and dearest or the law on my tail.

I get the car going and head off. The roads are clogged, jammed, which is good. I have to concentrate on the wheel. No time for disordered, self-doubting thoughts. When I leave the M25, I drive through the Mole Valley and its fat green fields with fat cows and fat sheep. Its plump villages with plump houses and plump four-wheel drives parked outside. This is the England I grew up in. And nothing could be more English than the house my parents own. It's an old vicarage that's smaller than the house with the spare room but just as grand in its way. And nothing could be more

English than my parents themselves, who are waiting for me at the front door. They will have seen me coming up the long drive before I reached the house. It's that sort of place.

My dad knows how to hold himself with ramrod straightness, giving him a height that makes the eye linger. A silver fox is what mum teasingly calls him, a nod to his mostly grey hair. Before retiring he was an eminent doctor in London, and towards the end of his career owned his own private practice. He's the kind of man you don't meet much anymore. The strong silent type. Stoical I suppose is the correct word.

Mum is shorter, her ear-hugging hair more white than grey. Age has taken its rightful place on her face; scars and lines don't scare her, I know that first hand. She's the kind of woman you don't meet much anymore either. The kind who takes immense pride in her husband's and her only child's achievements but prefers to clap from the sidelines. She's certainly not the kind of woman who gets mistaken for her husband's mother.

He's Edward and she's Barbara. That's Barbara – never Babs. They both wear sensible country clothes. I don't know if they're tweed but it feels like they should be. A solid couple, married for six months shy of thirty-five years. A solidness I yearn to find with a man too. Naturally Alex pops into my head. I ruthlessly push him away.

'Hello, dear!'

My dad's greeting is warm, at the same time laced with a gruffness that's a warning of what's yet to come. No embrace, no lips meeting cheek. Instead he brushes back a lock of my hair just like he did when I was small.

Mum gives me one of her sunshine smiles as she kisses me on the cheek. She doesn't let go, running her palms feverishly up and down my covered arms. Her gaze runs over me, searching for changes. I wish she wouldn't; it makes me so uncomfortable.

When we walk through the house, I notice, as I always do, that the old vicarage is smothered with photos of me. Me winning prizes at school, receiving my first-class honours degree in mathematics, me winning gymkhana competitions and me with my arms around various horses' necks. It's all rather embarrassing but there's a discordant note in all these pictures too. An invisible fracture. There are no friends posing with me, no boyfriends either. And I'm thin, painfully so. I make Martha look like she could do with losing a few pounds. And I know too that all the photos of me at my thinnest – jutting bones, a face full of large eyes – are all discreetly locked away.

There aren't any photos on display of me as a baby. Mum said they were stolen along with so many other items during a burglary at a house they lived in when I was really small, a house I don't remember. The only other prominent photo is one of Dad in his young days at medical school. It's a boozy picture of him posing with two fellow medical students, all raising pints to the lens and wearing surgical masks as a joke.

We enter the tranquil, well-loved garden. A great spread of Mum's homemade shortbread, cinnamon biscuits and fruitcake with a pot of tea waits on the wrought-iron table near the scent and bloom of Dad's prized multi-coloured carnations.

Mum deliberately places a slice of cake onto my tea plate first. It's more of a slab really, her silent way of keeping me fattened up. Her gaze locks hard on me as she waits for the moment. The moment I tear off a corner and pop it in my mouth, which I dutifully do. I chew.

'Great cake, Mum.' I dramatically lick my lips. 'You'll be giving Mary Berry a run for her money.'

Mum looks ecstatic, a glow of pleasure warming her eyes. If she were anyone else, she'd probably be clapping her hands in feverish delight like a meme recycled across social media. I'm lying of course. The cake has the consistency and taste of a congealed mass of sugar and fat mixed with Plasticine.

Tea is poured and my parents indulge in idle chit-chat about the warm weather, the neighbours, Dad's exploits at the golf club. But it's all fake. I know what we're really here to talk about. It's as predictable as my parent's visits to the parish church on Sundays. I don't miss the pointed glances they exchange with each other.

My dad starts the ball rolling. 'So, how are you today, my dear?'

He uses the same line he no doubt did with his patients.

I take a gulp of lukewarm tea before answering. 'I'm fine.'

And so it goes on with my mum joining in. 'Are you eating properly?'

'Yes. Three meals a day, the well-balanced way.' I shove more sugar, fat and Plasticine, stuffed with currants and sultanas, into my mouth to underline my response. This time the cake sticks to the back of my bottom front teeth.

'And you're sleeping OK?'

'Yes.'

Coiled turmoil twists my tummy. I don't blame them for what they're doing, but being put under a microscope is no fun. It's bloody irritating. My tongue manages to dislodge mashed cake from my teeth but there's a stubborn bit that refuses to budge.

'You're sure?' Mum this time. My parents are a tag team who won't let up.

'Yes.'

'So, you're still taking your medication at the right time?'

'Yes, I am still taking my anti-depressants.'

Mum winces like I knew she would. She can't cope with the word 'depressed' being attached to her only child. I don't like to torment her with it, but it's the only way to change the direction of our way too personal conversations sometimes.

It works; she starts asking about my job. That's usually safe ground; they know how hard I work and how well I'm doing. I tell them I'm probably going to be promoted again and headhunters are sniffing around, offering me jobs with bigger bucks. My parents beam with pride. I beam with satisfaction too. Why not? I'm good at my job. Too good, some might say, because I don't have any close friends at work. I don't have *any* close friends.

Then my mum pretends to remember something. She slips her cup onto its saucer. 'Oh, by the way, dear, have you had a chance to go and see Doctor Wilson yet?'

I nod, pushing my plate with the majority of cake still on it to the side. 'I've seen him a couple of times.'

My parents exchange glances again, this time worried ones. My dad looks off into the distance, to the weather-beaten yellow swing at the bottom of the garden. That swing is my definition of happy. My dad pushing with care while I go up and down, higher and higher, squealing as my hands cling on for dear life.

My dad turns back to the table, eyes darkened with pain.

Mum's eyebrows arch, her face a picture of concerned confusion. 'That's strange, dear, because your father met Doctor Wilson at a dinner recently and he said that you hadn't been in touch yet.'

If there's one thing I hate more than lying to my parents it's being caught out lying to them. Shamefaced, I mutter under my breath, 'Yes, well, I've been very busy.'

'Your father and I,' Mum presses on, as if I'm still the kid in the swing who needs to know when it's time to come back down to earth, 'really think it would be a good idea to go and see him. He's an old friend of your father's. They were at medical school together. He's one of the most eminent psychiatrists in London. People pay good money for a consultation.'

If she'd left it at that, I'd have thrown in the towel and consented to seeing Doctor Wilson. Unfortunately, she adds, 'Especially after what's just happened.'

I forget all about the unwritten rule of not losing your temper in families like mine. It's vulgar, not the done thing. I crack. Don't remember picking up the cake. Mum's precious cake flies through the air, lands on the grass, breaking apart. As broken as I feel.

'What happened four months ago was a mix-up, easily done. OK?' It doesn't sound like words coming out of my mouth, but the bawling of a child who wants to be heard, desperate to be held. 'How many more times! I didn't mean to do it deliberately!'

I quiver with rage. I want to stop, but can't. 'For sodding hell's sake! Ask the quacks at the sodding hospital, it was a sodding mistake!'

My mother shakes with horror, her disbelieving gaze darting to the empty cake stand and back up at me again. My dad has his stern face on. I can easily see how scared his medical students must have been of him back in the day.

His voice is harsh and grim. 'I'll thank you for not using that kind of language in this house, Lisa. I'll thank you for not insulting your mother when she's only trying to help you. And I'll thank you for not referring to members of my former profession as *quacks*.'

My head hangs in shame. Tears sting the bottom of my eyes. Why can't I just be like everyone else? I see the way my colleagues secretly look at me at work. Lisa the machine who doesn't even take lunch breaks most days; she can't be human. Be normal.

'Ed.' My mother speaks quietly, almost serenely. 'Give her some space.'

'I'm sorry,' I blurt out, finally lifting my head to make eye contact with the two people who love me most in the world.

My mother composes herself. Calmly takes the reins. 'It's fine dear; you're upset, we understand. No one's suggesting you…' The next words were obviously in her mouth but she swallows them back with a bob of her throat muscles. Changes tack. 'We know you didn't mean for it to happen; we know that.'

I don't see how she could know that. Even I don't know what I was really doing that day.

My dad, with his medical training, does not utter a word. Sometimes it's a mother's tonic that is the best medicine of all.

'If you went to see Doctor Wilson, he might be able to help guide you through your problems,' Mum coaxes, 'and offer you ways to cope with them. He's a brilliant man, isn't he, Edward?'

My dad's stern face has gone. So has his straight-backed attitude to life. His shoulders are rounded with the posture of an old man. 'Yes. He's brilliant.'

I yearn to reach out to him. Touch him. Hug him tight. I've always been a daddy's girl. There's a bond between us that was forged at the bottom of the garden on a plastic swing.

I make up my mind. Don't have the heart to cause them any more pain.

'I'll see him. Make an appointment.'

I don't want to see this Doctor Wilson. Yet another member of the medical profession dissecting me. It feels like I've seen every counsellor, therapist, psychiatrist, psychic healer and phoney shrink within a twenty-mile radius of London. How can I forget the session with the guy swanning around in a purple kaftan, wearing a necklace comprised of shells that looked like they were hauled off Brighton Beach, who laid his sweaty, meaty hands on me to drive out my problems? That's how desperate I had become to sort out my shit.

When I was released from the hospital, four months ago, something shifted me in a new direction. I can't explain fully what it was. Maybe I finally realised I couldn't go on like this. That's when I decided.

I don't need guidance and help.

I just need the truth.

Nevertheless, I'll visit Doctor Wilson if it will keep Mum and Dad happy, get them off my back.

We carry on for the remainder of the evening as if nothing has happened. That's what happens in families like mine: if embarrassment comes calling, invite it inside, permanently disable it and then sweep, and keep it, under the carpet. Our time together ends with a promise from them to visit me in London in two weeks' time. Only when I get back into the car do I realise something about their upcoming visit.

I haven't told them I'm moving to Jack and Martha's spare room.

Three

Martha and Jack are waiting for me at the front door the day I move in, a carbon copy of what my parents do each time I visit them. The sight makes me nervy as I climb out of the Uber with my single piece of luggage. I wasn't expecting a greeting party, like a welcome mat to dust the dirt from my shoes before I'm allowed to enter. *Of course they would want to welcome me into their home*, I reason to myself.

I'm so jittery it's a wonder I can move. I've spent most of the night tossing and turning, worrying myself to death about this move. I've shared a home with other people before, but this will be the first time I'll be living with the people who own the property. Martha smiles and waves at me while her husband rocks slightly on his heels.

There's nothing to worry about. These are good people.

I paste a super bright smile on as I confidently walk towards them. Martha surprises me with a big hug. Her warmth and delicately scented perfume wrap around me. I'm slightly awkward in her clinging arms, but some of my tension melts away.

She gently releases me, but doesn't let go, instead links an arm through mine. 'Welcome, Lisa,' she pronounces dramatically, as if she's live in front of an audience to hand me an award.

She certainly is dressed for the part. Last week, during my viewing, she was all chic woman about town; now she embodies the host of a very exclusive house party. Cocktail dress, ice-pick thin ruby-red heels and expertly contoured make-up that stops just short of resembling a mask. I wonder if she's going out. Or whether she's one of those 'sleeping beauty' women who insist on being done up to the max in bed, always on twenty-four hour looks call. Beside her I'm the picture of scruffiness in my faded stonewashes and long-sleeved green plaid blouse, with super short hair on top of my big-eyed owl face.

She gazes at me like I'm an adored family member. 'We want you to be very happy in our home. *Your* home.'

Your home. It hits me then that I'll be living in a place that's not really my own. A place already occupied by the people who own it: two strangers.

'I'm surprised that you were able to give notice so quickly on your old place,' Jack comments.

My hand tightens on the handle of my luggage. 'I've been sofa surfing at a friend's. Finding a place to stay at a decent price is murder in London. You don't know how grateful I am to have found your room.' I end with a genuine smile this time.

I am truly grateful. This move means everything to me.

Jack quickly takes my case as Martha's arm ushers me inside. The hallway brims with much more light today so I notice the framed prints and pictures on the wall. I have this insane urge to stand still again on the red and black rug in the heart of the house, but Martha propels me towards the stairs. She lets go of my arm.

'Jack, do the honours,' she requests softly. There's laughter in her voice, bordering on that of a giggly teenager.

I follow him up. Then I hear a high-pitched creak behind. Martha is following us up the stairs. Once again all the doors are closed, including the bathroom this time. There must be a window open somewhere because a cooling breeze licks at our heels as we progress along the first landing.

My room. I decide to claim it as Jack opens the door. The natural light that bathes it today is overcast. The air is still in the spare room, closing the walls in, making it seem smaller. And that blasted, annoying air freshener still lingers like an unwanted roommate who doesn't pay their share of the rent.

Jack wheels my luggage towards the bed and gives me a front door key. Martha remains in the doorway.

Jack looks at my luggage. 'You travel light.'

'Yes, most of my gear is in storage.'

'Waste of good money, Lisa. You should bring it all over here, we've got room.' Then he hastily adds, 'That's all right, isn't it, Martha?'

Martha clucks her tongue at her husband. 'Give the girl a chance to breathe, she's just got here. We can talk about storage another time. I'm sure all Lisa wants to do now is settle in.'

I hastily inform both that it's fine; the storage deal I've got works for me.

It's a strange thing but whenever you go to view a house, a flat or a room you never notice the little faults even though you're looking out for them. It's only after you've moved in that they jump out at you. The previous night there had been a short, sharp summer shower and now I can see drops of water around the skylight and the ceiling around it shows signs of damp. I point the problem out to Jack.

He studies the skylight for a while as if that might dry it out. 'I thought I'd fixed that. No matter, I'll get a stepladder and have a look at it.'

'No rush. Whenever you're ready.'

The last thing I want is to give the impression I'm going to be one of those demanding tenants, bitching and moaning about every tiny detail.

Then I remember. 'Is there a key for the room?'

Martha answers, her fingers locking together loosely in front of her gorgeous dress. I notice the ultra-red polish on her nails. 'None of the rooms in the house have keys. Myself and Jack decided that the only way we can have another person living in our home is on a principle of trust.'

I should really insist on a key. Surely that's pretty basic in these types of arrangements? How else am I going to guarantee my privacy?

But I quickly agree with her. 'Yes, of course.' I'm not happy about it but I don't want to make a big drama about it; I can't lose this room.

Then Jack gives me some reassurance by pointing at the door. 'There's a bolt on the inside, so you can have privacy.'

He comes to stand beside his wife. Seeing them side by side, I can't help but think how odd they look together. All the cosmetics, Botox and fillers in the world can't disguise how much older she is than him. His tatts and man bun will never be a match for her elegance. Instantly I feel bad thinking such bitchy thoughts.

Then I remember. I don't care about Jack or Martha. The only thing that matters is the room. It's mine.

'There are rooms that are private.' Martha lists them, tagging on a reminder about the garden.

Which reminds me: 'I met your neighbour after I left the other day. An older lady. She said something about her garden…'

Twin tension stops them in their tracks. Now why did I say that? I don't want them to think I'm going to be trouble or stick my beak into their business. And it is their business – whatever is between them and their neighbour has nothing to do with my time here.

Jack recovers first with a loud scoff. 'Don't worry about the old bat. She don't know what she's saying.' He touches his temples to indicate she's not the full ticket. 'Lost her marbles years back, that one.'

Lost her marbles… A chill runs through me.

Martha tells her husband off, very gently. 'Don't call her an old bat, Jack. We're all going to end up at that age one day and I, for one, want to be spoken about with the respect that should be given to an older person.' Her green gaze twists to me. 'Still, I'd stay out of her way if I were you.'

That seems to be the perfect point to bid them thanks and goodbye.

They don't leave; they remain in the doorway, frozen statues gazing at me. Like characters from *Westworld* waiting for their circuits and wires to be connected. A confused, uncomfortable sensation creeps over me.

Then Martha pops on her carefree smile like a light bulb. 'Anything you need or don't understand—'

'Ask me,' Jack cuts in, wearing a lopsided grin.

Martha playfully punches him on the arm. Then both turn to each other and laugh. Holding hands, they leave me to my new home. I hear the quiet, moaning music of the landing as they walk across it, of the stairs as they go down. Their voices are low with the quality of rustling paper as they whisper back and forth on the way. I suppose it must be a bit uncomfortable for them having someone else in their house. It's not something I think I could do. How do you relax knowing there's a stranger within the four walls of your home?

First order of business is the mirror. I walk over to it and flip the glass around. I won't be looking at the full-length reflection of my body it provides.

My phone pings. A text from my dad. He's been putting me through text hell since my visit. A text last evening to say how nice it was for him and Mum to see me. He included Doctor Wilson's personal number without comment. I replied without mentioning the number. An early text this morning to thank me for thanking him and the phone number. Again. I didn't reply to that one.

I open his message. No pretence lurking behind good manners this time. Only the number.

I haven't contacted Doctor Wilson because I'm hoping if I leave it for a few days he might get run over or retire and save me the trouble of having to go to see him. Nasty thoughts, but that's how much I don't want to see him. I copy the number into my phone and make as if to call it but then change my mind. Perhaps if I leave it for another few hours, Doctor Wilson will decide to emigrate in the meantime.

I step out onto the landing, closing the door quietly behind me. I stand there for a few minutes. Soak up what I can see and hear. Some people think that houses can talk to them. I want this house to talk to me.

There's very little on the top floor that's new. The light fittings are chandelier type contraptions with multiple bulbs. They're made out of what looks like gilt that's flaking in places. My room's door is old-fashioned, wood panel with a brass handle. It would brush up a real treat if stripped and varnished. The wallpaper has been there for years and is peeling away at the top.

I listen hard. But the top floor is silent. It's got nothing to say to me except that Jack and Martha have let this place go a little. Maybe they aren't as cash-rich as I thought which explains why they need a tenant.

I go down the stairs to the landing of the middle floor. I look up and down, close my eyes, smell the air. Listen. I only hear Jack and Martha somewhere downstairs. This house has nothing to say to me. It's silent. Perhaps another time.

I can wait.

Four

I start to unpack and hang things up. Tops are always long-sleeved, trousers full-length, shoes open enough to display the tops of my feet. I have a few private papers I decide to put in the bedside cabinet but the drawers won't shut properly. I pull them out and find lots of junk has fallen down the back. It includes takeaway menus, business cards for cabs, an old flannel. And there's an envelope. It's unsealed with a folded piece of paper inside.

My ears prick up. I'm sure I hear a creak on the staircase that leads up to my room. I listen intently but don't hear it again. *Stop being such a ninny.* I know in old houses the wood expands on hot days and then contracts at night. That's what the noise must have been. Maybe I should go and check? I half get up, the envelope still in my hand. But I stop myself near the door. *Stop being paranoid. You wanted the house to talk to you and now it is – except it's the language of old wood that you can't understand.* I try to shrug it off, but the gut-wrenching sensation of my first night in a strange house won't disappear.

Instead I retreat back to the bed and pull out the folded paper inside the envelope. It's a letter. Handwritten in a neat and precise professional style. The blood drains from my face, leaving me cold. I see straight away what type of letter this is.

I jump when the creaking sound is back outside. This time it's not on the staircase; it's on the landing near my room. It stops again. My breathing is heavy in the room. A few moments later there it is again. The uneven squeak of something heavy pressing against wood.

I put the letter back in its envelope and hide it under the mattress. I hurry over to the door. Put my ear up against it. Listen. There's silence.

Bang.

The thud of the knock against the door vibrates through me. I reel back in shock, panting wildly.

'Who is it?' I can't keep the trembling from my call.

'Only me.'

I relax. It's Jack. I flex my fingers by my side and catch my breath, trying to compose myself. I think about telling him to go away, but then he adds, 'Just wondering if you've got a minute?'

I open the door – not too wide, though – to see what he wants. But I suspect I've made a mistake straightaway. I should have told him I was in bed. He's in tailored trousers, highly polished shoes, freshly ironed white shirt with a gold chain dangling around his neck. He smells of soap and too much spicy aftershave. He looks like he's going on a date. Maybe he and Martha are going out. Both of his hands are hidden behind his back.

'What is it, Jack?'

He produces one of the hands like a magician. He's holding a stapled wad of paper.

'The lease. You've forgotten to sign the lease.'

He's right. I was so eager to move in that I hadn't stopped to think about getting all the legal stuff done and dusted.

'Oh, right.' I stretch out a hand. 'If you leave it with me, I'll read and sign and get it back to you in the morning.'

'That's alright, I'll wait. Me and Martha are keen to get all the i's and t's dotted and crossed.'

He pushes the door open with his shoulder and I let him do it because I'm too embarrassed not to. How many terrible things have happened to women because they're too embarrassed to put their foot down? It's only when Jack's in my room that I realise what he's got in his other hand. In his fist is a bottle of champagne and between his fingers are the stems of two glasses.

Smiling like a grown-up boy, he waves the bottle at me. 'Bought you a little present as a housewarming. Can't move in without blessing your new room. You read the lease, I'll pour us a couple of glasses of bolly.'

He closes the door and manages to pull the bolt without me even noticing he's done it. I could say something but decide the best policy is to get the lease signed and him out of the door.

I sit down, wilting, on the chair at the desk while Jack sits on my bed. He bounces up and down on it.

'Comfy!' He pats the bed as his tongue snakes out, wetting his lips. 'What you doing over there? Don't be shy, come and sit with me. Woah…!' The champagne cork rockets upwards and scuffs the ceiling while the fizz gushes over the floorboards.

I stay where I am. Jerk my widening gaze down to the lease. My hands are shaking and I'm scared stiff. Jack doesn't appear so charmless and harmless anymore. I remember the touch of his rough flesh against my skin.

'Where's Martha?'

'Martha?' He repeats it as if I'm talking about an alien. 'She's gone out. Don't worry about her; no one wants her at a housewarming party anyway. She knows what side her bread's buttered on when it comes to me.' I don't believe him. I've seen the way she flicks furtive glances at him, the way of a woman deeply in love. Poor Martha.

He looks at me with a hint of reproach. 'You're staying over there then?'

'I'm reading the lease.'

'Don't be long or the fizz will go flat.'

My fizz has already gone flat. What should I do? I'm in *his* house and the door's bolted. He's nearer to the door and if I run for it he might get there first. Plus, I'll have to use valuable time to undo the bolt. My mind is running riot. He might not even be thinking of attacking me, but when a man you barely know pushes his way into your space with alcohol and locks the door, anything can happen. I think of the awful, unfair tragedy that happened to a girl who had worked in my office. Lonely after her divorce, she'd gone on a date with a seemingly respectable guy who had drugged and raped her. Rape scars victims' lives. I'm so vulnerable. Even if I scream, we're so high up in the house; who will hear my desperate cry for help?

I gather my courage. 'Jack, I want you to leave.'

'What?' He appears startled, like he really doesn't understand why I want him to get out.

'What you're doing isn't fair to your wife.'

He raises his glass. 'The only thing I'm doing is offering you some bubbly – which I might add cost me a fair bit in the pocket department – to toast your new home.'

I sign my name with a flourish on both copies of the lease without reading them properly and stand up. Stretching my arm out as far as possible, I hold his copy out to him; I don't want him anywhere near me.

'Here's the lease, with the i's and t's dotted and crossed. Now please leave.'

Suddenly his attention shifts sharply to the door. 'Did you hear that?'

I wish it was the sound of me punching him in the face.

Instead, I turn my ear towards the door too. Can't hear anything. Jack clumsily puts his glass down on the bedside cabinet and hurries over to the door. The Jack the Lad pose has deserted him. With the quiet know-how of a burglar he eases back the bolt to minimise the sound it makes. Opens the door slightly.

Now I can hear it. It's Martha calling his name. It sounds as if she's in the hallway. He stiffens and then holds his finger to his lips to indicate silence. For the first time, I become angry. He's making it look like I'm complicit in his out-of-order visit.

I've had enough of this. I stomp over to him and slap the signed lease in his face, so he has no alternative but to take it.

Ball him out, that's what I should do, but I just want him gone. He creeps out of the door and along the landing and down the stairs.

He calls Martha's name, followed by 'I thought you were out for the evening?'

I don't hear her response.

I shove the bolt and ram the desk chair under the handle so Jack can't make a return visit. I sag on the bed. That was frightening, really frightening. What scares me the most is not Jack but the isolation of being in another person's home. You take them at face value, on trust as Martha had put it. The reality is I don't know these people who I've rented a room from at all.

***

I remember the letter I'd found which I'd stashed under the mattress. I retrieve the envelope and sit at the desk. It's slightly curled at one edge so I guess it's been hanging around in the bedside cabinet for a while, although it's not discoloured with age. I take out the letter. I won't be shocked this time because I know what it is. I read:

To whom it may concern,

This is one of the last things I leave in this room. I'm not going to give my name because it's not important and it may mean dragging the innocent into the decision that I have made. Enough innocent people have been hurt already. I'd respectfully ask the authorities not to inquire any further into my identity or background. It doesn't matter. I'm just a man who's made mistakes and has now decided to pay for them in the only way that seems appropriate, that is to say with his own life.

There's no need to ask too many questions. They can't help you or me. I'm gone now. Leave me to rest.

As I am familiar with the fate of pauper suicides, I understand I won't be getting a funeral in Westminster Abbey. However, I would like to request that a minister of the Church of England is invited to say a few words over me before I'm sent off to whatever rest I'm going to.

I would

The letter stops abruptly.

It's a suicide letter. A farewell to a life. At the bottom are a few lines written in pencil. They seem to be written in a foreign alphabet but as languages aren't my thing, I can't figure out what it says.

Did someone take their own life in this room? Not someone, I correct myself, but a man who refuses to leave his name. Is that why there was the subtle reek of cheap air freshener during my viewing to mask the rotten odour of a recent death? But Jack was clear; there'd been no tenants in the room before me.

I scan the top of the letter again – there it is in black and white: *'This is one of the last things I leave in this room.'* This room. Unless Martha and Jack purchased the cabinet and the letter was already stuffed down the back. I shake my head; the cabinet looks like a well-loved piece of furniture which has been here for some time, and the letter doesn't appear to be that old.

Why would Jack lie about there being another tenant before I came?

Adulterer? Liar? There was a lot stacking up against Jack here.

Did no one care for this unnamed man? I run my fingertips across the writing because I care. A lump of hurt knots in my throat. I know what it's like to be teetering on the edge. In this moment a strong bond develops between me and this faceless, nameless man. I can't stuff him in the back of the drawer again as if he doesn't exist. I correct myself – didn't exist. That would be cruel.

'There's no need to ask too many questions. They can't help you or me. I'm gone now. Leave me to rest.'

I can't respect his wishes. Can't stop the questions from coming. Who are the innocents he talks about? How did he hurt them? What were the mistakes that he made? My mind starts racing and racing. *Slow down. Slow down. Slow bloody down.* I find my pills and take one. Two would be too much. I'm bone-weary, need to sleep.

With a heavy heart I fold the letter and leave it on the desk. I want to find out so much more about this man who took his own life.

***

I look at the bed and sigh – it's time for me to face my own truths. Own demons. We all have them.

After I put my pyjamas on – all my nightclothes are long-sleeved, long-legged – I take out my mobile and headphones. One therapist had advised me that one of the best ways to get to sleep is to exhaust the body. Get myself so physically tired that when I lie down the weariness lures me into a world of slumber. The therapist had given me a vigorous bedtime exercise routine, which I'd binned at the first opportunity. I don't like that type of exercise; it's so artificial and boring. Instead, I had developed my own way of doing things.

I put the earphones on and push play on the music library on my phone. The tunes of the ultimate North London girl, Amy Winehouse, is my music of choice. 'You Know I'm No Good' blasts into my life. The first strike of the drum booms inside my body. I start dancing like a woman possessed, rapidly moving from one side of the room to the other. Her throaty, sexy voice propels me along. I'm sweating, a solitary rhythm beating in my head. *I will sleep, I will sleep. I will sleep.* By the time Amy stops I'm breathing hard, panting. I don't want to catch my breath; I need to use it to sleep as fast as possible.

With the beat of the song still strumming in me, I take out my other night-time friend – my scarf. It's made of the softest silk, plain lilac except for the black thread of patterns at the top. It was a present from mother on my fifteenth. For most people birthdays are special, their day, but I've always found them difficult. They're harder still for my poor parents, faced with a stubborn girl who half-heartedly celebrated. Funny, they had given me such great gifts over the years, but it's this scarf that stands out. Maybe it's because it's a bit like me: not flashy, happy to do its job without standing out.

I sit in the middle of my new bed. Stretch out my legs. I tie the scarf around the right corner of the bed and then double tie it around my ankle. I lie down.

I will sleep.

To whom it may concern.

My leg twitches against its bond. I dare to close my eyes.

Five

I wake up. My heart rate picks up as I frown at the ceiling, at the white walls around me. Squint at the morning light streaming through the skylight. Where am I? What is this place? Am I back in hospital? I'm panicked, my gaze roaming as I try to figure it out. Then I remember. I am in the room. My new home in Martha and Jack's house. I always feel disorientated that first morning waking up somewhere new – a hotel room, a plane, even my old room at Mum and Dad's.

My eyes slide down the bed to my leg. A huge sigh of relief punches out of my mouth. I'm still securely tied. I check the clock on my phone, sitting on the bedside table. It's 7:10am. Time to get up and face the world of work. I untie myself, gently fold my scarf and tuck it under the pillow. The radiator gurgles, which I'm assuming means that the heating is coming on. Thank goodness for that because the room is quite chilly despite it being summer.

Note to self: ask Martha or Jack if they can set the boiler to come on earlier. No, not Jack, not after the stunt he pulled yesterday.

As soon as I stand, the heading-south-fast sensation of needing the loo hits me quickly. I squeeze my muscles down below as I shove my feet into my closed fake-fur cuffed slippers in a rush and find my shin-length cardigan that doubles as my dressing gown. I open the door and quickly make my way to the next landing where the bathroom is. Jack had neglected to give me a tour of the bathroom but I recall it was the only door that was open on the landing below.

I'm desperate to go when I enter. It's very stylish with its black and white chequered floor tiles, art deco style mirror – a sister to the one in the hallway – tan-coloured cabinet with two fluffy towels neatly folded on the top. I can't see the bath because the shower curtain is drawn across it. Either Martha or Jack have been in here recently because steam clings and slithers down the walls.

At the toilet I reach under my cardigan, start to pull my pyjama bottoms down… and the shower curtain swishes back. With a cry of alarm, my jim-jam bottoms drop to my knees as I fall sideways heavily into the wall.

My landlord and lady peer at me from inside the filled bath. Martha's delicate hand holds the shower curtain, hiding their bodies so all I see is their heads, his slightly above hers. They look like Punch and Judy ready to begin their puppet show.

'I'm… I'm sorry… really sorry,' I choke out.

My face heats with embarrassment. I should've knocked on the door to check that no one was inside. Idiot!

Poor Martha looks mortified, while Jack… He gives me a cold, half-scared stare. I know what he's pissing himself about – me confessing to his wife about what he did last night. I suspect he knows I'm not going to say a word; I need the room too much.

His wife turns to him. 'Darling, didn't you tell Lisa about the bathroom arrangements?'

'I didn't think I needed to because it's all in the lease.'

Second note to self: hit head against wall for being so stupid and not reading the lease.

'I'm really sorry…' I start apologising again, totally understanding what Elton John meant about sorry being the hardest word.

Martha's hand waves my words away. 'It's us who should be begging your pardon. I'm sure you can understand that we want our own space in such delicate areas.'

Delicate areas reminds me that Martha and Jack are no doubt in their birthday suits in the bath, and my jim-jam bottoms are still down. Panic sets in as my gaze slams down. I draw in a deep breath of relief; my long cardigan has hidden my flesh. My trembling hand yanks my bottoms back to my waist in what feels like one second flat. Mumbling more 'sorries', I can't get out of there quickly enough.

Despite the pressure on my bladder, I head back upstairs to my room. Once inside I slump onto the bed. My face still burns with bonfire intensity. That must rank in the Top Ten Embarrassing Moments of My Life. And fancy not reading the lease before signing?

'Never put your name to anything unless you've gone over it with a fine-toothed comb and then a brush,' is the very wise advice that Dad gave me when I got my first job.

I ease off giving myself a hard time. The only reason I had signed it without reading was to get that prick Jack out of my room.

I find the lease folded in the bedside drawer and take it downstairs with me to find a more private toilet and shower room.

At the sight of the loo my spirits plummet. It's like a modern-day outhouse with an old-fashioned toilet: high tank, flush chain. The sink beside it is cracked. There's a small, frosted window that faces the forbidden garden. I suspect it was a proper outdoor toilet at one time that had been extended later on as an attachment to the house.

The shower room that's opposite is a bit of a step up with its contemporary fixtures, but its crammed, goose-pimple freezing, and there's the slight tang of mildew in the air.

I could complain… but heavily decide against it. I try to see the positives; at least I have a loo and shower room all to myself.

I sit on the toilet and go over the lease carefully. Come to the section I should've paid more attention to:

Licensee's obligations.

Most of it is bog-standard stuff except for:

Use of the toilet and shower room on the ground floor.

No food permitted inside the room. No alcohol.

The only visitors permitted in the room are the licensee's parents with prior notice to the licensor. NO ONE ELSE is permitted to visit the licensee in the house.

No visitors. Where was I living – in a Victorian boarding house for impressionable young girls?

I am starting to realise that the reality of living in someone else's home means you have to adjust your expectations. I lean back on to the cold pipe behind me, which makes loud, gulping noises. There's no point jumping out of my pram about it. I'd signed the agreement. No one had forced me. I resign myself:

Someone else's home.

Someone else's rules.

***

'Lisa.' Martha calls my name as soon as I enter the house later that day.

For a moment I get confused and think it's Mum calling me. I give my head a tiny shake to clear my mind. I can't hold back an irritated huff. I don't want to play the dutiful tenant. I'm exhausted from work. My trouser suit is heavy, as if there's another human wearing it too. All I want to do is crash in my room. And think about the suicide note. I can't get it out of my head. Can't stop thinking about its faceless author.

Then I notice something strange in the hallway. I stare in mouth-dropping disbelief. It's my suitcase and some shopping bags crammed with my belongings. I don't... don't understand. What's happening?

My trousers flick back from my legs, displaying the tops of my feet as I stride through to the dining room to find Jack and Martha sitting at the wooden table. They stare at me like two concerned parents who've discovered something illicit in their teenager's bedroom. Now they're getting ready for the awkward parental advisory explicit content chat.

They both get up when I come in. Martha seems tired, the skin across her face more stretched than ever, her cheeks a strange colour that the plastered blusher can't disguise. Jack stands slightly behind her. His wife appears to cower in his presence.

Neither says anything, so I ask, 'Is there a problem?'

There obviously is. My packed bags suggest they're going to try and throw me out. But it's not happening; I'm totally going to make sure of that. I feel like I'm stuck in an alternative universe. Yesterday was all sweetness and light between us, well except for… That's when I notice the bottle of champagne Jack had brought up to my room – yes, *my* room – the night before for his 'party' sitting on the dining room table. The two glasses, still half filled with stale fizz, are next to it. I tighten my lips.

Martha's voice is thready. 'OK, Lisa, I'm going to keep this brief because I don't want any upset and I don't see the need for it.' She looks at Jack for support but the only thing he can offer is his innocent expression. 'Jack and I have been talking and we feel that it would be best for all concerned if you found somewhere else to live. We'll refund your deposit and rent; that's not a problem. But we'd like you to leave. Today.'

I go straight on the attack. 'Why?'

The anger inside me begins to boil. These two have had the audacity to put their hands on my belongings when I wasn't here. That's not on, but I keep that to myself. Turn down the anger to a simmer.

Martha sounds hesitant, almost as if she's been given lines to read out but hasn't learned them properly. She looks with sorrow at the evidence on the table.

'While Jack was trying to repair the skylight in your room today, he discovered these on your desk. We've made it very clear in the lease that both alcohol… and visitors, unless they are your parents… aren't allowed. This is a clear breach of the agreement you signed. I'm afraid we can't allow you to stay. So, if you'd be kind enough…'

I suspect that Martha knows full well how the champers ended up in my room and who my visitor was. I'm tempted to lay the naked truth before her but she looks so forlorn that I feel sorry for her and decide I can't. Anyway, I don't want to burn any bridges unless I have to.

I catch Jack's nervy gaze. He sharply looks away.

'The bottle was a gift from a colleague at work when I said I was moving. I brought the two glasses with me and filled one up while I was sorting my things out. It got lost in the chaos when I unpacked so I filled a second. I hadn't read the lease at that stage, never mind signed one. So, as you can see, this is all a misunderstanding.'

That would be plausible if they're acting in good faith. But it's clear they're not. Or rather Jack isn't.

Martha looks at her husband again and then turns to me. They've clearly decided that she's going to be doing all the talking.

'That may be the case, but it's still a breach of your lease. And anyway, we just don't think this is going to work out. It's nothing personal. You're a very nice girl.' She hunts for an explanation. 'We just feel you're a round peg in a square hole.'

I'm staying; I'm in no doubt about that. But I'm curious to know what's really behind this. I'm sure there are some dumb girls who are happy enough to jump into the sack with Jack, but I can't believe he normally responds in such a vindictive way when he's knocked back. It's a numbers game for guys like him. You win some, you lose some. Then I remember the look on his face when I asked him to leave my room. I think about what might have happened if Martha hadn't come home when she did. Perhaps I've given him too much benefit of the doubt.

'Listen, Martha, I don't care about pegs and holes. All I know is that I've signed a lease for six months. I'm going to honour it and so are you. And I'm going to warn you now that I work in an industry with lots of very smart lawyers and my ex-boyfriend is one too.' Why am I dragging Alex into this? 'If *you* decide to break the agreement we've signed, I'll speak to them and I'll see you in court.'

At the word 'court' they both shudder slightly. Martha seems to be nearly in tears. 'There's no need for threats, Lisa. Why can't you see that this just isn't going to work? There are lots of rooms in London. Why don't you go and find one somewhere else?'

I'm firm. 'Because I've found this one. I've paid a deposit and the rent and I'm staying. Now, is there anything else?'

Jack's not looking innocent anymore. In fact, he's staring at me with something approaching fury. He's obviously not used to women fighting back. Perhaps that's what living with an older woman like Martha does for him. Gives him the illusion he's the king of the world.

Neither of them says anything more so I turn to go.

But before I do, I say to Jack, 'Did you fix the skylight?' He shakes his head very slowly so I add, 'I'd be grateful if you could do that as soon as possible.'

I look over at Martha with accusing eyes. 'Yesterday you talked to me about trust. You said it was one of the reasons my room didn't have a key. I trust you both.' Not Jack though; I don't trust him as far as I can kick him. However, I'm a realist. I need to destroy as much ill will as possible before I exit the room.

I walk out. I don't hurry to show them they don't scare me. I collect the bags and suitcase in the hall and take them back to my room.

As soon as I close the door I collapse back against it. The scene downstairs was the last thing I had expected on my second day in this house. But at least I had the measure of Jack now. A spoiled boy who hides behind Mummy's skirt when he gets his fingers all sticky in a jam.

'Did they try to kick you out too?' I whisper to the man who left the farewell letter, as if he's in the room.

I'd decided to call his last words a farewell letter. Suicide is such a harsh word. The 's' and 'c' sounds fall from the tongue like the slices of a knife. His farewell still sits on the desk where I left it the night before. I feel terrible about leaving it in the open. Almost as if I've disrespected the last wishes of a man who left this earth in one of the worst ways possible – by his own hand.

I fold it with care and place it gently under my pillow near my lilac scarf.

I also carefully re-read the lease. Read it again. Check my belongings to make sure I have nothing that's in breach of it, like a visitor hiding in my purse. They've got free access to my room when I'm not in it and I'm already expecting Jack to come back and start digging around in an effort to find something else he can use to try and turf me out. But I'm not going to give him the chance. I should really have asked someone to check the lease first before I signed it but it's too late for that now. Although given the way they both blanched when I mentioned the courts, perhaps they won't try that route.

I look around the room to make sure I haven't missed anything.

The damp near the skylight is getting worse. There's now a patch stretching down the bowed ceiling towards one of the walls. I decide I'm going to keep on at him about that until he fixes it. I've got no intention of yielding any ground, although I know he almost certainly won't mend it. He's probably hoping that if the room becomes a health hazard that will be enough to drive me out when the cold weather comes.

Wrong again.

I hear whining creaks on the staircase leading up to the landing outside. They stop. Then the whining starts again, followed by soft footsteps on the landing itself. I'm not in the mood for round two with Jack's predatory intimidation. This time I will scream the house down.

I grab the chair by the desk and jam it under the door handle. I take out the pepper spray and personal alarm I purchased at lunchtime today. My heart is thumping with such an intensity I'm sure I can hear it. My hand squeezes tight on the spray. There's a long pause before there's a gentle knock on the door.

'What do you want?' I say between gritted teeth.

'I was wondering if I could have a word with you in private?'

But it's not Jack. It's Martha.

Six

I pull the chair away and unbolt the lock. Hesitantly, I open the door slightly and discover my visitor is alone. There seems to be no reason not to let her in. It's her house after all. Once inside, Martha notices the pepper spray and alarm in my hands.

She laughs grimly and says, 'There's no need for that, Lisa. You're worried about Jack? Don't be, he's harmless. All smoke and no fire.'

I'm slightly embarrassed, although still on my guard, but put the spray and alarm on the mantelpiece. Martha's barefoot, the illusion of her height from her heels gone. She's still dressed to impress for a posh evening out in a pricey black number. Perhaps she always is. I don't know what perfume she's wearing, but it's a hint of delicate-sweet, not overpowering.

It's near twilight; the only natural light in the room is from the dormer window and skylight. It's quite gloomy. Perhaps because of that, I can see how bewitching she must have been as a young woman. Her cheekbones and forehead make a fine setting for those dazzling green eyes. Martha must have been quite a heartbreaker in her heyday, a real scene-stealer, which only makes me wonder how she ended up with the husband she did.

Martha must be nervous because she wanders around the room inspecting things like a prison warder while I look on. She pauses by the desk as if expecting to find something. She looks up at me, still slightly shaky from the scene downstairs, but then she gives me an alluring smile.

'Do you mind if we have a chat, Lisa? You know, woman to woman?'

'Not at all.' She can 'chat' to me as much as she likes, it isn't going to change a thing; I'm not leaving this house. This room.

Martha sits down in the chair by the desk and crosses her shapely legs.

'I don't do this often…' she warns in advance and gives me no time to respond before pulling out a packet of cigarettes.

I don't let my surprise show. Martha plus cigarettes is not an equation I would have imagined. She appears too refined for something as dirty as a cigarette to be hanging out of her dainty mouth. Then I witness her smoking – she takes it to the level of performance art. Her red lips pout as she lights up. Smoke rolls and curls up around her so she's poised with the natural glamour of a star of a noir film from Hollywood's classic period. A star whose lover has just shot her husband and is worried the FBI will come looking for them. She doesn't ask me if I mind her smoking or if I want one. I do mind.

But this is her house not mine.

'Can you answer a question for me?'

'Of course.'

Smoke obscures part of her face. 'Why aren't you just packing your bags and leaving? I would in your position.'

'I've already told you. I've signed a lease and I intend to stick to it. It's not easy finding a charming and cosy room like this. As for the business with the champagne and the…'

She cuts me short. 'I know full well how the bubbly and glasses ended up here. Jack brought them up, didn't he? Because he thought I was out for the evening. I'm not stupid.'

I'm surprised she admits this. 'Then you know I've done nothing wrong. Even less reason for me to leave.'

'I would have thought it was more of one. I wouldn't want to live in a house where the landlord comes racing upstairs on my first night, armed with alcohol and a condom. Actually, forget the condom, he's not that sensible.'

I'm stunned by her knowing knowledge of her husband. Why would she stay with a man like that? Doesn't she feel humiliated?

'I know my rights. I'm not going to be driven out.'

Martha gets up, goes to the window and throws her cigarette out. When she sits down again, she immediately lights up another. Her hands have a faint tremble now. 'Did you sleep with him?'

I'm slack-jawed with shock. 'Of... of course not.'

She stretches the fingers of her free hand. 'I wouldn't blame you if you did. He's a great-looking boy. And to be honest, while I've got my faults, I'm not a hypocrite. I've strayed a time or two in my time. I'm not in a position to criticise anyone else for it.'

'I. Did. Not. Sleep. With. Him.'

This woman-to-woman chat is too personal and very uncomfortable. I wonder where Martha is going with all this. She clearly doesn't want to be here discussing infidelity. Her whole manner shows that. I bet Jack has sent her up here with a message of some kind but I can't work out what it is. It can't be to order me out. I've already made it clear that's not happening.

Martha seems lost in thought. Then: 'How old are you?'

'Twenty-five.'

She nods. 'I'm forty-three.' She pauses for a moment before adding, 'All right, forty-eight.' *And the rest* I'm dying to add; she's definitely a woman somewhere in her fifties. 'You know, it's not easy being the wife of a much younger man like Jack. Having the world mistaking you for his mum or thinking your husband is some kind of gigolo. It's not easy at all.'

I can't help but cringe, remembering mistaking her for his mother.

'I can imagine.'

She turns from wistful to hurt. 'No, you can't. You can't even begin to imagine. You know, when I was your age, I had men following me around like dogs. All I had to do was throw a stick for them and they'd go racing after it, barking at the top of their voices. They carried my stick back to me between their teeth before sitting up on their hind legs with their tails wagging and their tongues hanging out. Now...' Her voice crackles with bleakness. 'Now, they're laughing at me behind my back. You can't even begin to imagine what that's like.'

I feel sorry for her – how can't I? No wonder she's injecting chemicals to recapture her youth.

The room is turning dark now. Martha is becoming a shadow.

'Listen to me, Lisa. I'm not telling you to leave or asking you to leave; I'm begging you to.' Her tone borders on frantic. 'Pack your bags and go tonight. I've got a couple of hundred pounds downstairs in a bureau; you can have it and move to a hotel if you like. Jack's a great guy, but sometimes he can be…' Her gaze flicks up as if the words she needs are floating in the air. She makes eye contact with me again. 'A bit stubborn if he doesn't get his way. I don't want either of you to feel awkward in my house.'

'So is this your house not his?' I jump in.

I don't need to see the heat rising in her cheeks to know my question has got her blood up. She rises to her feet, her features a twist of strain and fury. 'If you're suggesting that he's only with me for my home and money you're…'

'I'm sorry, Martha. That was uncalled for. I'm just grateful to have a corner of your amazing house.'

She remains on her feet looking unhappily at me. 'We've been together for four years. Just me and Jack, alone in *our* house.'

And the man who was in this room before me, I want to add; I don't.

'It wasn't easy letting another person move in. But his work's been a bit up and down lately, and he doesn't like taking money from me. He wants his independence. So, we agreed to get a lodger so he has another stream of money coming in.' Her expression becomes hooded. 'I'll be truthful with you, I didn't think through what it would be like living with a younger woman in the house with my much younger husband.'

God, she looks so vulnerable. Like I'm about to bash her whole world apart.

I quickly stand, but keep my distance. 'Let me assure you that nothing will ever happen between me and your husband other than the professional relationship between a landlord and his tenant.'

Martha thinks for a moment. 'It's not just you, it's Jack as well. His feelings have been hurt. I don't want there to be a strange atmosphere between you.' She waves her palms. 'Maybe the best thing is still for you to go.'

'Do you know how hard it is to find somewhere to live in one of the most popular cities in the world? I've got a professional job on great wages yet I still can't afford a place of my own. If I leave tonight I'll end up in a hostel, in a room crammed with other people. I can't do that.' I take a breath. 'There's a light at the end of the tunnel for all of us. If it doesn't work out after six months, you don't offer me another lease and I leave. Simple.'

'I'll tell you what I'll do.' Her tone has perked up. 'I'll have a word in Jack's ear and smooth it all over. Yes, that's what I'll do.' The last part was said for her own benefit, accompanied by the balling of her hands. Why was the thought of speaking to her husband making her tighten her hands? Making her so tense?

Martha does that floating walk of hers towards the door. 'Did you know that this was once a servant's room? Can you imagine having to work all hours downstairs and then being worn out at night and having to climb all the way to the top of the house?'

I wanted to answer, '*I know the feeling well; I have to trudge downstairs to the toilet and back again every time.*' I keep it to myself and force my lips to smile.

'Martha, don't worry, everything will work out fine.'

Seven

I wake up in the chilly dark as a sweating heap on the floor, my left leg twisted up on the bed. The knot of the scarf has tightened, the material digging painfully into my ankle. Tears of despair trickle down my face. I feel defeated; the dreams have started again.

Some people get migraines. They know when they're coming and the only answer is to try and avoid trigger factors and take painkillers. When they kick in anyway, the only cure is to lie down in a quiet place and wait for them to pass. I don't suffer from migraines; I suffer from cycles of bad dreams instead. Sometimes these cycles last a few days and sometimes a few weeks. After that they stop for a time, often for months or even years so I think that they're all over for good.

Then they come back with a vengeance. I know when they're coming and what the trigger factors are, but there are no prescription drugs to help, and I can't lie down in a quiet place and wait for them to pass because lying down in a quiet place is when they attack.

The reason I'm frightened is because this house has got 'trigger factor' written all over it.

I've had these dreams for as long as I can remember. As a small child I would wake screaming for my very life and my parents would rush into my bedroom fearing I was being attacked. And I *was* being attacked, but only in the horror films that were rolling in my head. My parents would gather me close, Dad soothing me, Mum silently weeping. During these nightmare cycles, I suffered in the daytime too. That was partly because I was so tired, but also I wasn't entirely sure whether what had happened in my childish imagination hadn't actually happened in the real world. My parents and teachers became so alarmed at my state during these spells that they packed me off to see a child psychologist.

She tried to hide it, but it I saw her puzzlement at my stories of monsters armed with knives, axes, swords, daggers and gigantic needles chasing me round the house trying to kill me. And the pain, God the pain. And the other nightmares, the abstract ones that make no sense at all, filled with changing shapes and colours, closing in on me, carrying death on their coat-tails.

The only way she could find meaning in it was to diagnose me as a disturbed, high-functioning misfit who was probably being bullied. Naturally, she gave my parents and teachers a slightly sanitised version.

My new home is the perfect environment for a cycle of nightmares. By day it's an imposing Victorian pile, but at night it becomes a slightly creepy Gothic mansion you could imagine a vampire taking a nap in. By day it's a quiet place where you can rest or get some work done. At night, there's every kind of noise going on. The woodwork lengthens and shortens, becomes wet and then dries out. That creates creaking that sounds like someone breathing in and out as if the house was alive.

Suicide note.

Jack coming onto me.

Jack and Martha trying to kick me out.

A hostile neighbour.

Martha was right. I should pack and get out.

No. That isn't an option.

I haul myself back into bed again. Loosen the bond on my leg. Reach for my phone and earphones. Press play. Close my eyes. Sink into Amy Winehouse's 'Wake Up Alone'. It's a profoundly sad song but the melody lulls me, soothes me, cleanses away the terror.

My body starts to unwind, my breathing soft and regular. I'm drifting…

But in the darkness, I sense they're waiting for me. Those outsized figures, twice my size, outlined in a recognisably human shape. They're peering in at me through the dormer window and down through the skylight. Hiding behind the closed door of the room. But I know they're there. I see their ghoulish, murdering faces. Knives and needles in both hands. They're waiting. Waiting for me to fall properly asleep so they can steal their way in and deal out death while I twist, turn, bleed and scream for my mum.

With a startled flick of my head I wrest myself from this half-sleep. The earphones are still in my ear. Still woozy, I press play. Amy begins to caress me again. My body drops into the dead weight of relaxation. I sense I will sleep this time.

The murdering figures have gone. But I know they're patient. They'll be back on another night and that night will be soon.

***

I freeze as the first-floor landing creaks beneath my slippers the next morning. Damn! The last thing I want is to wake up Martha and Jack. Not that I'm scared of them. I simply could do without the aggro of a confrontation with the husband. Although I'm praying that Martha was able to reason with him and he'll stop bothering me or holding it against me. I wait a moment. No sounds coming from any of the rooms nearby.

I'm wrung out as I travel on tiptoes down the stairs. I don't know how many hours of sleep I managed to get but it isn't enough. I feel like a zombie. As soon as I reach ground level the smell of bacon hits me. Someone has been up and about. I suspect it's bad boy Jack; I don't associate Martha with bacon, but something a bit more upmarket like smoked salmon and scrambled eggs. I think about peeping in to check the coast is clear... screw it; I am paying good money to live here and am not prepared to creep about like an unwanted ghost. As I walk off, I'm sure I hear a door closing upstairs. No doubt Martha starting her day. Thankfully there's no sign of Jack in the kitchen. I visit the loo and then take a long much-needed shower. Feeling slightly more refreshed, I make a cuppa, some toast and head back out of the kitchen.

I don't go back upstairs; instead I walk into the long lounge with its eggshell-blue walls, marble fireplace and large mirror that makes the room appear twice as big. There's an impressive black piano at the other end. I repeat the same exercise I tried on my first evening here. Close my eyes and concentrate, trying to see if the house has anything to say to me. Then I open my eyes and soak in every feature of the room. But there's nothing.

I do the same in the heart of the house, on the luxurious red and black rug in the hallway. The house isn't saying a word here too. Perhaps I'm too upset to hear these four walls. But it doesn't matter anyway; there'll be plenty of other times. Time is something I've got plenty of. As I climb the stairs, I grin to myself. This house has already said a few things to me without realising it.

As soon as I get into the room, I pull across the bolt on the door and place the chair under the handle. Kick my slippers off, pivot half round and freeze. Tense. Was that a noise? A spine-chilling sensation washes over me. Something, someone, is watching me. Goose pimples push my hair to attention on my covered arms.

I lower my breathing. Don't move a muscle.

There it is again. A slight rustle and a faint clatter of wood like a small stick being run over the floorboards. I turn fully in alarm. My darting gaze finds nothing. There's so little furniture that it's difficult to see how anything can be hiding. I tread softly around the room and that's when I see it. A grey object, like a feather, out of the corner of my eye. Then the faint clatter again.

A shudder of epic revulsion ripples through me. My worst nightmare. A mouse. I cover my mouth, am powerless to move. Its tail is firmly clasped in the metal wire of a trap. It heads towards the blocked-up fireplace but thinks better of it. It tows the trap behind it like a sledge and puffs its desperate way under the bed.

The room is silent. I'm too petrified to cry out. I don't know where it comes from but I've always had a memory of a dead mouse with large dead eyes staring at me. It's almost touching me. For some reason I can't get away. It's going to pounce on me, run its diseased feet and filthy nails over my cringing skin, the tail brushing over my screeching lips. I'm as immobile now as I was in the memory.

I had asked Jack if there were any mice in the house when I came to visit, hadn't I? Scratching under the bed replaces all thoughts of my landlord. It propels me into action. I leap across the room. Boot the chair away from the door and fumble with the handle. I slam the door shut panting, panting and panting. One small creature against big, old me? I know it's stupid, but I can't handle it.

'Ja…' I begin to bellow. I suck it back despite the crippling fear.

I know he'll be able to sort this out, but the last thing I need is a touchy-feely man in my room again.

Then again, I can't spend all morning hyperventilating with terror outside my room either; I need to get to work. It crosses my mind that If I get a broom I can shoo it out onto the landing where it can take its chances until Jack arrives – Martha's probably too frail to deal with it. Or even better, my little visitor might have made its escape and be gone by the time I get back in. They're little Houdinis these things, so I'm hoping.

When I return, armed with a broom from the cupboard under the stairs, I carefully open the door and slip inside with my back to the wall. I go down on my hands and knees and peer under the bed. My little friend is still in hiding. It makes no movement as I stare at it. Perhaps the mouse is too scared to move, just as afraid of me as I am of it. I'm seized with horror as I lock with its eyes. Wide open, as terrified as mine.

My old memory comes storming back. Large dead mouse eyes staring back at me. I scream and scream and scream.

There's a commotion on the landing below and the thump of heavy boots on the stairs before the door flies open and Jack storms in.

He looks down at me and is curt. 'What's the matter with you? Oh, right – it's a mouse is it?'

I struggle to my feet, angrily pulling my arm away when he tries to help. 'You told me you didn't have a mouse problem.'

He looks both innocent and contemptuous at the same time. 'Did I? I don't remember that. Of course there's mice in this house. Loads of them. This is a Victorian house, babe, you try finding one in this city that doesn't have them.' He takes the broom out of my hand. 'Now, where is the little blighter? Ah yes, there he is. Hey, what do you know? He's got his tail stuck in a trap. That should slow him down a bit.'

With a sweep of the broom the mousetrap, with the mouse still attached, comes spinning out from under the bed. I jump back in petrified panic, holding my palm flat against my furiously beating heart. Jack picks up the trap and holds it at shoulder height. My mouth twists in disgust. He presses it towards me with the mouse suspended underneath by its tail, desperately trying to turn itself the right way up. I can't tell if Jack is trying to torment the animal or me. Probably both. He can tell how upset I am.

'What are you doing that for?' I croak. Seething heat enters my voice. 'Do you get a kick out of being cruel to animals? Take him out front and let him go.'

Jack tuts. 'Can't do that, what if he comes back?'

I've had it up to here with this moron. 'You put it in my room, didn't you?'

'You what?' he replies scornfully. 'Stop talking bollocks. The missus has told me point blank to stay out of your way and that's what I was doing until you decided to bring the roof down as if Freddy Krueger's in town.'

I don't believe a word of it. How else would a mouse stuck to a trap have got to the top of the house? He probably caught the live mouse somewhere else before pegging it on to the trap and leaving it in my room for me to find. It's a piece of grotesque theatre by him against me.

That must've been the sound I heard upstairs when I reached the ground floor: him creeping out of his bedroom with the mouse and then creeping up to my room. What a bastard!

With a sound of disgust ringing from his lips Jack disappears from the room, but a few minutes later he returns with the mouse still on the trap in one hand and what looks like a length of lead piping in the other. Very carefully, he puts the helpless mouse back down on the floorboards. He gives me a look with a glint in his eye before raising the pipe and bringing it down with unspeakable violence. The animal is not so much killed as obliterated. It's a tangled mush of fur and flesh with drops of blood scattered around on the white painted boards.

I gasp in both horror and anger.

'What did you that for? Why didn't you let it go?'

'Kindest thing to do, Lisa…'

He takes a plastic bag and brushes the remains into it along with the trap. He gets to his feet and gives me a beady look which I know is not so much cruelty or baiting as an implied threat.

I say nothing but give him an angry look of defiance as he leaves.

When he's gone, I go to the bathroom – *their* bathroom – and fetch a sponge. I scrub and scrub and scrub until every trace of the tiny drops of animal blood and fur have been erased from the white floorboards.

Eight

I hover, pace, hover some more, then make myself still in front of the door to Doctor Wilson's studio. All that dithering has made me ten minutes late for our first appointment. I really can't face it. Shrinks, therapists, head doctors. They don't work for me. Worst still, a session with one can tumble me backwards into the dark side where only frightening things await, control slipping out of my clawing fingers.

I take a breath that fills up the empty cavern of my chest. Remind myself I'm doing this for Mum and Dad, sort of like an early Christmas present for them. Grin and bear it is the name of the game. No doubt the good doctor is a great guy, a leading light of his profession by the sound of it, but I know he can't help me. He can't. No one can now.

Except for me.

I don't know why Wilson calls his consulting rooms his 'studio' – he's supposed to be a psychiatrist not a rock star. Perhaps it's the trendy new word that shrinks use for the places they do business in. His *studio* is in upmarket Hampstead, housed in a pretty detached cottage. The Mercedes parked out front roars big money. I guess his client list must include messed-up millionaires, poor little rich kids and the like.

Even after I've rung the buzzer, that need to bolt tugs, won't let go. But Wilson is too quick for me; the door is confidently pulled back before I know it.

Despite my unease, I nearly burst out laughing. He's the image of Sigmund Freud: close-cut hair, neatly trimmed grey beard. Even his glasses look like pince-nez. The image bursts when he opens his mouth. He speaks the Queen's English, doesn't have a German accent.

'Lisa? It's a pleasure to meet you.' He has one of those deep, careful voices, the type where every word is considered before it leaves his mouth.

It's a Saturday morning, so the reception and waiting room are deserted and we're here on our own. He asks me a few questions about my parents' health as we go; it seems he hasn't seen them for a while. In his consulting room, I have to hold back the laughter again. He has a psychiatrist's couch, the real deal. Very expensive – gleaming in fact – upholstered jet-black leather.

'You've got a couch.' I can't stop myself from sharing my disbelief.

He doesn't take offence, instead smiles warmly, lines creasing at the corners of his eyes. 'Some of my clients seem to expect one and I don't like to disappoint. Try if it you like. Or, if you prefer, there's a perfectly good chair over here.'

I can't stop myself. I climb on board the couch like it's a fairground ride. Settle in, lean back and sink into the comfort of its welcoming texture. I might appear as snug as a bug, but I want to get this done ASAP so I refuse his offer of tea, coffee or bottled water.

Before I know it he's in his own chair, fingers woven together in his lap. 'Do you mind if I record some of what we share today?'

I shake my head. What does it matter what he writes down? I know what questions he's going to ask and I'm ready to rattle the answers off and then go. I do worry, though, that I might lose the run of myself while I'm going through my story by numbers.

He starts: Can I tell him something about myself?

No problem. I reel off my prepared CV.

I'm a nice middle-class girl from Surrey, an only child who grew up in idyllic surroundings with loving and stable parents who provided me with everything. Totally everything. I excelled at whatever I did at a private school that described itself as 'outstanding' in its prospectus. I became one of those rare girls who go on to study maths at university before moving into high-end software work in the financial sector. I rose up the ranks fast. I'm disciplined, focused and hard-working. I don't have any real friends, but hey, who needs them? I've had one proper boyfriend. Yes, one, that's right. I've never been abused – so don't go down that road – and I've never taken drugs or had any substance or addiction issues. That's it. That's me.

I notice he's making a lot of notes, far more than are justified by what I've revealed. It occurs to me that perhaps he's just making a shopping list. Perhaps he's no more eager to waste his Saturday morning talking to me than I am talking to him. Perhaps he's just doing it to humour my parents. Then I remember he's a friend of my dad's so he may well know more about me than he's letting on. My fingertips dig into the leather.

'I see.'

A two-word comment is not what I expect from him. Follow-up questions surely. He asks none. He finishes making notes.

Without thinking about the implications, voice bitter and hoarse, I almost yell, 'I need to make one thing clear straight from the gate. I'm not mad, OK? I'm not mad.'

Where had that come from? The 'M' word was the last thing I wanted planting roots during our session.

The doctor's gentle smile is there again. 'I think you'll find, Lisa, that there are very few members of my profession who use the word "mad" these days. And if there are, they should be struck off.' He sighs slightly and studies what he's written. 'Your father mentioned something happened four months ago, an incident, that he thought you might want to discuss. Is that right?'

It would be typical of my dad to refer to what had happened as an 'incident'. A blip. Almost as if it's something everyone does at one time or the other.

I lift one shoulder. 'If you like.'

'It's not what I like, Lisa, it's what you like.'

I suppose we're going to have to discuss this. 'Sure, let's talk about the "incident".'

'Do you want to tell me what happened?'

I don't want to but I do anyway. I take a deep breath that's audible in the room; I don't want my voice to tremble. I can't stop the coldness that covers my skin. I detach myself. Start talking as if I'm delivering a report.

'Well, I suppose I'd been feeling a bit low and I'd got some pills for it. I'd had a really bad night. I've had cycles of bad dreams every so often since I was a kid, and I was at the end of one of those cycles of nightmares. I hadn't slept at all, so I took the day off work. At lunchtime, I helped myself to a vodka to cheer myself up along with some of the various pills in my medicine cabinet. And then I took some more and washed them down with more vodka. Then some more and then some more. I don't really know what I was doing, really. I was exhausted and very rattled by my dreams. I suppose I must have passed out. I was found on the bathroom floor. The next thing I know I'm down the hospital getting my stomach pumped.' Now comes the hard bit. 'They – the hospital, Mum and Dad, especially Dad – decided it was a suicide attempt.'

I feel the ghost of the faceless man who wrote the farewell letter lie down on the coach next to me. It's not uncomfortable, almost as if he's giving me strength.

The doctor is still making copious notes. 'And was it?'

'Was it what?'

'A suicide attempt?'

I sigh and think about the question. 'I don't know really. Maybe it was. My parents certainly seem to think so. Now I have to check in and visit every so often to prove that I'm not dead.'

'Have you contemplated suicide in the past?'

I close my eyes. It's a difficult question to answer but I do my best. 'Not... exactly. But sometimes I just wish I wasn't here, you know? Perhaps I should have mentioned I suffered from an eating disorder in my teens. I think sometimes that was just an attempt to disappear, to go away somewhere. From time to time, I just wish death would come along and sweep me away to a Shangri-La of peace and quiet. A place where bad dreams are banned. You know, what it says on Victorian gravestones: "Where the wicked cease from troubling and the weary are at rest".'

The doctor shares a new smile. 'That's the Bible, the Book of Job.'

'Poor old Job. I sympathise with him.'

'Have you had any professional help with your problems over the years?'

'Yeah, loads.' Truth be told I could write a book on it. 'Even when I was messed up in junior school my doctor dad was trying to work out what was wrong with me and consulting his friends in your profession. My parents were at their wits' end so they sent me to see a child psychologist. Nice lady. Always wore Vivienne Westwood skirts. She asked me if I was being bullied by the other children and I said I wasn't. So she decided it was bullying that was causing it even though I'd just told her I wasn't being bullied.' I glance sideways at him. 'No one can help me, I'm afraid.'

'What about your father? What does he think?'

'My… father?' I utter slowly. My mind flashes back to my parents' garden. Dad pushing me tenderly on the swing.

'Yes,' Doctor Wilson continues softly. 'You said he tried to help when you were very young. You mention him more than your mother. He's also a highly distinguished doctor with many friends in the field. So I'm wondering what his opinion is? Has he given you one?'

I'm silent. I wasn't expecting this. I'm also acutely conscious of the fact that my parents have never in my life been disloyal to me and I don't want to be disloyal to them. Especially my beloved dad. Like all children, I find my parents irritating from time to time but they've never stabbed me in the back. I've already edited my story to avoid appearing disloyal and I don't want to start now. I try to think of something to say but disloyalty seems to lie in every direction.

Abruptly, I sit up and swing my legs over the side of the couch. 'I'm sorry doctor, I've got to go.'

His face is a picture of empathy. 'Of course, if you wish.'

'I've wasted your time.'

'Not at all.'

I stand up. I'm a little unsteady on my feet and I'm avoiding Doctor Wilson's X-ray gaze. I have wasted his time. If I were one of his mixed-up millionaires he would've earned a couple of thousand out of our little chat. Instead, he's seen me on his free Saturday as a favour to my mum and dad and made nothing out of it. And now I'm walking just when things were getting interesting. As I creep towards the door, I ask him if he can do something for me.

'Of course.'

'I'm really grateful for you giving up your time, really I am, but I'm not coming here anymore.'

'I understand.'

I'm still avoiding his eyes. 'I was wondering if, when you bump into my dad again or speak to him on the phone, whether perhaps you could tell him I'm still coming for these sessions? It would make him and Mum relax, you know, feel more at ease. Stop worrying.'

Doctor Wilson smiles sympathetically. 'That wouldn't be very ethical of me, Lisa. I mean ethical in the personal sense rather than professional. Look, why don't you sit down again for a moment?'

I sit on the edge of the couch.

'These sessions aren't about your parents or me and my time or anyone doing anyone favours. They're meant to be about helping you. If you think by coming to see me it will help then come again next Saturday. I'll be here at the same time next week regardless. I always have plenty of work to get on with anyway.'

'I don't think you can help me.' My voice trembles for the first time in our session.

'Possibly not. But I have a lot of experience of these issues so possibly I can. I'd say something else too. You can't betray anyone by honestly telling me what's in your heart or in your head.'

I don't know what he means by that. Whatever, it makes no difference. I'm not coming back but I still say, 'I'll think about it.'

Doctor Wilson escorts me back through the building and out onto the doorstep.

As he opens the door, I face him. 'I used to feel like I was frozen in time. Couldn't move forward.'

'Used to?' He looks at me quizzically. 'You said "used to". Has something changed?'

'Goodbye, doctor.' I take a step outside. Turn back to him. 'Sometimes I think I'm living someone else's life. That this isn't the life I was meant to have.'

Before he can answer, I scurry down the street like an escaping thief.

Nine

People rush past me as they leave the tube station, their feet moving in that well-known London rhythm. I can't get home fast enough. Compared to them I'm sluggish; the muscles in my legs appear to have been replaced by stones. I'm tired. God, I'm exhausted. An invisible hand has pulled my plug. It's not work that's wiped me out, it's the farewell letter I found.

'To whom it may concern.'

It's the last thing I think of before I mercifully find sleep and the first to greet the start of my day. I can't give the man the rest he'd begged for. Maybe it's my own brush with trying to end my life – or whatever that traumatic incident was – I don't know, but I can't leave my invisible roommate alone. Obsessive. That's what one of my past therapists called my personality. Once something takes root in my head I can't let go. It grows and grows until I'm sure my mind's not my own. Now I've got a dead man queuing up with all my other problems.

It's been almost a week since the mouse incident. Martha came to my room to apologise and to assure me that Jack would never do the horrible thing I was accusing him of. Funny, she seemed to have her eyes wide open about her husband's infidelity but not much else. I'd let her say her piece, hadn't argued and had shown her to the door. I hadn't seen Jack and that's the way I want to keep it. As long as he doesn't try any more stunts we'll rub along fine.

Another commuter brushes, none too gently, against me. I pick up my pace as I move down the high street. Turn the corner onto the street where my new home awaits me. As I get closer, I see Martha and Jack's neighbour pruning roses in her front garden. I haven't seen her since our unforgettable meeting when she'd accused me of laughing with Martha and Jack about her garden. Jack claimed it was the rambling of a mad woman. I can't help wincing. Mad is such a nasty word. A label that sticks for life.

What is clear is there's certainly no love lost between her and my landlord and lady.

What if…?

I walk with renewed purpose to reach her.

She stops clipping and gives me the evil eye. The corners of her mouth sag with sour displeasure. Her summer trousers and earth-smeared shirt are baggy against her small frame and, despite the warm weather, she still wears her woolly hat with the knitted flower. Age has taken its inevitable toll on her face, but there's no sign she's lost her marbles, as Jack so eloquently put it, in her sharp brown eyes.

'I'm Lisa,' I introduce myself, rustling up a lengthy smile.

She doesn't smile back. In fact, there's now a twist to her mouth and brows that communicates her irritation.

An insistent meow takes me by surprise. I look down to find a tiger-striped, well-fed tabby wearing a collar and silver name tag rubbing itself against the woman's leg. There's another tabby behind, the pattern of its fur blotched and swirling, snatching its paw back and forth as it plays in the dirt.

'Betty.' My new neighbour addresses the cat attached to her leg. 'Stop being such a mummy's boy.' Her voice is full of affection. 'Go and play with Davis.'

Betty and Davis. Ah, Bette Davis. The cat's name ends with an 'e' no doubt. The cat purrs as it slinks away, curling itself up on the flagstone tiled path as if the idea of frolicking in the dirt is too scandalous to contemplate.

'What do you want?' the woman says, glowering, her eyes narrow.

'I've just moved in next door.'

A grunt of disdain comes from the back of her throat. 'One of their lot, are you?'

'Their what?'

'Friends.' She spits it out like it's the most poisonous word in the world. I'm surprised the roses don't wither and die. 'I thank you kindly, missy, for having the good manners no doubt your mother bred in you to take the time to say good day, but if you see me again, I would appreciate it if you just went on your merry way.' Her pruning scissors click shut by her side.

'No.' I rush to enlighten her. 'They're not my friends. I'm just renting a room at the top of the house.'

The skin on her face relaxes, sagging further, as she takes her time assessing me anew.

'Well, if I was you,' she growls with volume, no doubt hoping it's loud enough for her neighbours to hear, 'I'd have a bottle of holy water on hand to deal with the evil of those two.'

I lower my voice, hoping that will be enough for her to take the hint I'd rather not draw Jack and Martha's attention to me speaking to her. 'You don't get on with them?'

Bette is back, caressing its owner's leg. 'I think you mean *they* don't get on with *me*. I've lived on this street for sixty odd years, since I was a little girl. This house belonged to Papa and Momma and one day it will be passed on to my grandchildren.' Her mouth does its familiar twist. 'Although, the way my Lottie's bunch have been eyeing me lately, it seems like they're willing me to meet my maker any day now. Cheeky bloody young people. Told Lottie she should've taken the strap to the lot of them years ago. If they're not careful I'll leave it all to Bette and Davis.'

I can imagine how that will play out in her family. A mega court battle, feline versus human.

'Umm… I didn't catch your name.'

'Because I didn't throw it,' is the snap response. Then her creased face lightens up as she gives me a crafty smile. 'That's what we told the boys back in my day. I might've loved a good old dance at the Palais or in Soho but I was not fast and loose with the elastic of my knickers.'

My lips twitch at that. This lady has real character. I like that.

There's now a twinkle in her eye. 'The name's Patricia or Patsy. Never Trish though. Knew a Trish once; had a voice like a foghorn and a devious character that should've sunk with the *Titanic*.' She glares back up at the house. 'She would've fit in with those two like three monkeys stuffing their faces with bananas on a branch.'

'Patsy.' I decide to get chummy with her. 'What happened between you and Martha and Jack?'

'I'll show you.' She moves briskly towards the front door.

I can't believe my luck. I quickly follow with the cats purring close behind. She leads the way through a hallway that's full and fussy with a wooden wall table and Victorian-style coat and hat stand, walls jam-packed with family portraits and more modern photos of smiling children, no doubt who grew up to be adults who can't wait to get their hands on her house. We end up in the back and it's not a kitchen, like next door, but a cosy conservatory bursting with summer light. Patsy opens the French doors and gestures with her hand at the garden. It's an eye-grabbing confection of flowers of all colours, butterflies and bees. The scent of the blooms is strong. A blue and grey mosaic table with matching chairs sits by the door and in the far corner is a bench shaded under a fig tree. What a serene place.

But why has she brought me here?

Seeing the question and frown on my face, she moves close to me. Whispers, 'Even the trees in the garden have ears.' She points with a crooked finger and winks to the fence that borders Martha's and Jack's.

'I've played in this garden since I was this high.' She places a hand just above her knee. All her fingers appear slightly bent; a classic symptom of chronic arthritis. 'A couple of months back, his lordship in there shows me street plans that claim – *claim* – the bottom of my garden belongs to their house. These so-called plans show that their garden doesn't stop at the bottom but includes a considerable stretch of land all the way along the back, past all the houses, right to the bottom of the street.' She scoffs. 'What do they need more garden for, eh? He's out there all hours of the day and night, doing what? Their garden's a bloody disgrace.'

I think of Jack grabbing my hand roughly as I tried to go into the garden on my first visit to see the room. Martha claims he's just a touch territorial. But is it more than that? Has he got something to hide?

There's a tremor in Patsy's voice now. 'The bastards took my back fence down one night when I was away visiting my daughter for the weekend. Cowards.' Tears glisten in her eyes. 'The police said there's naff all they can do about it. I'm not like the others on this street who have caved in.' I can almost hear the creak as her back stiffens with resolve. 'They are not getting away with it. I'm taking them to court, all the way to the Bailey if I have to.'

I don't have the heart to tell her that the Old Bailey tries murder cases.

'My lawyer, my nephew, is here at this very moment writing up the notes on our meeting on his laptop. Well, he's not my nephew really. I've been a friend of his grandmother's since we were young girls out on the town. Which reminds me, I need to make him a nice cup of tea before he sets off.'

That surprises me. I hadn't sensed anyone else was in the house.

As she potters around the kitchen I commiserate with her over her troubles. And I do feel huge sympathy for her; it can't be easy losing part of your home. However, I must focus on what I came to speak to her about.

'Do you remember any of the people or families who lived next door?'

Patsy tips a spoonful of fragrant tea leaves into the teapot. 'Course I do. There were the Latimers, Morrises, Patels.' A solitary bony finger rubs against her lips as she searches her mind. 'Ah yes, the Warrens. Christ Almighty, the kids were like wild animals. Should've been behind bars at London Zoo. The Peters. The Mitzes. Or was that across the road? I get a bit mixed up sometimes.'

Before she gets into a proper muddle I ask, 'Do you know if they had a tenant in their house before I came?'

Patsy looks confused as she stirs the tea in the china teapot. Her expression settles as her mind ticks over my question. 'I think there was one. Yes, a man. I didn't see him much...' Her voice trails away as her threadbare brows surge together.

'I remember seeing him from my bedroom window, roaming the garden like a prisoner walking the yard. You know, like he had the troubles of the world pressing down on both shoulders. Never caught his face.' Her tiny teeth worry her bottom lip as she puts the lid on the teapot.

My jubilation at finding out there was a previous tenant nosedives when the older woman adds, 'Mind you, Queen Bee in her brass castle had blokes coming in and out of her place like it was Piccadilly Circus. All times of the night as well. It only stopped when she got her hooks into that dumb toy boy she parades around on her arm.' Her tongue clucks in disgust. 'Fancy a woman her age taking up with a young lad like that. Her fanny better be topped up with Botox because getting between the sheets with her isn't going to be a pretty sight.'

I can't stop the laughter gurgling out of me this time. It feels good. So good. I can't remember the last time I pushed my head back and roared with joy.

Patsy beckons me close with the crook of her finger. Her breath warms my cheek. 'There definitely was a man there. Already living there when she dragged that Jack indoors with her. I don't recall when he moved out.'

So Jack had been lying to me. Why would he do that? If a tenant had killed himself in the house Jack wouldn't get into trouble with the authorities. What was he covering up? Did it have something to do with the garden? Question after question swirls with the destructiveness of a hurricane in my mind. One after another, backing up, demanding an instant answer.

Faster, faster, faster.

Breathe. Just breathe.

One, two, buckle my shoe.
Three, four…

I can't slow down. Can't. The sharp teeth of desperation sink into my nerves. Where are my pills? Bollocks. They're in the house. In my room. Sweat beads along my hairline. Vertebra after vertebra freezes until my spine is a column of ice. The bottom of my feet hurt along their familiar lines of pain. I'm shaking. Trembling. Seams falling apart.

Patsy stares at me, wide-eyed with concern, the same way that Mum does.

A man's professional voice breaks through my suffering from the kitchen doorway. 'I've written a comprehensive account of…' He abruptly stops as his gaze finds me. 'Lisa?'

Seeing him should tip me over the edge. Instead my control slips back into place.

'Alex?'

Ten

The problem with the past is sometimes it has a nasty habit of headbutting its way in to your future. Me and my once-upon-a-time boyfriend stare at each other. It's uncomfortable. Neither of us knows what to say.

Patsy's inquisitive gaze darts from Alex to me, back to Alex. She makes no comment except, 'I've made a lovely pot of white tea, Alex. My friend always brings me gorgeous white tea back from Sri Lanka. When you're ready…'

Bette and Davis prowl excitedly after her as she leaves us alone.

We just stand there, staring. I'm drinking him in. God knows what thoughts are going through his mind as he assesses me. Alex is neatly turned out as usual – slim-fitting charcoal suit, black tie, snowy-white shirt. I wonder if he still wears odd socks.

'Don't want to be a member of the herd,' was his cheerful explanation.

Alex breaks the booming silence. 'Lisa, what are you doing here?' There's a wow-wonder sound in his voice, as if he thinks I've been conjured up by a magic trick.

I wrap my arms protectively round my middle. 'I live next door.'

I have no idea why I'm telling him this; we'd finished nearly six months ago and that's how I wanted to keep it.

We'd met by pure chance at the end of last year. He was part of a team from a high-powered city bank representing a Russian client with very deep pockets who was doing business with my firm. I hadn't noticed Alex at first; I was too busy doing my usual practice of working myself to the bone at my computer. He came to my attention on his third visit when two of the women who worked beside me decided to rope me into their 'look at what's just waltzed through the door' whispered gossip-fest.

'Nice buns, hun,' Cheryl had remarked with all the lip-licking yumminess of eating the best meal in town. 'He's only thirty, I hear.'

'And that height,' Debbie cooed, no thought to being a married woman. 'I wouldn't mind climbing that. What do you think, Lisa? Would you let him become your tree?'

I'd tried to ignore what I considered to be two grown women tittering away with the hormonal overload of adolescent schoolgirls. Besides, my number one rule at work was to do exactly that – work. Colleagues were acquaintances not friends. Friends inevitably drifted away. They never said it, but it was there after a while, imprinted in their disbelieving eyes. *Your weirdness we can do without.* But the women wouldn't leave me alone until I was forced to look at wonder man.

I surprised myself by being riveted. It wasn't his looks, his bum, his climb-me quality. It was the way he threw his head back, ever so slightly, and laughed. I have a weakness for men who love a laugh. Laughter makes you forget, puts your troubles behind you, at least for a time.

Later that day, lunchtime, we'd taken the lift down together.

'I'm Alex,' he surprised me by saying. 'You're one of the software crowd.'

I blushed hot and deep. Men didn't notice me; my neck-to-toe clothing put them off. Who was it who said you needed to put something on display in the window to get a man's attention? Well, my window had the blinds down and curtains swished across.

Somehow – who knew how it happened – I ended up showing him one of the more memorable lunch haunts. He wouldn't take no for an answer when he insisted I ate with him, the corners of his eyes crinkled with smile lines as he persuaded me. Over two plates of hummus, baby spinach salad and warmed, wholemeal pitta bread, we'd got to know each other. And that's how it had started, to Cheryl and Debbie's open-mouthed, catty astonishment: three months of dinners, cocktails, movies, Alex teaching me to laugh again. Of course, I knew that the problems would start with taking things to the next level: discovering each other in bed. At the age of twenty-five I'd never laid my body bare to a man. It was my secret shame I kept hidden for my eyes only. Nevertheless, I decided that Alex was The One.

I force myself back to the present. That night is what makes me push past him and stride out of Patsy's house. And walk away. I don't need to be told that he's my neighbour's lawyer who is helping her get back her slice of England's green and pleasant land.

'Lisa,' he urgently calls after me from the front door.

I shut his words out as I shove the key into Martha and Jack's lock. Slam the door. Wish I hadn't when I remember the last thing I need is to alert the landlords that I'm back. I remain where I am, listening. Then I hear the door to Patsy's front door close.

I'm glad that Alex didn't come after me, I convince myself. Then why do I feel so achingly bad?

I rush upstairs, down two of my pills and lie on the bed.

***

The first thing I hear when I enter the house two days later is raised voices. Or rather a single voice. It doesn't sound like a man or a woman, it simply sounds like cutting anger. I can't make out what's being said, being shouted. I don't want to either. I grew up in a home where there were never any open displays of anger. No confrontations. If my parents had an issue they needed to discuss – never problems, Dad insisted, always issues – they would close themselves in his study and talk it through. Even the worst disturbances of my childhood were conducted in hush-hush tones.

Crack!

The vicious sound jumps me back to the present. That was the slap of flesh on flesh. That bastard had hit Martha. I waver, not sure what to do. I could go storming along the hallway, fling open the door to the kitchen and rip his head off. Or… I think and think. Confronting Jack could make things worse for Martha. Also, do I intervene when I'm living in their house? How far do you get involved in the personal lives of others when you're a guest – albeit a paying one – within the four walls of their home? Because this isn't really my home, it's theirs. Their space. I'm the interloper here.

Still, I feel crap about my decision as I tramp up the stairs. What does a cultured, elegant woman like Martha see in a violent Neanderthal like Jack? I bet he was all sweetness and light at the start of their romance, whispering sweet nothings, bombarding her with gifts. Then, as soon as he's got a ring on her finger and has his boots well and truly planted in her super expensive house, he shows his true thuggish colours.

I reach the top floor and my steps drag. After the incident with the mouse and its bloody finale, I think I can see and hear the little grey bastards everywhere, so I want to give advance warning to them that I'm coming. A loud knock on the door, stamping my feet on the floorboards, that sort of thing, so they run for cover if they have the nerve to be around. I'm still on the fence about Martha's explanation that Jack didn't put the mouse there to freak me out.

I turn the handle and cautiously remain on the threshold, watching. My blood thrums wildly through my veins as I check out the room. Everything seems to be in its place. No odd sounds. Still, pulse quickening, I go on an intense search of every nook and cranny. I straighten with relief when I find nothing out of the ordinary. Or, as Mum would put it, everything's ship-shape and Bristol fashion.

As I walk towards the bed there's a strange tearing sound behind me. My terror alert dials frantically up to ten. The air shakes out of my slack-jawed mouth. My gaze kicks sideways to the door. I want to run. Get out of there while I can. I don't want to deal with *whatever* this is.

My breath lodges in my throat as I turn ever so slowly. Look down at the floor. I frown. There's nothing there. The noise comes again, drawing my attention to the wall on the far side, under the skylight. My gaze quickly goes up. Ah, there's the problem. The finger of damp that had once pointed towards the wall has expanded and now looks more like an outspread and webbed hand. The damp from the rain has caused the white lining wallpaper, near the dormer window, to peel back and flop partially down. Underneath is beige-coloured wallpaper with the imprint of a tiny raised flower. The type of showy stuff modern telly makeover shows insist is a no-no.

Bloody Jack! He's supposed to be some kind of handyman, isn't he? He should know better than anyone how destructive water can be to a property. Perhaps he's hoping he'll have driven me out by the time the top floor starts to collapse.

I could go downstairs and tell Martha this time. No, she wouldn't want to see me after what I heard happening downstairs.

Instead I try to fix it. Well, temporarily at least. I jump up and try to slap the paper back into place. Dismal failure. As it flops back down it unpeels even further. Suddenly the hairs stand to attention on the back of my neck – there are black markings on the wall.

I step closer. Peer harder. Is it writing? Yes, it is.

Neat handwriting. Black ink. It's smudged in places by the damp and some has disappeared on the back of the lining paper. But it's clear enough. Or at least it would be if it were in English. It's in a script. Alphabet would be the correct term, I suppose. I don't think I've seen it before, although there's something familiar about it. There's an ancient quality to the shapes and the lines of the letters.

Is this the work of the man who wrote the farewell letter?

I hurry to retrieve the letter from under my pillow where I keep it with my scarf. Once I'm facing the wall again, I hold the letter up to compare it. Both sets of handwriting look like dead ringers to me. I'm no language expert, but the pencilled message at the bottom of the letter looks like it's written in the same language as the writing on the wall. I realise the writing on the wall triggered my memory of this line in the letter.

The wallpaper is cold, almost wet, to my touch as I gently peel the rest down. I can't help but hold my breath – the writing goes right down to the skirting board. I step back slightly, the same way I do when I view a great piece of art in a gallery to properly view the line, tone, colour, background and foreground. I can't tear my eyes away from the writing. It's like the graffiti of a condemned prisoner awaiting execution in his death-row cell. Is this what this room became to my nameless man? A cell? A place where the only freedom was through death?

I'm chilly and sweaty at the same time. Cold and heat. I can't stop shaking. I reach out to touch his words… snatch my hand back. What if I accidentally rub some of the writing away? Lose a vital part of the story?

I make myself turn my back. Get practical. I need to move fast here. At the rate the rain's coming down, this find could all be gone in hours. I'm rather like an archaeologist whose dig has uncovered something important while the diggers are waiting to move in. Or, perhaps more likely, a detective whose crime scene is about to be disturbed.

***

I go back downstairs. Leave the house. Walk and walk in the now spitting rain until I find the high street. It takes me about ten minutes of checking the names on the fronts of shops until I find the hardware store. I leave armed with a box containing a lightweight folding ladder, adhesive and a door chain. The box is awkward to carry but I manage to get it back to the house.

I don't stick the wallpaper back into place straight away; instead I pace. I need to get the writing translated. What about an app on my phone? I spend the next hour going through all manner of language apps but nothing suits my purpose.

I know I'm becoming too obsessive but I can't help it. Don't want to help it. I pop a couple of pills to slow my mind way down as I think. Who can I ask to be my translator? Who do I know who might recognise this language? I scroll through names.

I slump on the bed when I realise who's the obvious person to ask.

Hell! I don't want to ask this person, but what choice do I have?

Eleven

Amy's 'Back To Black' is my go-to, get-me-to-sleep music of choice tonight. I dance round and round the room, the sassy rhythm pumping loudly through my earphones. I soak up the breathless beat, my jim-jams tugging against my skin as I flail my arms and legs in all directions, willing my body to exhaustion so once I hit the pillow I'll sink into a world of blank oblivion.

When the music ends, I stretch and arch my back, a light sweat coating my face. Run my fingers through my short cut. Weariness shakes inside me. Good. I allow a small smile to curve my lips. Not giving the tiredness a chance to flee, I skip over to the door to check my new chain. Test the handle. Safe for the night.

In the dark I tie my leg to the end of the bed and then fall onto my back. And wait for sleep to claim me. I focus on breathing.

One, two, buckle my shoe.

Three, four, knock at the door...

I stare at the writing on the wall. Hypnotised. Can't look away. The author has a strong hand. Each letter energetic; bold strokes. Such funny shapes. Such jagged, edged lines. A patchwork woven in the deepest black ink. I reach out to touch its upright, elegant beauty. I gasp as it starts to grow. Big and threatening. Its lines stretch into long, long legs. Its shapes swell into mouths with sharp teeth that transform into gigantic knives. It jumps off the wall, out at me. I scream. Try to run away. Too late. A blade slashes me in the back. I fall. Agonising pain rips through me. I beg for mercy. The knife is a huge needle now heading for my face...

I slam upright in bed, breathing horribly. I jam my hands protectively over my face. Nothing happens. My hands fall

71

cautiously back in welcome relief. Just another crappy dream. At least I'm still in the room, leg tied to the bed.

Something brushes against my cheekbone. Instinctively my hand comes up to wave it away. Maybe I imagined it. There's a funny, low-level irritating sound that my ears don't like. I ignore it. Something dive-bombs against my forehead. Something crawls in my hair. Another in the inside of my ear. Panic grips me as I desperately wave my arms madly around and jump off the bed. Except I cry out in pain as the top half of me tumbles upside down to the floor, the rest of me still tangled on the bed where my foot remains tied.

I pant and pant as I lunge forward; I shift on my bum until I reach the end of the bed. With shaking, desperate fingers I untie the scarf. Jump up. Now I hear them. A buzzing roar all around me. I can't see them as I stand alone in the dark. Shock holds me in place. I cry out as they twitch against my face, back in my hair, up the legs of my pyjamas.

One squiggles and buzzes on my bottom lip. I knock it off with fury and spit in the air. I hate creepy-crawlies, with their legs, hair and wings. My terror rises. I need to get out of here. Now.

I don't even think to put the light on as I rush to the door. They're there waiting for me too. Buzzing, touching. Are they eating their way into my skin?

Open the door. Get the fucking door open. NOW. My hands pat against the wood, searching for the handle. I find it. Turn. Nothing happens. I frantically pull. And pull. It won't budge. Why won't it open? I don't understand. It's a door; its function is to open.

I turn around. Lean my tense back flat against the door. There's nothing for it – I will have to face the horror in my room.

Click. I switch on the light.

Disbelief locks me tight.

Swarming. Round black bodies; manic-moving wings swarming all over the room. A black cloud turning this way and that. Disgust heaves in my belly. I fight not to chuck up. How did they get in here?

Is this the latest dirty trick from psycho Jack? It's that thought that makes me calm down. I refuse to let him run me out.

I woman-up. Face the door and see the chain. In my panic I'd completely forgotten that I'd bought it; no wonder the door had refused to open. I reach for it, but my hand freezes. If I open the door, screaming for help, that will give Jack a smug satisfaction I won't let him have. Not again. He'll see me practically on my knees begging for help. Screw that!

I drive the terror down somewhere deep and stare dispassionately at my new roommates. I suspect they're nasty blowflies which means there's something dead in the room. I can't stop the ripple of chilling dread that shivers all over me, bringing goosebumps to the surface. I know what I have to do. I'm going to have to find the dead thing.

My gaze darts around the room; I'm thinking where it might be. Chest of drawers? Wardrobe? Under the bed where the mouse had hidden? Desk? That's when I notice a few flies bursting out of the small fireplace. Now I know where they are coming from. There's nothing for it. I'm going to have to rush right into them.

I don't think about it, just do. I gag as their bodies bombard me as I drop to my knees in front of the fireplace. I push back the lid on the fireplace.

I screech as the dead body of a pigeon falls out. I fall back on my bottom. The flies are going crazy. The dead bird is a sickening sight. Much of its body appears plucked of its feathers, its colour the ripe pink of rot and… maggots. My gag reflex kicks into gear again. I cover my mouth as I stumble to my feet. I get the skylight open so they can literally start buzzing off. Next, I take the carrier bag from inside the small basket bin. I put my hand inside it. Slowly, as if walking a tightrope, I approach the repulsive pigeon. The only way to get rid of the flies is to remove the dead creature that is giving birth to them.

Hand cupped inside the bag, I swoop down and pick up the bird through the plastic. It feels so cold. So dead. I tie the mouth of the bag and head for the door. Release the chain. Open the door quickly and close it. I take the stairs with quiet, determined steps. Reach the front door. Once I'm outside I dump the pigeon in its plastic grave into the bin.

I rock back on my bare feet as the cold night breeze, laced with my shock, settles over me.

I go back inside the eerily quiet house and am in my room in less than a minute. The logical part of me admits that decaying pigeons is an everyday hazard of open chimneys. In that scenario this will have nothing to do with Jack. But inside, I suspect it's him.

This would be the moment most would pack their belongings and go. Allow that bastard Jack to have them fleeing in the night.

Not me.

I look over to the wall where the writing is.

I won't go.

Twelve

I flinch when I enter the pub in Soho the following day. The light isn't muted and warm, but bright and loud like the mainly sparky young crowd inside. It's too packed, music and chattering voices competing to be heard. I almost do an about-turn and leave. Then I spot Alex propping up the end of the bar. He spots me too. I gather my resolve and remind myself why I am here.

He's not his usual, smiley self. Definitely not happy to see me; I can't blame him after I turned my back on him the last time our paths crossed at Patsy's. Mind you, it was him who dumped me not the other way around.

I walk over to him and have no alternative but to get close and personal with the press of bodies close by.

'How are you keeping?' I start with a safe question.

His response takes me to a place I don't want to go: 'I'm sorry about the way things ended between us. I should have handled it differently.'

'I don't think there's any good way to end a relationship. You're either into someone or you're not and you decided you were definitely not into me.' Blatant bitterness is my tone. Instantly, I wish I could drag it back; I've never been good at dealing with being hurt.

He looks incensed as his face inches closer to me. 'That's not fair. Given the situation, what the hell was I meant to do?'

'Seriously? You want us to start singing "Reviewing the Situation"?' I seethe in a rush, conscious of the people nearby. I draw in a deep, deep lungful of air. What's the point of getting pissed? I'm not here to be railroaded by the past.

'I need you to do me a favour, if that's possible.' I congratulate myself on my renewed calm.

He remains wary and alert. 'Of course. If I'm able to help you I will.'

'You speak a number of languages, right?'

'Yessss.' He strings the word out along with suspicion.

I plonk my bag on the bar and pull out my phone. Open it and slide it across to him. 'Can you read that?'

It's a photo of the line in pencil at the end of the farewell letter. Alex picks up the phone, his brows twitching together as he inspects it.

'It's Cyrillic…'

'What?' I rack my brains. I don't ever remember hearing of a country called Cyrillica or Cyrillicland. Learning languages at school was a bit like enforced torture. My shtick was numbers, not the written word.

His gaze darts momentarily at me, then back to the screen. 'It's Russian.' Ah! 'I've been speaking it since I was a kid. My grandmother is Russian. It's her belief that every child in my family should learn it or she thinks it will be lost. She's probably right.' He wears the ghost of a smile, openly displaying his affection for his grandmother. They must be close.

I'm fascinated. We'd never progressed to the stage of talking about our families. Along with a grandmother he must have a mum and a dad. Does he have brothers and sisters? Of course, Patsy had told me that she was a friend of Alex's grandmother's and considered him to be an honorary nephew. I can't keep the longing from my eyes as I glance at him. Quickly, I avert my gaze and stare down at the phone. I need to keep my emotions at bay; well, at least from Alex.

'Can you read it?'

'Yes.'

A sharp breath of frustration escapes me. He can be a bit literal; sometimes he needs a bit of a nudge. 'I know you can read it. Can you tell me what it says?'

'Ah, yes, of course.' He's embarrassed but smiling. I like his smile a lot. Wish I could freeze him in this moment, wrap him up and take him home.

'They're lines by the Russian poet Etienne Solanov. He was a friend, a sidekick, of Pushkin's.'

I think of pretending I've heard of him but decide against it. I've barely heard of Pushkin. 'Who was he?'

Alex knows of course. 'He was a minor poet who enjoyed a reputation for a while as "Russia's death poet". You know, if you were going off to war or in a condemned cell or considering suicide, you kept a book of his poems on you to pass the time.'

'And what happened to him?'

Alex laughs. 'He had an affair with someone's wife to provoke her husband into a duel and then allowed himself to be shot by the outraged guy. I think he was twenty-six at the time.'

'Well, I bet he was a wow at parties. What does it say?'

Alex studies the lines. '"Others may wait for their candles to be blown out. I'm merely blowing out my own".' Alex looks at me. 'Blimey, that's bleak.'

Was my farewell man talking about his own candle? Blowing his life out? I keep my dispiriting thoughts locked away.

I choose safer ground instead. 'How do you know so much about this poet's work?'

'My grandmother is a big fan. She's got his entire collection in Russian as well.' His expression becomes wistful. 'She would read it to me when I was a teenager.'

'Sounds like you've got a good relationship with her.'

His face glows, no doubt wrapped up in memories of him and the woman he obviously loves so well.

'Gran came to England with practically nothing. Found herself in the East End. She worked in the rag trade on very poor wages, but when she tells me about her life she never complains.' His voice fills with quiet emotion. '"All good things come to those who wait". That what's she used to tell me.'

All good things come to those who wait. His beloved grandmother was wrong. In this life you can't afford to wait. Sometimes you have to go out there and snatch it.

'Can I ask you to translate something else for me?' I tentatively ask.

'No problem.'

I choose the words of my request carefully. Plunge in. 'I wasn't able to bring it with me. It's in my room.'

'Woah.' He stops me. 'Are we really going *there* again?'

'Going where?' I'm dumbfounded. What's he rattling on about?

'If I go there – your room – where's it going to lead? We'll end up in bed and I don't need the drama.'

Room. Bed. Drama.

Comprehension hits. Is that what making love with me was? Drama?

My head rears back in rage. 'You know what, Alex, when your gran was teaching you all that fancy poetry she really should've left a slot to teach you some manners. I'm not interested in your body, got it? The Russian I need translating is not written on my duvet.'

His hand flashes furiously in the air to underline his gritted words. 'Lisa, I can't get involved in all this craziness again. The weirdness. The mad behaviour.'

A bucket of ice-cold water would've been warmer than the irate words he throws at me. 'Don't call me that.' I'm upset now, trying my best to cling on to my temper. 'I. Am. Not. Crazy.'

'I'm not saying you're mad...'

Mad. Mad. Mad. It marches through my head, an unwanted occupier I can't get rid of.

'Is she mad?' Mum's trembling strained voice had asked the doctor while I was in the hospital after the *accident*. I was in a semi-conscious state, Mum having no idea I could hear all the hushed talk around me. I'd wanted to bawl my eyes out. Sink and disappear forever into the mattress beneath. Destroyed. Devastated. That's how I'd felt. That's how the man in my room must have felt too. I can't cope with Alex pushing it in my face now as well.

I grab my bag. 'Alex. Sod. You.'

I'm gone. My anger and me push past people. Someone bitches at my back at my rudeness. Sod them too. The cooling air outside hits and I rapidly suck it in, my chest rising and falling with an ocean of unwanted emotion. I completely forget about my mission, my intent only to get away.

His hand catches my arm. I pant heavily. Alex turns me to face him. The street bustles by us, so he steers me to an empty corner next to a packed sushi bar. Our gazes clash, dive away from each other. We both shuffle our feet, back in the uncomfortable zone.

I speak first. 'I didn't mean to kick off in there.' I swallow. 'I know I'm not your usual run-of-the-mill girlfriend, but I am who I am and refuse to apologise for that.'

His palm in the air stops me. 'I'll come over and read it for you.' His expression darkens. 'From what Aunty Patsy has told me, your landlords seem to be fully paid-up members of the psycho club. A proper pair of nasties.'

'It's Jack who's pulling the strings. Martha's a deluded, older woman enthralled by a young, tasty pair of buns.'

'No time like the present. Let's go.'

He starts walking off. My fingertips touch his arm with enough pressure to make him stop. Now for the really difficult bit. The part where he really will think I've lost the plot.

'I'm not allowed any visitors, apart from my parents.'

'I don't understand. How are we going to do this?'

I nervously wet my bottom lip. 'I'm going to have to sneak you in.'

***

My phone rings just as I reach the entrance to Piccadilly Circus. I step away from the heaving tourists taking in the delights of London.

It's Dad. A groan escapes me. I suspect he'll be checking up on whether I've been to seen Doctor Wilson.

I make my tone bright and breezy. 'Hi, Dad. How are you?'

He clears his throat; never a good sign. 'I'm fine, as is your mother. Just a quick call to remind you that we'll be visiting you on Wednesday.'

I suck back the curse that's ready to bolt off my tongue. How could I have forgotten that we'd agreed on them coming to visit?

'Dad, work's really hectic this week. I'm so busy. I'm really sorry but we're going to have to rearrange.'

I am living in a dream world if I think Dad is going to let me off the hook. He doesn't disappoint. 'Your mother is looking forward to seeing you.' Pause. His voice is soft. 'We both are. Call it a parent's indulgence; we need to see you with our own eyes.'

I consider verbally fencing with him until I get my way, but there's something in his voice. Something that I'd last heard from him as he whispered to me, holding my hand, in the hospital – guilt. I gulp down the sorrow whelming in my throat. That my wonderful father should feel guilt about me trying to kill myself, if that's what I'd attempted to do, something he had nothing to do with, that I had done alone, fills me with grief. It's not fair. Not fair that parents suffer when their children bring about their own suffering.

Sometimes I want to snatch that terrible day back and start all over again.

'Of course, Dad. Can't wait to see you both.'

After the call I head down the steps of the Underground station. I pass a large poster advertising a new computer. Its strapline is 'the writing on the wall'.

How am I going to get Alex into my room?

Thirteen

I'm making an instant latte in the kitchen when Martha glides in. I've never seen a woman walk like that before, as if she's barely touching the ground. She's wearing a fifties-style summer dress: pastel green with small strawberries dotting it.

'Lisa.' Martha gifts me with one of her radiant smiles. 'I'm glad I've caught you because I want to ask you something.'

Before I answer I scan her face to find evidence of Jack hitting her, but she's so heavily made up I can barely see her skin. Then again, he might not have hit her in the face. This is my chance to quiz her about it. Tell her what I heard. Provide female solidarity. But I don't.

'What do you want to ask me?'

'I saw a fly, one of those nasty ones.' A visible shudder goes through her. 'Sometimes we get dead pigeons stuck in the chimney. Poor things can't get out, die and… well, before we know it one of the rooms is filled with flies.' Her fingers flutter in the air like fly wings.

So I had been wrong. Jack hadn't put the pigeon there to torment me. Maybe he was finally leaving me in peace.

I perk up. 'There was one. I sorted it out. I didn't want to trouble you by saying anything.'

Her neck stretches. 'I want you to be happy here. I've been asking Jack for the longest time to put mesh wire on the chimneys to stop the birds falling in.' She sighs. 'I suppose he'll get around to doing it in his own good time.'

She takes out a packet of oatcakes from the cupboard, smiles and heads for the fridge.

Maybe it's her back being turned that gives me courage. 'Why do you stay with him?'

Her arm freezes inside the fridge. Then she moves, taking out a tub of fat-free cream cheese. She won't meet my eyes as she picks out a dinner knife and small plate from the dishes and cutlery drying by the sink.

'Have you ever been in love, Lisa?' Martha finally asks as she places the plate on the island. Her voice is tender and calm.

I'm lost for words; it isn't how I expect her to respond. But I give her the truth. 'I've only had the one boyfriend. It was a disaster. I like him… liked him. He decided I wasn't the right woman for him.'

Head still down, Martha opens the tub of cream cheese and starts to spread in small, controlled swipes. 'I contacted Jack the Lad, the handyman with a van, to do some work for me. Oh, how he made me chuckle.' A tinkle of laughter floats from her. 'Call me an old fool, but he made me feel sweet sixteen again. All tingly inside, bursting with energy.' I know the feeling well; Alex had made me feel the same. 'When women get to my age, the world writes you off. I want love just like the next person.'

'I heard him strike you the other day.' I surprise myself with my bluntness. I could've been more gentle. Taken my time to build up to the moment. But how do you build up to a moment of vicious violence?

Martha looks at me now. 'I'm sure you're mistaken.' The fear in her eyes tells a different story. 'Maybe it was a sound from outside. Or kids mucking around on their way home from school.'

If she won't admit that her husband is an abusive pig what do I do? I can't make her say it. Maybe it's too painful to talk about with a virtual stranger. I'd felt exactly the same during my initial session with Doctor Wilson and all the other we'll-fix-her-therapists that I'd seen over the years. Dragging a terrible trauma out into the open is like ripping your guts and heart slowly, agonisingly, out of your body and placing them on public display in all their gory ugliness. Once they're out you can't pretend they're not there. You still might deal with them but they aren't going away.

'If you ever need to talk, Martha, I'm here. And if you can't face calling the cops I'll do it for you.'

As I turn to leave, her palm cups my arm. I wince slightly as one of her nails scratches my skin. 'Thank you.'

Then I remind myself I am dealing with my own troubles. This time I'm going to get the answers so I can put them behind me.

Forever.

***

I turn into the avenue where I now live. A couple of kids skateboarding in the middle of the road are enjoying what has been reported will be the last of the summer. No one else is out and about. It's not the kind of street where neighbours hang over fences to chat or sit out on the front soaking up life.

My phone goes off.

'Alex?' I'm surprised to hear from him. We'd agreed I'd make contact when the time is right. It's been three days.

'Bond. James Bond.' Alex uses his best Sean Connery imitation, which is a bit crap really. I can't help smiling. He continues in character. 'I can slip into the evil organisation run by arch-criminals Martha and Jack by scaling the walls or abseiling from a helicopter.'

I laugh out loud at that. He always knew how to press my funny button. It was one of the things that attracted me to him. I miss it. Miss him.

'M, Miss Moneypenny and Pussy Galore are out to lunch.' The joy disappears as I get serious. 'Why are you calling?'

'I'm driving over to Aunty Patsy's and thought it might be a good time to do the deed.'

I shake my head. 'Now's not a good time. I'll call you, OK?'

Pause. Then: 'Fancy popping over to Aunty Patsy's in about twenty minutes?' He coughs. Well, more a nervous clearing of the back of the throat. 'Maybe we can have a cuppa and a chat?'

Thought I was too weird for you? Too mad? I don't say it.
'I'll call you.'

I end the call. The last thing I'd expected was for Alex to try and resurrect the past. Maybe he wants to be friends? I think on that as I reach the house. No, there can be no friendship between us; not the lasting sort. He's seen my body and knows my night-time secret which will always be unspoken between us.

There's no sign of Martha or Jack so I head to the kitchen and pour a small glass of orange juice. When I look out of the window, into the garden, I see Jack right at the bottom. I peer closer. He's talking to someone. Maybe Martha... No, it's a man. I can't see the guy's face but he's wearing light-blue jeans and a heavy jacket. Jack passes something to him. The man looks furtively around as if worried someone might see them. Like me.

I quickly step to the side, out of their line of vision. I'm curious. What is Jack doing out there? What's with him and the garden?

I head for my room. Dump my bag on the floor as soon as the door is closed and head over to the window to observe the garden from my high vantage point.

The dormer window is open. That's odd; I didn't leave it open. Has Jack been in my room again? Or maybe I'm mistaken and I did leave it open? Truth is I can't remember. Keeping a safe distance, I peer out. There's no sign of Jack or his visitor. They've either left or been obscured by the heavy trees at the back.

Well that's the end of that.

It's chilly so I pull the dormer window, but there's a piece of old material stuck in the frame that stops me doing so. I wear an expression of confusion; how did the material get there? Probably blown there by the wind.

The window isn't going to shut with the material in it so I pull it away. It's damp and greasy to the touch and there's a faint whiff of cat's piss. Only when I pull harder do I realise what it is. A cat's tail.

Startled, I jerk my hand back. Paralysed, I stand there not sure what to do. I can't leave it out there. Grimacing, I touch the tiger-striped tail again, tighter this time, and drag the body into my eyeline. It's clearly dead. Its paws are tucked under its body and its eyes are wide open as if in terror or shock. Its jaws are slightly apart and there seems to be some kind of foam smeared around the mouth. The animal isn't stiff so it's not been dead long. Now it's lying on my windowsill.

I know at once this is Jack again. There's no way this cat could have climbed up this high and put its tail in the window frame before deciding to die a natural death. The foam around the mouth suggests it ate something rotten or poisonous.

I grind my teeth in disgust and horror. Fear too. Because I know enough about life to be able to see that someone who's willing to do this to a helpless animal will also be willing to do it to a human being. I'm determined to stay in this room but for the first time I'm really scared, even more than when Jack came up for his 'party'.

Then it gets worse. Around the cat's neck is a collar, an expensive one in embroidered leather. There's no address and name tag attached. Suddenly I know who the cat is. I should've recognised her from her tiger-print coat.

It's Bette from next door.

Fourteen

Jack's pulled off a double whammy. He's sent a warning to the neighbour about what will happen to the other cat if she doesn't back off in their dispute over the garden, while sending a warning to me about what will happen if I don't move out.

I leave Bette on the windowsill and hopelessly sink onto the bed. What should I do? It would be disgustingly cruel not to tell Patsy what's happened to her beloved pet, but at the same time I can't face being the one to tell her. And there's another thing. I'm living with Jack and Martha. Patsy is going to immediately draw one of the same two conclusions I have: that this is their latest demonic chess move in their tug of turf war and she might suspect I'm in on it. For a moment it crosses my mind to give Bette a decent burial somewhere and say nothing.

But I know I can't do that. I'm not like that. I'm not cruel. I'm not Jack.

I find an expensive scarf from among my things and gently wrap Bette up in it. I take it next door. On the way, I meet the cat killer in the hallway. He looks at me sourly. I'm glad to see the reddening bruise on his face. Hope that was Bette fighting back. 'Why you staring at me like that for?'

I let rip. 'You know what? You're a murdering bastard.'

His jaw drops south. 'You what?'

I rush past him and out of the house because I know if I don't I'll hit him again and again. Give him a taste of the same medicine he dishes out to Martha. I don't hesitate at Patsy's door; I know if I do I'll turn around again and run away.

She opens with a bright smile and a twinkle in her eye. 'Hello, Alex's Lisa.'

I open my mouth. No words come out.

Patsy goes breezily on. 'I'm glad you called actually because I was thinking about you today. I do remember something about the fellow the Devil and his mistress rented a room to next door.' She pulls the door wide. 'Why don't you…?'

Her gaze zeros in on the scarf cradled in my arms. The blood drains out of her face as she gazes at me. Then back at what I hold. The cat is well covered – I made sure of that – but part of its tail is sticking out of the side.

'What's that?'

Patsy doesn't give me the chance to answer as she flicks the scarf back, revealing her cat's still face.

'Bette,' she shrieks, her arms shooting into the air and shaking in horror.

Patsy clutches her head in grief, and then, with the care of a mother for her newborn, takes her cherished cat from my arms. Patsy seems to shrink; her face changes colour and her lips quiver but no words come out. She holds her adored cat as if it's a sacred object for a few moments before going back indoors and closing the door.

I'm not sure what to do. The poor woman is in shock and I want to help. And let's be honest, although I know she's going to be devastated, I want an opportunity to ask what she remembers about the old guy next door. Perhaps I am cruel after all. I stand for a few moments unsure what to do before a decision is made for me.

There's screaming like a banshee from within the house before the door flies open and Patsy emerges carrying a heavy walking stick. It's pointed at me.

'Get off my land!'

'But Patsy…'

I don't get a chance to finish, explain or offer condolences, as she takes a swing at me with the stick and it just misses my face. She's not Patsy to me anymore. She chases me out onto the avenue and I make my escape across the road. But it's not me she's after as she marches up the drive to Jack and Martha's. Patsy's screaming threats at them before she even reaches the door, swinging her walking stick as she goes.

She hammers on the door with her stick and pushes the letter box open. 'Come on, come out, I know you're in there! You pair of utter bastards, killing a defenceless animal! What kind of scum are you?'

A pissed-off Jack leans out of an upstairs window. 'Oi! Get off our land! We've got an injunction against you! Get off our land before we have you put in prison, you mad old bat.'

His neighbour hunts around for something, probably to throw at him. 'You miserable coward! Why don't you come out here? A cat's about your size, isn't it? You piece of worthless offal.'

By this stage other residents are out on the street. The skateboarding kids are also looking on, one of them filming everything on his phone, no doubt to giggle and laugh at with his mates on social media. How utterly disrespectful. I want to snatch it from his hand. Poor Patsy is beside herself with grief and this kid thinks it's a roll camera, action and share moment.

Truth is, I don't know what to do. Patsy thrashes the door with her stick but her frail arms and arthritis get in the way of making any dents.

Martha has now appeared at the upstairs window.

Jack's unruffled voice tells her, 'Call the cops – mad girl next door is having one of her witchy, funny turns again. They should put her in the nut house where she belongs. Woman's an embarrassment.'

But there's no need to make a call. The police turn up anyway.

Jack sends Patsy such a look of unbridled fury she stumbles back from the door. 'If you called the cops—' he begins to yell.

'I never. I swear I didn't.' Patsy looks terrified. That's strange. Wouldn't she want the police to sort this out?

Two officers, a man and a woman, get out of a car and walk up the drive. The male officer gently takes the stick from Patsy while his colleague puts a gentle, but restraining, hand on her arm.

'Take her away,' Jack yells. 'She shouldn't be on the streets with normal people anyway. Nutter…'

The officer with the stick looks up. 'Can you come down please, sir? We want a word.'

'Not until you lock her up, I can't.'

I notice that Martha doesn't utter a word.

Patsy breaks down, sobbing and wailing as the officer steers her bent figure back onto the avenue. I cross the road to help but that's a mistake.

Patsy glares at me with such naked hatred I instinctively step back. 'She's one of them. Arrest her. She's one of them.'

I back off and realise that my phone is ringing in my pocket. It's Alex again.

'What the hell is going on over there? I've just had Aunty Pats on claiming the neighbours have murdered someone. I've had to call the police.'

So that's what Patsy had been doing inside.

'Jack killed one of her cats.'

Alex is baffled. 'He's murdered a cat?'

'Yes.'

He's got his lawyer's hat on. 'It's not really my field but I'm pretty sure you can't murder a cat.'

'Bette, her tiger tabby, is dead. I found it in my room.'

'You think Jack put it there?'

My voice rises slightly, shaking as it does so. 'How else do you think it got there? It was awful.'

'Do you want me to come over?'

'Definitely not. I'm sure Martha and Jack know who you are and if they see you with me…'

'I hear you.'

I look up as the door to Patsy's house closes. I can still hear her weeping and sobbing the name of her dead cat over and over again.

'Bette. Bette. Bette.'

***

89

'How could you do something as shit as that?' I round on Jack as he stands next to Martha in the hallway. 'I know you've fallen out about the garden but how could you? How could you?'

He levels a steely stare at me. 'How do you know about our business with her and our garden?'

His question takes me unawares. I try not to stutter. 'I met her by chance the other day and she just told me. She seems to like to talk.'

He straightens his man bun, which has tilted to the side in all the earlier uproar. 'I'll tell you what I told fruitcake next door. I didn't touch her pussycat.'

'Then how did it end up dead on the windowsill in my room?'

He moves menacingly close to me. Martha tries half-heartedly to stop him. I stand my ground. 'If you don't like it you know what you can do: pack your gear and leave.'

Oh, he'd love that. Not a chance.

I shake my head in disgust and leave the room. As I near the stairs, the front door knocker goes.

It's the male officer.

'Are you Lisa?'

I nod.

'I need to have a word with you.'

***

That night I double knot my scarf around my ankle and lie down. The house sounds restless. Wood cries as it creaks on another floor and the pipe in my radiator ticks and gurgles.

What a nasty day. Thankfully the talk with the police had been short, with him taking me at my word that I'd only found the cat, already dead. I hadn't accused Jack of doing it because the truth was I had no proof. Unless Patsy pays for a post-mortem of her cat – I'm not even sure if you can do this – no one will ever know if Bette was poisoned.

Poison. Is that what Jack has in store for me next? Surely not. Dead animals seem to be his thing. Nevertheless, I make up my mind to only eat ready meals and pre-prepared food and keep drinks in my room. I'll hide the drinks away in the wardrobe, conscious that if Jack discovered I've broken the agreement not to keep food in my room it will give him the excuse he's been looking for to boot me out.

And that isn't going to happen. I will not allow it to happen.

A mouse brutally bashed in the head, death flies, poisoned cats, a grief-stricken, shrieking neighbour; my subconscious doesn't need any help tormenting me tonight. No need for my usual girly groove with Amy tonight; I don't need music to get me to sleep. I'm beyond tired. My bones feel like they've fled my body, leaving me a flopping mess.

I'm drifting… drifting… I can hear Patsy wailing over the loss of Bette. I wake with a start and realise it really is her shouting outside. I go to the open window. She's in her garden, clearly distraught, shouting 'murderer' at the top of her voice as if to no one in particular, like a drunk. Then it stops. Or am I dreaming? No, I'm not. I hear her back door slam shut. My gaze lingers on the shadowy spot where I found the corpse of her dead pet. I feel sick and my heart is pumping as if I'm running in terror.

I go back to bed. Tie my leg. Lie down. And sleep.

Bette is on the windowsill. Her fur's matted, tangled and greasy with blood. Foam licks at her mouth and whiskers. She's sitting up, staring at me. Her tail swishes to Amy's 'Love is a Losing Game'.

'Murderer,' she mouths at me.

And again. 'Murderer.' Bette mouths 'murderer' at me and then again. I can feel my fingers digging into the duvet and my leg thrashing and pulling against my mum's birthday scarf.

This is how it begins.

Bette whispers, 'Scream all you like, no one's coming… You're dead, just like me… You're dead'.

Bette looks up at the skylight because someone must be there, and then behind her, and then at the door, because someone is coming. She leaps away through the dormer and then around whoever I sense is waiting out there on the roof.

My heart's bashing against my skin, almost ripping out. I have to get away.

Get away.

Or it will be the end.

In the house a woman and children scream. The woman's scream is like an animal howling in pain. Desperate footsteps pound in the bowels of the house and on all the stairs, where the noise merges to one continuous drumbeat of steps. There's more screaming. Everyone's fleeing and I have to flee too.

On the landing below, I hesitate. There's a whirl of shapes and figures around me and they're wielding knives and needles and screaming at me. I call out for my mum but she doesn't come. Where is she? Down in the hallway are the dead. Piles of them, covered in blood with anguished and shocked expressions on their faces. I can't go down to where the dead are. Unbelievable pain grips me. I'm screaming. I'm falling.

Falling...

My eyes flash open. Oh God, I don't know where I am. I'm shaking, panting, finding it hard to fill my lungs with air. I realise that I'm crouched down with my back against the wall on the second landing in the dark. My arms are locked tight, with the power of a lifeline, around my raised knees. I close my eyes. I'm in despair. Devastated. Can't believe it. I'm sleepwalking again. Or, as I call it, awake-sleep; I remember what happens in each episode. It's as if I'm awake, forced to follow where my feet take me, but I don't have any control to stop it. It always ends the same: I fall asleep somewhere that isn't my bed and wake up feeling like it's the worst day of my life.

That's why I tie my scarf to the bed. To stop me from the dread of awake-sleep. Since I'd invented my homemade remedy of tying my leg to the bed the awake-sleep had vanished. Only a few times had I woken to find myself on the floor beside my bed, but at least I was still in the room.

I had told Doctor Wilson about the nightmares but nothing about this or the real root of my problems. I am convinced if I had he would indeed think I'm mad.

I bow my head; hopeless tears leak down my cold face. Why is this happening to me again? Why? I'm so scared.

Something ice-cold touches my naked arm. I cry out as I desperately try to find out what it is. A small hand.

'It's just me.' Martha's head looms before me as if it there's no body attached. Am I still in the land of awake-sleep?

When she speaks again I know I'm not. 'I'm going to put on one of the side lights.'

No. No. My panic rises. I mustn't let her. She'll see... Warm orange bathes the landing. Bathes my exposed skin.

I want to turn away so I don't see the 'O' her mouth makes as she stares at my body. At the scars that slash across my arms and legs.

I refuse to look at them, but say, 'They're ugly, aren't they?' My voice rasps, barely above a whisper.

I hold my breath, waiting for what she will say. Alex had been the last person to see them while we made love. He was steadfast that it wasn't the reason we'd parted company; I didn't believe him. Who wants a girlfriend who looks as repulsive as me?

Martha surprises me with her comment. 'Let's get you back upstairs. Don't worry about Jack, he's dead to the world.'

I allow her to help me to my feet. I'm grateful for the arm she curves round my waist, giving me the much-needed strength to help me climb the stairs. The door of my room is shut. That's what frustrates me about the awake-sleep; it's as if the part of my brain that deals with small, everyday tasks still works – close the door, walk down the stairs, switch on the lights.

My room is peaceful, quiet. No writing on the wall on display. No Bette, thank God. We both ease down onto the bed. The scarf hangs off the bed like a forlorn flag never to be raised up again. *Traitor*, I want to yell at it. *How can you have let me down?*

Martha pulls it towards her. Runs it through her hands. 'This is a beautiful.'

'My mother gave it to me.'

She turns her body to look fully at me. 'Your mother?'

The chill of whatever time it is settles in my bones. 'She gave it to me when I was a teenager. Mum never said it was a family heirloom, but it seemed to have some special importance to her.'

'I never knew my mother.' Martha looks sad. Her face is made up as meticulously as if it were daytime. 'My father did his best, but it was a rootless existence, being dragged from place to place. When I was a child I'd make up stories that if I had a mother I'd be settled, living in a proper home. You know, breakfast, dinner and bedtime stories always at the same time.' She takes a breath. 'How long have you been sleepwalking?'

I run a hand through my hair. 'Since I was a kid. It's not sleepwalking to me because I remember everything I do.' I smile ruefully at her.

'How did you get the scars?'

I gasp even though I know her question was bound to rear its head. 'More childhood shit. Look, if you don't mind—'

'You don't want to talk about it. I understand.' She gets to her feet, the scarf still in her hands. 'I'll keep what happened tonight between us girls. No need for Jack to know.'

After the door clicks closed behind her, I get up and do something I haven't done in years. I flip the full-standing mirror to face me. I've kept it turned away from me since I moved in. I peel off my nightclothes and force myself to stare at my reflection. I know each of those scars off by heart. The three on my left leg, the one on the right, the two on my right arm and the biggest of all, the long one, a magnified lifeline across my stomach. Some are long, others short, the longest jagged. Puckered, discoloured. Macabre. The original freak show.

At the group therapy session my parents had forced me to go to as a teenager to win the battle against my eating disorder, the therapist said the scars were the symptom not the problem. She was wrong. They were part of a set of problems that had blighted my life. Problems I wasn't prepared to sit back and do nothing about anymore.

I put my jim-jams back on. When I get to the bed I notice that Martha has left the scarf in a series of knots. It takes me a while to have an uninterrupted length of material flowing through my fingers.

Time to sleep.

I tie my leg to the bed.

Fifteen

I ring the buzzer of Doctor Wilson's studio. I had no intention of making any follow-up visit. But then, during the day while I was working on a project at work, something occurred to me that made me change my mind.

My dad had said that Doctor Wilson is an old friend of his, dating back to their days studying medicine. That had to mean their relationship dated back to before I was born. And that might mean he'd know or had heard something along the way that might answer a few questions. What if Dad had asked his advice about me privately over the years?

However, there was a wrinkle in my logic. Until recently I'd never in my life heard Doctor Wilson's name mentioned at home or ever seen him at my parents'. Then again, my parents aren't big social entertainers.

And what was it Mum had said during my last visit to see them?

'He considers himself almost a part of this family.'

Bubbling with anticipation, I'd called Doctor Wilson to ask if there was any possibility he could fit me in this evening? Not in the least surprised by my change of mind or my urgent request to see him, he'd readily agreed.

I'm eager to begin our session. I might be able to tease those longed-for answers out of him. Deduce them from his reaction to what I say. I realise that I'll have to be careful because I don't want him to think I'm just here to collect evidence and he's obviously a very clever man. On the other hand, I'm past caring. If it comes to it, I'll just ask him flat out: what do you know about my childhood? What do you know about how I really got these scars?

Doctor Wilson comes to the door and takes me to his consulting room. This time I accept his offer of tea: chamomile to keep me nice and calm. I think about taking a chair this time so I can study his face but I don't want to arouse suspicion. Soon I'm back on his couch, my hands clasped like an obedient patient. The man from my room doesn't join me this time.

Once again, Doctor Wilson opens his notebook and has his pen at the ready.

He begins. 'At the end of our last session, at the door, you said you feel as if you're living someone else's life. That your body doesn't seem to be yours. Am I right?'

'Something like that.'

He writes and talks. 'Why is that?'

I'm careful about what I say. 'Apparently, on my fifth birthday, we were holidaying on a friend's farm down in Sussex. While the adults sat around a table in the garden, me and the other kids were playing chase in the farmyard. I climbed onto some farm machinery and fell into it. I was very badly injured and rushed to hospital where I was kept for several months while I recovered. As I was only five, I wasn't a very good patient. I couldn't understand what had happened, what was happening and why I couldn't go home. I was also in a lot of pain. The nights were especially bad on a dark ward with strangers all around me. With children weeping in the small hours and the shadow of adults passing on the floor by my bed. When I was better and went home again, I was OK for a while. Then the nightmares began.'

I deliberately pause. 'What I've just told you is what my parents told me. I don't remember anything – I mean *anything* – about it.'

I steal sly glances at his face to see if there is any reaction. There isn't.

He pointedly observes, 'You sound as if you doubt their story?'

He's good. I've said nothing to suggest that but he knows I don't believe it.

'I don't.'

'Do you have *any* recollection of that day at all? Anything that would suggest your parents' version of what happened isn't true?'

I don't answer him directly. 'I've got a very clear memory of three things but I don't know if it was on that day. I hear a woman screaming. Actually, not screaming, it was more like howling, like a wounded animal.'

I stare desperately at the ceiling as the horror of it shreds my mind. It's so terrible, like her guts are being ripped out, her life torn forever apart.

I make myself carry on despite the taste of bile in my throat. 'Then there was silence. Children start screaming – high-pitched, deafening – in terror. Then there was silence. Finally, I remember a man screaming but his screams are different. A sobbing kind of screaming, like his heart's breaking. Then there was silence.'

Now I'm silent. I catch a glimpse of the doctor's face. His mouth twists to the side; his eyes blink rapidly as he thinks.

'None of what you remember is incompatible with your parents' account, is it? If you'd fallen into machinery and been seriously injured, women, men and children would be screaming. Your mother would have been distressed, no doubt manifested in her screaming. If that had happened to my child, I certainly would be.' His gaze becomes more forceful. 'I hope this isn't too personal a question, but do you have scars on your body?'

The way my gaze jerks away from him tells him all he needs to know.

'Do you remember anything else that would give you a reason to think that their story is wrong?'

I whisper, 'No. I just know it is.'

Doctor Wilson places his pen very carefully on his notebook. I steel myself for the mind-can-play-tricks-on-us pitying lecture.

But he surprises me with, 'Have you discussed this with your parents?'

I instinctively roll my eyes in desperation. I hate eye rolls. Such a dumb expression. 'How can I? I'd be calling them liars to their faces. I'm not going to do that. They pride themselves on telling the truth even when it's not in their interest to do so. Honesty is the best policy and all that.'

'So why would they change the pattern of a lifetime of behaviour with you, the daughter they love?'

I can't answer that, so don't.

'And the farm in Sussex. Do you know where that is? Could the people your family were visiting confirm your parents' story?'

The strain of this conversation presses on me with the mighty weight of a boulder. I've accused my parents of lying when they never lie. And I'm feeling deep in my bones what's happened at Jack and Martha's. It's all getting too much.

Tears are in my response. 'I remember a farm in Sussex but the people there are dead now. Apparently.'

He sees my distress. 'Would you like a break, Lisa?'

'I don't know.' I wipe a tear from my cheek with the back of my hand. 'How long have we got left?'

'I haven't got a clock on. We can take all the time you need. Go for a walk in the garden if you like.'

***

I'm glad for an escape to the garden. I can breathe there. Doctor Wilson is obviously a rose lover because I smell them before I get out of the door. Row after row of neatly trimmed bushes with firm crowns that spray scent like mist from a perfume bottle. They stand on a carefully mown green lawn. I gather myself together. The flowers are all fresh yellows and pure whites like cream. Colours that calm me. By the fence is a fountain with clear running water gliding from some stone classical figures. There's a bench next to it, which I sit on. Collapse on, more like.

I know I've passed through some veil of fire by telling Doctor Wilson that I don't believe my parents' story about my fifth birthday. I've never told anyone that before. I've always been scared of the consequences, of what might happen if I spoke out. Sometimes, I've believed their version myself; how else do I explain the scars on my body? Now I've said it out loud I feel liberated even though it doesn't help very much. I want to know what actually happened. Then I'll be free. And now I've come this far, I'm not going to stop trying to find out. There's no going back now.

When I get back to the doctor's consulting room, I don't retake my place on the couch but sit down in the chair that he offered me the previous Saturday. He seems surprised but not uncomfortable.

'Doctor Wilson, can I ask you something?'

I think he's probably been expecting this question. 'Of course.'

'This accident when I was five, you knew my parents then. Do you remember this accident I had? Do you remember them talking about it at the time?'

I search the doctor's face. No reaction again. I feel crushed this time.

'I don't. Let me explain why I probably wouldn't. I knew your father at medical school and we've stayed in touch since but we were never really close friends, more colleagues. I've met him over the years at conferences and professional gatherings but we don't really socialise together except very occasionally. There have been long periods during our somewhat distant relationship when I didn't see him at all and your accident may well have fallen during one of those periods. Also, you know what families like ours are like; they're very private and they don't like a fuss. That's the English way.'

'But you still keep in touch with my dad now? I'm sure he's checking up with you to make sure I'm coming to see you and to find out how it's going.'

'Yes, that's partially correct. We speak, but it would be a breach of your confidentiality if I told him anything about our sessions including whether you are seeing me or not.'

Even though I know he's professional to the core, I still ask. 'Is it possible then that the next time you speak to him you could make some discreet enquiries about this apparent accident and see what he says?'

The doctor is horrified. 'No, it's not, Lisa; I'm a psychiatrist not a private detective. That's out of the question; it would be a gross abuse of my position. If you have any issues with your parents' version of what happened, I urge you to speak to them.' He hesitates slightly before adding, 'Although I will say one thing that might help you. You suspect your parents' version of what happened isn't true. However, one part of it is very likely to be true. They say that this accident happened on your fifth birthday?'

'Yes.'

'In my experience, when people invent stories they tend to avoid specifics because they can be checked. If they say that this incident happened on your fifth birthday, they're unlikely to have invented that. It would more likely be a random date.'

That had never crossed my mind before. But I'm not done yet. 'Thank you, that's very helpful. Can I ask you something else?'

He looks a lot less eager to help this time. 'If you wish.'

'Supposing I told you that my so-called suicide attempt was actually a real one? That if I don't get any answers to what happened on my fifth birthday, I'm never going to get any peace and, consequently, sooner or later, I'll be walking off Beachy Head with a bottle of pills in one hand and a bottle of vodka in the other? Would you speak to them then?'

Even to my ears this sounds nasty. But then emotional blackmail always is.

'Are you saying that it was a real attempt to end your life?' He turns my words back to his agenda. Probably one of the first strategies he learned in shrink school.

But I'm clever too. 'You know exactly what I'm saying.'

He closes his notebook. 'I've already explained my position on this, Lisa. If you have any questions to ask they need to be addressed to the people who can answer them. And that's your parents, not me.'

As far as I'm concerned, we're done for the day. We say our goodbyes at the door. He tries to hide it, but I see the expression flame and then die on his face. He doesn't want me to come back.

Sixteen

'How do I look?' Martha asks me as I sit in the dining room, following it through with a giddy, girly whirl. Her evening dress is sexy indigo-blue, off the shoulder with slits on both sides to showcase her well-toned legs. She is passionate about going to the gym at least twice a week and it shows.

Since the awful business of the cat next door's death, I've been keeping to my own space, primarily to stay out of Jack's way, and having my meals in the dining room when I know they won't be there, but this evening is different. Martha and Jack are going out. One of Martha's friends is hosting a lavish birthday party. I need to be present downstairs to make sure they leave.

'You look gorgeous.'

She leans forward and whispers, 'Jack says I'm putting too much in the window.' Her leg peeps seductively through the slit.

'Never you mind what he says, you have the time of your life.' Martha deserves that and more with the crap he's putting her through.

Talk of the Devil. Jack shouts from near the front door: 'Are you ready? We'll be bloody late at this rate.'

His wife's radiance dims. 'Be just there, love.' Then she reminds me: 'Remember, don't lock up or we won't get in.'

'Marthaaaaa,' he screeches.

Martha says goodbye and leaves to join him. I stay put as I hear the engine of the van as it revs up and drives away. Give it two minutes. Take out my mobile. Text:

Ready.

A thumbs-up emoji pings back.

Anxiously, I wait by the front door. What's taking him so long? The nerves kick in. What if something goes wrong? What if... A silhouette dims the door outside. I open up quickly and yank Alex in.

'Steady on, Lisa.'

'What took you so long?'

He appears flustered and is back to looking suspiciously at weird, mad me. I get in there before he can.

'You're not going to bloody well back out?'

'I know what I said, but this' – he indicates the hallway and the house with his hands – 'is... odd. Strange.'

For some unknown reason we're huddled almost head to head and whispering.

I ignore his comment and turn to the stairs. 'We need to go upstairs.'

'This isn't some suburban, swingers sex party?' He sounds cheerful and hopeful now.

'In your dreams.'

I can feel his gaze taking the house in. 'If Patsy hadn't told me about the couple who live here I'd say you've fallen on your feet. This is an incredible house.'

We reach my room. I open the door. I feel a strange sense of pride at his glow of appreciation as he looks round. The light in his eyes dies when it falls on the scarf on my bed. We're both stuck in the memory of our last night together.

'Lisa...' he tentatively begins, but I'm not dealing with *that* tonight. Besides, there isn't time for that.

I swipe up the scarf and bundle it under my pillow, smothering our past; for now, at least.

'I want to show you something.'

My heart's thumping as I move towards the wall. Alex wears a cagey expression; he's worried about my state of mind. Thinks I've flipped. I don't blame him. I might feel the same if someone took me to gaze at what appears to be a blank wall. On the tips of my toes I reach high, tuck my fingers into the wallpaper's edge and pull. There's the sucking strain of paper disengaging from brick. Slowly the paper pulls back from the wall and unravels down.

'Bloody hell,' a dazed Alex utters as he steps closer to the writing. 'What is this?'

I can't tell him it's a dead man speaking to me, a house revealing its secrets, because he really will call me mad and not take it back this time.

So I go with a partial truth. 'The rain leaked through the skylight and the wallpaper came down. And there it was.' I give him my most innocent look.

'Fascinating.' He can't take his gaze off the writing.

I stand next to him. Both of us are caught up in the writing on the wall.

'Can you read it?' I finally ask.

He doesn't answer, instead points a finger and runs it in the air, following sentence after sentence, his mouth moving silently.

I don't want to rush him, but… 'Tell we what it says so far.'

He darts an irritated sideways glance my way. 'Give me a…'

We both freeze at the noise of a vehicle coming closer to the house. I peep out of the window.

Bloody hell. It's Jack.

Panic punches me in the gut. I start panting. What am I going to do?

'Alex, you need to hide.'

'What?'

I need to shock him into action. 'That's Jack. He's back. Might come up. Remember what Patsy said he's like. He killed her bloody cat.'

But Alex stands his ground. 'I don't see why you aren't allowed any visitors. This isn't a prison. If you give me the tenancy agreement I'm sure I can—'

The front door slams downstairs.

I plead with him. 'Alex, please hide under the bed.'

He takes me very gently by the arms. 'This is not a farce, Lisa. This is your room. You pay good money to live in it. If Jack comes up here don't open the door. Simple. You have a bolt and a chain to keep him—'

Urgently I place the pad of my finger on his lips. There's footsteps on the landing below. Our ragged breathing is the only sound in the room.

The wooden boards under the carpet downstairs moan with the tread of feet. The hinges of a door squeak below.

Silence.

Me and Alex stare into each other's eyes. His shoulders tremble faintly so I know his heart is beating as fast as mine. His palms are warm with sweat as they tighten around my arms.

The hinges protest again. The door closes.

We wait. And wait.

There's movement again downstairs but the footsteps are closer this time, as if they're moving towards the flight of stairs that lead to my room.

Please, make him go away. Make him go away.

Silence. But this one's different; I imagine Jack breathing as he stands at the foot of the stairs.

I let out a huge, drawn breath of air as the footsteps retreat. Go downstairs. The front door slams. Me and Alex continue to stare at each other. I should go to the window… but I can't let go of the spell I'm under. There's always been an intensity between us. I can't name it; that something special, I suppose.

If it was so special, why did you break up? the cynical part of my mind reminds me.

I pull myself free and go to the window just as Jack's van heads out again. I stay put, not ready to face my one-time lover just yet.

'Lisa,' he softly calls.

I spin around, all business. 'You were about to read what's on the wall.'

He looks hurts… no, wounded, like his favourite computer game has been taken from him. I sternly remind myself he was the one who dumped me, not the other way round.

We give the wall our full attention.

Alex speaks. 'I think this is kind of like a diary of events. It begins again with a line from Etienne Solanov: "When you're not to blame but the blame is yours, eternal sleep will soothe your soul".'

I'm spellbound again, this time by his voice, as he continues…

Seventeen

Before

It was the worst possible day to be out on Hampstead Heath. It was spring, the sun was shining and there was a gentle breeze. Flowers were blossoming, leaves were budding and everything around them was a brilliant green. It seemed as if half the population of London was out on the Heath and they'd all brought children with them. Those children were all running around shouting and squealing, being happy and cheerful. John's own kids seemed bursting with life, full of joy as if they were a part of the nature around them. Even his oldest, the boy, didn't look as serious as usual that day. John's own father had decided his grandson was going to be a scholar so he called him 'the Russian'. The two younger girls were the 'English ones' because they laughed and played all the time. All three of them were being adorable that day.

His wife didn't always match her two daughters' gift for enjoying life but even she seemed to have caught the mood. While sitting on the blanket that was laid on the grass, she rubbed her bare legs, shielded her eyes from the sunlight and said, 'It's enough just to be alive on a day like today, isn't it, John?' And he'd nodded without saying a word.

It was all wrong.

It should have been winter. The Heath should have been empty of people. A gale should have been howling and blasting the grass; sleet should have been slashing its way across the skin. The view over London should have been blanked out by dark mists. Or it should have been summer. One of those summer days when the heat is about to break and heavy clouds rise into the sky, choking the sun with darkness, followed by rumbles of thunder and flashes of lightning. Children should be scared and running for cover, not running around playing with balls. It was ridiculous.

It was totally wrong.

The two girls decided they wanted to fly the kite they'd brought with them. John tried to smile. 'Oh, I'm sorry, ladies, I forgot to bring it.'

They thought he was joking. The oldest reminded him. 'It's under your arm!'

And so it was. He'd taken it out of the car and then forgotten he was holding it. The youngest girl tried to unroll the string but she couldn't. So the older girl snatched the kite and she tried too, before a squabble broke out between her and her brother, who thought he should be in charge, because he was the oldest and he was the boy and he should be flying the kite. At the same time, the little girl said no, she was there first, it should be her. John was forced to break the fight up and launch the kite himself, and to remind his three children that they could all have a go and to play fair with each other.

'Alright, Mr Kite Flyer, that's enough. Come and sit down.'

He turned to see his wife putting out the picnic on the blanket. But he didn't want to sit down. Even sitting down next to his wife felt like a betrayal, a sign that everything was going to be alright. And everything wasn't going to be alright. And it wasn't going to be alright for these children either. Maybe if they were a bit younger or a bit older, they would be, but not now. He'd floated that idea to himself over the past few months. They were too young to understand. But that wasn't going to fly any more than the kite in the hands of that little girl over there.

'Are you coming to sit down then?' Her voice was more insistent this time. So he sat down; one more betrayal to add to all the others. 'Are you alright?'

'Yes, of course I'm alright. Why wouldn't I be alright?'

'I don't know. You tell me.' She looked beautiful but fragile because that's what she was. Beautiful but fragile.

Even when he'd first started dating her, her best friend had warned him: 'You'll find your new girlfriend can be out on the window ledge a little sometimes; you know, slightly overemotional, a bit fragile. Lovely girl, of course.'

It sounded like green-eyed jealousy at the time. He was the handsome eligible bachelor with the exotic Russian roots and she was the girl every guy in college wanted to be with. In fact, it probably was jealousy with her friend. But it was true all the same.

And now this.

'I'm fine.'

She used her hand to lift her hair out of her eyes. 'I think you're working too hard. You should spend more time at home with me and the children. You don't need to be doing all these hours really. I sometimes think you prefer working to us. Is that true? Do you prefer working to your wife and children? My best friend is more of a father and husband than you are.'

She'd given him the perfect opportunity. *Go on, tell her.* He planned to say what the real problem was that evening when they got home from the Heath and those tired children were safely tucked up in bed. It was simple really. *Look, there's something I need to say…* He was absolutely going to do it. But then he'd absolutely been going to do it the previous weekend. And the weekend before that. And he knew deep down he wasn't going to do it now, or later either. He was too weak to do the right thing and too weak to stop doing the wrong thing. He was no different to his grandfather, the man who pretended to have been an officer in the Russian Imperial Guard, a war hero who fled his country after the revolution. When really Granddad was a draft dodger who'd run away to the West to avoid getting killed in Russia's war or anyone else's.

The children got fed up with the kite and raced back to see what there was to eat. The youngest grabbed John's leg so she could lean over and peer at what was on offer on the blanket. His wife had lost interest in whether he was alright and working too hard because she was tending to the children. He rubbed his face with his hands and lay back on the grass to catch the sun. The girl sat on his belly to eat a sandwich.

Perhaps he wouldn't need to do anything at all. Perhaps everything would sort itself out on its own. Things usually did. Perhaps his wife would get fed up with him working all the time and find someone else. She'd get a lawyer and force him out of his house so she could move her lover in. The children would grow up blaming their mum for their ruined childhood and hate her new guy. In the eyes of the world he wouldn't be a pathetic man who couldn't make decisions; he'd be a tragic hero instead.

Or perhaps his family would be wiped out in a terrible accident and he'd be the lonely man by the graveside with the flowers and the tears who recited snatches of the Russian poetry he loved so much. Obviously, he didn't want them dead; that wasn't what it was at all. It was just that he wanted the whole problem to disappear and sudden death was one way it could happen. He really would be a hero then. No one would blame him for seeking solace in the arms of another woman. There was plenty of poetry around to justify that.

Or perhaps those things wouldn't happen but everything would still work out anyway.

But in the end it didn't matter.

He was convinced the best thing was to do nothing and to see what happened.

Eighteen

Alex stops reading. Neither of us says a thing. Honestly, I'm not sure why I'm not jumping about my room with excitement. Farewell man has spoken to me again. Fed me more information about his life to help me solve the puzzle of his death. Then I realise what I am experiencing. A huge wave of disappointment. I wanted the writing to tell me so much more. Answer all the questions after I had read the suicide – farewell – letter. What was his name? What mistakes had he made? Who are the innocents he mentions?

I finally speak, a whisper really. 'He didn't say what his name was.'

Typical Alex takes it all in his lawyering stride. 'Well, it's your typical Russian drama. Married couple plus kids, all seems to be brimming with rosy happiness on the outside, inside it's bloody turmoil. Whoever wrote this must've been writing a play. A very tragic, Russian one, which, from what I know, is the only kind there is.'

'It's tragic alright,' I answer quietly. 'It's no play; it's all true.'

Alex's face scrunches up in confusion. 'How did you figure that out?'

Now I have a decision to make: do I show him the farewell letter or not? The letter is so smothered in pain and regret, so private it seems like a betrayal to share it with someone else. How else, though, am I to get Alex to understand why I need to do this?

He's surprised when I go to my bag. I take out the letter and pass it to him.

He stabs me with his very troubled eyes when he's finished reading. 'What's this?'

It gushes out. 'It's a suicide letter, although I prefer to see it as a farewell. The day I moved in I found it stuffed down the back of the drawers in the bedside cabinet. The Cyrillic writing at the bottom is what I showed you in the pub. It's the same handwriting as on the wall. The same man. He's trying...'

The words go on and on, tumbling and tumbling, delivered in an awkward fashion that suggests I have no control. And from the dawning horror on Alex's face, maybe I don't.

He finally stops me with an adamant hand in the air. 'Did you say this was a suicide letter written by a man who at one time lived in this room?'

Quickly I nod. 'But Martha – well Jack really – insists that no one else rented this room before me.' I gulp. Swallow. 'I think he killed himself here—'

'What? In this room?' Alex is horrified.

'Yes. I need to find out why he did it.'

Alex passes the letter back to me with his fingertips as if it's impregnated with the worst type of disease. The way he's staring at me I know what he's thinking.

I explode. 'Don't you dare say I'm bonkers.'

'I wasn't going to. This is spooky. Disturbing. A man takes his life by his own hand where we're standing, leaves a suicide letter and writing on the wall in a foreign language, and you expect me to carry on as if we've just read a page from *The Guardian*.'

Frantically, I wave at the wall. 'There must be more writing on the wall. This is only the start of it.'

To demonstrate my point I start peeling the next section of lining paper, which doesn't reveal any more writing. It must be there. I can't stop.

'Lisa, stop it.'

Alex's commanding order makes me stumble back. I'm hyperventilating, racked with shakes. Although the room's cold my skin feels like it's on fire.

'This is creeping me out,' Alex says.

Alex heads for the door and is striding down the landing before I can call him back.

'Please, Alex, help me find the rest.'

He storms over to face me. 'There probably isn't any more. The poor guy probably topped himself before he could write any more. Why is this so important to you?'

I seal my lips shut. Then: 'I want you to help me find out who he was.'

He tuts with utter frustration and goes downstairs. I don't go down. Remain at the top. Alex is swallowed up in the half-dark, a shadow opening the door and leaving my life. Jack insists the tenant never existed, so how am I going to figure out who he was?

As I walk back upstairs I hear the ping of my phone. It's a text from Dad reminding me of his and Mum's visit. I don't answer. Instead, I lightly smooth down the lining paper covering up the writing of a dead man.

***

My parents sit on one side of the room, I on the other. Mum holds a mug of sugarless tea while Dad nurses a glass of brandy. They arrived for their agreed visit promptly at four, kisses and hugs at the door as usual. We've been talking, back and forth, in this strange, rapid chatter, especially Mum who has ended practically every sentence with a nervy cough. Talking about all those safe topics: my work, the weather, the state of the nation.

Now we're faced with a silence we all know too well. A moment of quiet where they are carefully sorting through what they really have come here to speak to me about.

It goes without saying that the last thing I need at the moment is a visit from my parents. As far as they're concerned, I'm effectively on suicide watch now. In the same way a criminal is always a criminal in the suspicious eyes of the world, a suicide risk is always a suicide risk even if you never were in the first place. So when people say 'So how are you in yourself at the moment?' what they really mean is 'Have you tried to top yourself lately?' So I let them come and hope it doesn't last too long.

My dad arrived carrying flowers from their garden while my mum brought a basket of fruit. Probably someone told her at church that fruit is good for suicidal people. Perhaps it is.

My dad breaks the silence. 'So how are you in yourself, Lisa?'

I know that my dad has my well-being at heart, that he loves me and only wants the best for me, but I'm tired of these questions. Each one is a needle poking all my vulnerable places, some of them places I've only recently allowed to come out of the dark.

'I'm fine.' I know what the next question is going to be, so I add, 'I've been going to see Doctor Wilson.'

That cheers Mum up. She wears an expression of blessed relief. 'I'm so pleased. I've been so worried about you.' She coughs lightly to settle the quivering emotion she lays bare in the room.

It's at moments like this that I am ashamed of thinking they have been lying to me about the past. About the accident when I was five. I am so lucky to have them. Maybe it's time for me to quit the past and stare, face forward, only at the future.

'I'm really sorry, Mum. I know you and Dad have only been trying to help me.' My head drops down. 'I must be a big disappointment to you.'

Mum's answer is stern and strong. She puts her cup down. 'Never let me hear you say that. Since the day you came into our lives you have been our greatest joy.'

Since the day you came into our lives. That's a strange way of putting it. Surely a mother would phrase it as something like 'The first time I held you in my arms.' *Stop it! Stop it! There you go again, reading things into things that aren't there.* Or as Shakespeare put it, 'Nothing is but what is not'.

'He's very good, isn't he?' Dad says with a certain amount of pride in Doctor Wilson's abilities.

'He has an easy manner and we talk,' I concede.

'He had a practice in California back in the nineties.'

My dad obviously thinks having a practice on the West Coast of America proves what a cracking shrink he is.

'Do you think it's helping?' Mum's question is so full of hope it's painful to hear.

I decide to say something that is going to be hard for me to say and for them to hear. 'We talked about whether I tried to kill myself or not.'

There. Out in the open. The source of a bad smell has finally been found.

Dad looks like I've sucker punched him and Mum, poor Mum, has the complexion of someone who's about to thrown up.

Dad recovers quickly, using his former doctor's voice. 'And did you?'

I'm honest with my parents for the first time. 'I don't know. I was stressed, life speeding so fast I found it hard to keep up. I wanted everything – everything – to slow down, stop even, but it wouldn't. The bad dreams were back, and the sleepwalking. I turned up to work looking like one of the walkers from *The Walking Dead*.' My gaze beseeches them to understand. 'I wanted it to stop. Stop.'

Mum must sense I'm on the verge of tears because her loving arms surround me. I hang on to her for dear life. Breathe in her comfort and security, the type that has been missing from my life for so long.

'We love you, darling,' she croons into my hair. 'Never forget that. We love you.'

Dad quietly adds, 'You could have come to us at any time. We're always here for you.'

Gently I move out of Mum's arms so that I can see his face. The strain and struggle of a lifetime is stamped across it. I get up and go to him. Sit down by his side and lean my head against his shoulder. His arm hooks me close.

'Do you remember that time we came up to London when you were ten?'

I nod against his shoulder.

'And we decided to go to Harrods? You kept saying you were bored, that you didn't want to see old ladies' clothes and old ladies' knickers.'

'Edward!' Mum rushes in, scandalised.

Our laughter rings through the room. God, it feels so good, for us to be enjoying our circle of three as a family again. If time could freeze this is what I'd want it to look like. Me in the middle, Mum and Dad either side. And we're smiling, eyes laughing, making the best of our life on this earth.

'Then you got lost,' Dad continues. 'We were both frantic. Next thing we know there's a store announcement asking for the parents of Lisa Kendal to come to the information desk.'

What I had never told them was that I'd been found in the beauty department looking through the make-up. It was one of the assistants who had spotted me running my fingers through the face powder testers and then smoothing each shade on to my arm. Our conversation has never left me.

'Where are your mum and dad, beautiful?' she'd asked, crouching down so she was at my level.

My mouth had dropped open in astonishment; her face was the most perfect thing my young eyes had ever seen.

I ignored her question and pointed to the powders. 'I'm trying to choose the right colour for me.'

The dazzling smile she gave me was as perfect as the rest of her. 'Now, why would you want to put any of these on your gorgeous skin?'

'Because of these. I want to cover them up.'

I rolled up my summer dress sleeve and presented her with my scars. I waited for the inevitable 'Oh you poor thing' or 'Scarface' as some of the girls at school taunted me. But this goddess did none of that. Not even a sharp intake of breath.

Her smile grew. 'Honey, beauty is only skin deep. It's on the inside where your true beauty lies. And here.' She took my small hand and laid it over my heart.

I should've made her words my theme song. Let them guide me through the difficulties of life. Probably would've saved myself heaps of heartache along the way.

'You know why I was so proud of you that day?' Dad says, bringing me back into the room. 'The man at the information desk told us how brave you were.' He kisses me softly. 'You'll always be our brave little girl.'

A thrill of pure happiness and belonging runs through me. This means so much to me. For so long I've believed I was the worst thing to happen to them.

We sit there together chatting, sharing memories and laughing when Mum asks, 'Don't you think it's a touch strange he never got married? I mean, he's such an attractive fellow.'

'Who are you talking about?' I respond.

'Tommy Wilson.' Ah, she's got her gossip claws into the good doctor. On the whole Mum disapproves of gossip, however, every now and again she can't help herself. 'Oh! You don't think that he's... well, you-know-what?'

'Gay?' I supply. 'It's not a banned word, Mum. Plenty of liberated gay guys out there, and if Doctor Wilson is gay what's the problem?'

Dad leans away from me and frowns at Mum. 'Can we leave Tom out of this conversation?'

'I'm just saying, dear. Didn't you say he was quite the ladies' man when you were at medical school? Very charming, very dapper and quite the dancer, wasn't he? And, of course, I suppose it helped that he was a student of female psychology. He probably knew the right levers to pull when he went out wooing the girls.'

It's difficult to imagine the good doctor as a babe magnet. My dad seems to think so too; he's wearing the stony face of the century.

But Mum doesn't catch on to his expression and adds, 'Perhaps he's never met the right woman or had his heart broken and renounced the fairer sex for a life devoted to the service of others.

I prefer to believe the latter of course; it's so much more romantic. Mind you, there was that time with that flighty piece—'

My dad snaps, 'Can you stop it with this silly nonsense, Barbara? You sound like a soppy schoolgirl.'

My mum looks shocked. I am too. I've never heard Dad let rip at Mum in such a fierce manner. He isn't one of those men who believes that a man is the head of the house. He prides himself on having a real partnership with his wife.

Mum glares back, her dander well and truly up. 'Don't you carp at me like that, Edward Kendal. Tom's not just your friend, he's mine too, ever since he helped us during Lisa's accident when she was little—'

Her mouth slams shut. A tense, anxious look travels between my parents.

'What?' My question is sharp and blunt.

Dad gets to his feet. 'We really must be going.' He looks across at Mum. 'Mustn't we?'

'Of course.' Mum's on her feet too. All the joy has drained out of her. She probably doesn't realise that she's self-consciously wringing her hands.

They are already heading out of the room and towards their coats near the front door before I can speak.

'Doctor Wilson helped you during my accident? When I was five?'

That look criss-crosses between them again. This time Mum appears on the verge of tears.

Dad shakes his head. 'Your mother is getting mixed up with one of the doctors who treated you in hospital after it happened.' He takes my mum's arm before I can ask anything else. 'Now, we must be off or we'll get caught in the rush-hour traffic.'

The wall is back between us. A wall built of brick after brick cemented with lies. Dad is lying; I can tell by the way he won't meet my eyes. I was right all along. Instead of the anticipated elation I'm gutted with grief. Why won't they tell me the truth? I want to scream at them, but Dad has already opened the front door and is escorting my shaking mother into the street towards their car.

Stunned, I remain rooted in the doorway as their car roars off and they leave me and the lies behind. I want to go after them, to demand the truth. It won't do any good though; Dad will stick to his story. During his time as a doctor he'd no doubt learned all the ways to deal with human suffering by shutting off his emotions. Why should his reaction to my suffering be any different?

What finally gives me the strength to move is remembering the lines in the farewell letter I found in the spare room:

There's no need to ask too many questions. They can't help you or me. I'm gone now. Leave me to rest.

The man who'd taken his own life was so wrong. I have *so* many questions. They can help me. I'm not gone. I *refuse* to rest.

If my parents won't give me the answers I know who can.

With determination I throw on a light jacket, grab my bag and open the door.

I jump slightly back when I realise there's someone blocking my path. My heart drops when I recognise who it is.

'What are you doing here?' my shocked voice asks Jack.

He's standing in the doorway of my house. Yes, my house. Not the one I share with him and Martha but the one I own in East London.

His gaze narrows. I know what he's thinking: if Lisa has her own home why is she renting the spare room in mine and Martha's?

Nineteen

As I stare at Jack I have the same feeling a child has climbing off a spinning roundabout: your eyes tell you the motion has stopped but your ears say it's still going on and you feel sick. That's how I feel. Sick. Literally sick.

He folds his arms, looking really pleased with himself. I should slam the door but I just stand there.

'Hello, Lisa.'

I stutter. 'J-Jack.'

He looks the house up and down. 'Nice place.'

And it is. A Victorian semi in fashionable Dalston in East London. I managed to buy it before the East London line transport link came this way, making property prices shoot up. Now the area is full of cafés serving up pine nuts and quinoa to hipsters. Jack and his man bun would fit in here a treat.

Ever since I moved into Jack and Martha's, I've had a cover story ready if they should ever discover that I have my own home. It's a good story and I've practised it in front of the mirror many times. Now I can't remember how it goes.

'No, it belongs to a friend. She's on holiday and I'm checking on it for her, collecting the post, opening and closing the curtains. You know… burglars.' I sound pathetic and I know it.

His voice drips with sarcasm. 'That's very good of you. It's nice to have friends who'll look after your place while you're away.' He's enjoying himself, the rat. 'Only it's the funniest thing – I knocked on the next-door neighbour's and asked them if Lisa lives here and they said, yes she does. Although, according to them, Lisa hasn't been around much lately. They thought she'd gone on holiday. Quite a coincidence your friend being called Lisa too…'

He's peering over my shoulder trying to see into my house. I pull my front door closer to me.

'What are you doing here, Jack?'

'Here's another funny thing. I was in town today and who should I see on the street making her way home? That's right, you! And I thought, maybe Lisa wants some company on her way back to our place but you were so quick I was having trouble keeping up. And then you were taking the wrong train and I thought, funny that, has she forgotten where she lives?' He sounds like a sneering teacher or policeman who's got someone bang to rights and is enjoying every last second of it.

'And finally, I caught up with you here. But you seemed to have company, so I thought, I'll wait until those people have gone before I knock and point out that you've come to the wrong house. Relatives are they? Parents maybe? Yeah, that's right; they're probably your mum and dad.'

Nerves dig into me at the mention of my parents who had minutes before been sitting in my front room. I had only come back to my house so that they could visit me. There's no way on this earth I can reveal to them that I'm really living in a spare room at the top of a grand, old house. They'd only start bombarding me with questions, wanting to know what the hell was going on.

I tell Jack a half-truth. 'Sure, this is my house. I'm renting it out to make some money. The couple you saw were coming to view the place with a view to moving in. Obviously, I need somewhere to live while I'm doing that so I took the room at yours and Martha's. Is that a problem?'

He ignores me. He looks my house up and down again and surveys my front garden. Then he turns back to me. The sarcasm is over. His voice is biting and menacing. 'What are you playing at, Lisa? What's your angle here?'

I've recovered a little now. 'I'm not playing at anything and I don't have an angle. Nor do I appreciate being followed around by my landlord. I'm pretty sure that counts as harassment. Perhaps I'll speak to a lawyer and see what he thinks.'

He lifts his hand as if he wants to place it around my throat and squeeze. All my instincts are to rush back inside my house to protect myself. But I refuse to do it.

His hand twists into a fist and falls by his side. 'You think I don't know what you're up to? Do you think I'm stupid? I know exactly what your little game is and I'm warning you now if you don't give it up, pack your bags and leave our house, I won't be answerable for the consequences.' He leans in close, his spit flying into my face. 'Do you understand?'

'What I understand is that I've got a lease that's legally binding for six months. Renting out my own home does not breach any rules of my tenancy.'

His lip curls, eyes livid, like I'm dirt on the street. 'Is that so? Let me remind you that there's more than one way to skin a cat. Did I say cat?' He slaps the back of one hand with the other. 'Oh, naughty me, that's a bit tasteless, given what happened to that old crone who lives next door's kitty.' He points his finger in my face. 'You've been warned.'

'Are you threatening me?'

He sends me one last expression of disdain before he turns on his heels and walks back down my path and slams the gate behind him. Despite my outward defiance I'm petrified. If I go back to Jack and Martha's who knows what fun and games Jack will have in store for me. I can't understand why he's so angry. What does it matter to him if I have a home already? He'll still be getting his rent. And he needs the money from what Martha has confided in me.

The answer is obvious. Jack's hiding something. Just like he's hiding what happened to the tenant in the spare room before me.

But he's not the only one holding secrets.

***

'Why did you pretend you didn't help my family during the accident that happened to me when I was a young girl?' I slap my damning question at Doctor Wilson as I sit on the edge of the chair in his consultancy room.

I feel a measure of triumph when he stops writing in that bloody irritating notebook of his. I feel like snatching it from his hand and ripping it into tiny pieces. He hadn't looked best pleased to see me, but I suppose professionalism didn't allow him to turn me away. Probably thought I might do something nasty to myself if he didn't allow me in, like I'd done four months ago.

'Have you spoken to your parents as I advised?' he calmly throws back.

This man is a master of his craft. No matter what I chuck his way he always knows how to slip it back into his gear to ensure traffic is flowing in the direction he wants it to.

I'm persistent, almost falling off the chair. 'And the way my dad talks about you… you're no casual acquaintance. You've been buddies for years.'

He deflects my accusations with a mere arch of his brow. 'Is that how you feel, Lisa? That people, all people, are lying to you?'

Now he's trying to turn my words against me, make me feel like I'm totally paranoid. 'You know what I'm talking about. I'm talking about you lying to my face. Telling me you weren't there during my accident and you know full well you were.'

He makes notes in his book. His head comes back up. 'Who told you this?'

'My mother.'

'Lisa, I have only met your mother on three separate occasions. Once was at your father's golf club—'

'Why are you doing this to me?'

'Doing what?' He actually writes that down.

Gritting my teeth, ready to do some serious damage, I lean down and pull off one of my shoes and throw it across the room.

He straightens. 'I won't have violent behaviour in here.'

'Don't worry, doctor, I won't hurt a hair on that lying head of yours.'

I pull off my second shoe and throw it across the room.

'I don't want to have to call the police but in this instance I may have no alternative.'

I'm not hearing him as I jump up on the leather couch. I point the soles of my feet at him. Point at the one set of scars no one ever sees. His skin loses its colour.

'They're ugly, aren't they? When I was young, I gave each of them a name in the tradition of *Snow White and the Seven Dwarfs*.' I place one leg across the other in order to touch my foot. 'This one's called Lumpy because it's quite uneven, like something tried to bite a chunk out of me. Now, this one's called Dumpy because it would get so painful in the winter when I was little it would make me fall. Dump me. Dumpy. Get it?'

'Lisa—'

I won't let him slow me down as I switch to my other foot. 'There's only one of my close friends on this foot, as you can see. It's called Forget Me. So small it's almost not there. But I can never forget it. Forget any of them. So disgusting.' My leg swings back down. 'I need you to tell me what really happened. What kind of accident can give me scars like this on the soles of my feet?'

He fetches my shoes and hands them to me. 'You do see how irrational your behaviour is. Normal people don't throw their shoes around.'

'Normal? Why don't you say what you mean, that I'm mad?'

He steps back as I slip my shoes back on. 'I don't think we should continue today. I do want you to come back tomorrow. Let's pick this up then.'

I'm about to agree when I notice it. The photo on his desk. How have I missed it before? It's the same photo that my dad has on his lounge wall, of him back in the day with two other medical student chums. This photo is slightly different; none of the guys are wearing jokey surgical masks. Their faces are plain for all to see. I notice Dad, looking handsome and ready for the world. I don't recognise one man, the other I do. Doctor Wilson.

He notices where my gaze rests. He moves across and coolly turns it down on its face. He stares defiantly at me. I could chip away at him about it, but there's no point. He won't reveal a thing, just spew out more of his blah-blah-blah shrink spiel. No matter. I don't really need his confession anymore.

At the front door, I tell him, 'With my scarred feet, I would tramp the streets of London trying to find the house that's in my memory. For years I did it. I couldn't stop.'

'What house?' He shakes his head, frowning hard in confusion.

'The house where I know the accident when I was five really happened.'

'Lisa, there is *no* house.' He looks at me with pity. 'The accident occurred on a farm like your parents have told you.'

'You're so wrong.'

He senses something different about my answer. His question is almost breathless. 'What do you mean?'

'I found it. The house.'

'Lisa?' He doesn't look like a doctor anymore but a man sucker punched in the gut.

'I'm living in the spare room in the house. The house in my nightmares.'

Twenty

I stare, deflated, at the plates of sushi rolls – spicy cucumber and tuna and teriyaki chicken – on my table in the café-style Japanese restaurant, knowing he won't come. Hell, I'd probably be a no-show too if I wore his shoes.

The door opens. My spirits lift; he's here.

I feel the need to stand up to greet him as if that will show him the ultimate respect.

'What's this about, Lisa?' Alex is more than unhappy; he's properly ticked off.

'Will you sit down?' I indicate the chair across from me. 'I ordered some sushi rolls. Chicken teriyaki.' *Your favourite.*

He doesn't take the unsaid bait and roughly takes a seat. 'I'm not hungry. I thought—'

'I used to live in that house. Martha and Jack's house.' There. Out of my mouth. Now Alex knows too.

I've told him what I told Doctor Wilson a few hours ago and still can't believe what I've done. That my secret is out. I was no random, would-be tenant like all the masses of others in London. I targeted the house, took the room so I could get inside.

My mind zips back to the unforgettable moment I finally found the house that has haunted me for as long as I can remember. As I told Doctor Wilson, for years I had tramped the streets of London obsessed with finding the house that rears like a raging monster in my nightmares. After the incident cum suicide attempt, I decided the only way to rescue my sanity was to put the brakes on my hunt for the house. Giving up something that had become as natural as breathing hadn't been easy. It had become as vital to me as another arm, another leg, a second brain. Gnawing away at me, never leaving me in peace, digging its teeth in until I discovered the truth. But the truth was that finding the house was tipping me over the edge. Yes, I'll say it: sending me mad.

It was a Tuesday full of summer showers when I came back to the office, after lunch, to find Cheryl and Debbie hunched over Cheryl's iPad. I'd almost passed both women when Cheryl had beckoned me over.

'Which of these spare rooms do you think Debbie should rent?'

I'd hesitated. The last thing I needed was a chummy-chummy chat about their personal lives. I knew that Debbie had split up with her live-in fella and obviously she was looking to put down temporary roots somewhere else. Space to get back on track.

I felt sorry for – and envious of – her; she'd managed to keep a relationship going for seven whole years. I couldn't keep one going for four months. Still, it couldn't have been easy to start life all over again. So I went over. Leaned down to check out the iPad screen.

Cheryl said, 'There's this cosy little number in Camden.'

It was a lovely ground-floor room, all white and light, with a French door leading to the garden and an impressive 1930s fireplace complete with mirror. The monthly rental was eye-watering.

'Or this…' Debbie tapped her finger against the screen and the photo of the outside of a house flicked up.

There are moments in your life when you can't talk, can't breathe, become frozen in time. My heartbeat raced as I stared at something on the front of the house. Everything trembled inside me as I recognised it: the circle engraved in the stone with the key inside. It was as if it were my own special key, just for me to enter the house I'd hunted for for so many years.

Neither of my colleagues noticed my strange reaction as Debbie brought up the photo of the spare room.

I didn't look at it, excitement mixed with disbelief and anticipation flowing through me as I straightened up and breathlessly informed Cheryl, 'Take the room in Camden. It's a touch pricey but Camden's super trendy. It's where all the stylish people are hanging out.'

I had to butter her up; the last thing I wanted was for her to take that room in my house. And it was mine. I'd been searching the streets of London for what felt like all my life to find it. I couldn't believe it. I could finally unravel the secrets of my past. Or what I thought was my past.

I left them and headed for the loo with my phone in my hand. Once inside I registered quickly with the accommodation website and got the house up on screen. I organised a visit to view the room.

I stared at the house in a daze. It was like finding an old friend. Or an enemy.

Alex is staring at me now, lips slightly apart, the same way Doctor Wilson did when I revealed my secret. The good doctor, who prided himself on having a detached manner, had covered his astonishment quickly, insisting I talk more. But I couldn't have talked more if I wanted to. I was drained, mashed, could barely think.

'I don't understand,' Alex finally says, with a tiny shake of his head. 'What do you mean you lived in the house? The house next door to Aunty Pat's?'

'No, I mean the house next door to Santa Claus in the North Pole,' I respond tartly. 'Of course I mean the house where I'm renting a room.'

'When did you live there?' I'm pleased to see he picks up his favourite sushi.

Now comes the hard part. 'I don't know.'

The sushi roll hovers at his mouth as he levels me with a sceptical stare beneath his lashes. 'I've been working with a very demanding client today, a real do-you-know-who-I-am wanker, haven't had a lunch break and all I want to do is down a half pint and go to bed.'

He does look tired. Dark circles are etched beneath his eyes and his skin looks like it could do with a shot of vitamin D.

'Remember what happened that night we went back to yours?' I say slowly.

Who can forget?

He reluctantly nods and pops the rice roll into his mouth.

Nerves pinch away at me. 'I have these nightmares. Sometimes sleepwalk. I've had them since I was a kid. They're always the same. A woman screaming, children screaming, someone running after me with knives that turn into wicked-looking needles. There's a mouse with the biggest dead eyes staring at me. It finishes with a man's scream. A very different scream. Next thing I know I'm in this car being driven away from the house.'

My tongue hurriedly wets my lips before I continue. 'The one thing that sticks out about the outside of the house is a circle in the stone with a key inside. I'm sure you've seen it when you visit your Aunty Patsy.'

His eyes narrow as he thinks. His eyebrows jump high in an ah-ha moment of recognition.

'It's a mason's mark. Whoever built the house… this is their mark, a signature if you want, to tell the world they built the house. I researched mason's marks and couldn't find one like it. It's unique. One of a kind. I figured if I could find it, bingo, I'd find the house, and I did.'

Alex swallows the rest of the roll, his Adam's apple bulging unevenly. 'That's some heavy stuff. Screaming and knives and needles. Mason's marks.'

'Remember the scars you saw on my body?'

He's one of the only people I know who doesn't look away with pity or disgust when my scars come up. Even when we got it on for the first time in bed, he didn't turn his face away. Didn't ask me if they would fade with time. Didn't ask about corrective surgery. Didn't ask.

He tells me, 'I never had a problem with the scars.' He sounds hurt.

'I know that.'

The scars weren't what had pushed him to dump me.

'Do you believe me about any of this?' I plead.

'I believe that you're having these dreams for sure, but the rest…' He spreads his hands wide. At least he's not running for the hills.

A little, humourless laugh comes out, leaving a burning sensation in my chest. 'I know it sounds crazy.'

'It's not that.' He becomes very animated, moving his hands, lifting his shoulders, gaze flickering around. 'It's just our minds can play so many tricks on us. Years ago, I got really plastered and woke up thinking I'd asked my girlfriend to marry me. I saw the scene in my head, reel after reel, as it had happened. It was real. I was shitting myself – she was lovely, but be my wife? Thank you, no. Turns out I never asked her; it was all part of my drunken illusion.'

'You with a wife?' I tease.

He rolls his eyes. 'I know. Cart me off to the shrink now…' The good humour drains out of him. 'Lisa, I didn't mean—'

'It's OK. Stop treating me like I'm a delicate piece of crystal. My parents have been doing it all my life.'

'Have you asked your parents about the past? The house?'

'I have and they deny it.' The seething anger is back. 'I know they're not telling me the truth.'

'And why would they lie to you?'

Now it's my turn to become animated. 'I've been all over that with my therapist.' I don't tell him I suspect that Doctor Wilson is holding out on me too. 'The man who killed himself and the writing on the wall,' I carry on. 'I don't know how to explain it. Call it a sixth sense, but he has got something to do with my past. What happened to me in that house.'

When I discovered the farewell letter it was as if another puzzle piece from my past had slipped into place. That's why I need to find out about the man who wrote it; the route to him is the pathway to my past.

'And you want me to help you find out if there's more writing on the wall and translate it if it's there?' Alex sums up correctly.

I'm not going to beat about the bush with him. 'Will you?'

He leaves me hanging and eats another roll. The adrenaline is up, pumping a hot course through me. If he doesn't lend a helping hand I don't know what I will do.

He licks the sauce from his fingers. Leans forward. 'Here's the deal. If the writing's in your room I'll help you. If it's not, I want you to terminate your lease and leave that house.'

Initially I'm outraged. Who does he think he is to order me about? Does he really think I can up and leave the house after finally finding it? I might as well cut my throat. But he doesn't need to know that.

'Deal.'

We shake hands on it.

'When do you want me to come over?'

'The landlords will be out tomorrow night, I think. Martha says they're off to see *Macbeth* at the theatre. I'll call you.'

I've been hunting down a house with a unique mason's mark on it for years and I've moved into it with the notion of trying to work out what really happened there twenty years ago. All on the basis that I remember a few screams and being driven away in a car afterwards. When I was five. It doesn't just sound nuts. It is nuts.

I'm not losing my mind, am I? Something really did happen to young me in that house. Didn't it?

***

I stare up at it. The house. The same way I did on my first visit here. Now my secret isn't mine alone it appears different. Its stone walls are no longer a biscuit-coloured picture of welcoming warmth; they're blackened by hostility, close-mouthed about the lives of the people – families – who lived here before. The ivy has switched from creeping to creepy, slithering and winding into position to strangle its host. The mason's mark with the key inside holds my gaze. It's the only part of the house that remains the same. It's my lucky charm. The North Star in my memory that guided me here.

When I open the door my one purpose is to get to my room as fast as possible because I don't fancy another verbal brawl with Jack about my real home. Then again, what can he do? I haven't broken any laws. I'd like to see him try to kick me out onto the street. Let him shout, yell, bully, threaten. I won't be leaving. As much as I try to beef up my courage quota, there's a seed of fear inside me that won't stop growing. I'm in plain sight now, my real reason for being in this house known by two other people, and Jack has rumbled that I have my own home.

Maybe that's why instead of going straight up I'm drawn to the black and red rug in the heart of the house. As soon as I stand on it, calm seeps up through my damaged feet, fanning out through my body. The warm, welcoming sensation takes me away from all the worries. Through my nose and mouth I flood my lungs with fresh air. I feel rebalanced, resettled, retuned.

Upstairs, I shut my door and use the chain. I don't switch on the light. Let my gaze dart around, searching for any more fun and games from Jack.

Everything's in order.

I should eat, but I'm not hungry. I move over to the wall, where the lining paper once again covers the writing, and place my palm against it. That's what I'd wanted to do when I found the writing: trace my fingertip over every letter, hoping they would communicate with me about the past. I turn to the other walls, almost tempted to take down each piece of wallpaper now. Peel back more secrets. I decide against it. I'll wait for Alex. I have a strong sense of dread about doing it on my own. Where this feeling comes from, I don't know.

I get ready for bed. Run the softness of my scarf through my fingers before binding my leg to the bed. I'm too weary to dance tonight but still need the rhythm of music to change the beat of my body into one ready to sleep.

I lie down. Put my earphones in place. Press play.

Amy's 'Tears Dry On Their Own' soothes me.

I close my eyes and hope.

Twenty-one

The following evening, when I get in from work, the house is still. No sounds to indicate anyone else is here. None of that subtle energy people give off that tells you they're around even when you can't see them. Good. Martha and Jack are already out. I can't hold back the satisfied half-smile.

I head to my room where I text Alex. Twenty minutes later his text pings:

At the front door.

I race down the stairs and pull him in. Worry lines crease his forehead and his eyes, and his hair has an edgy pattern that suggests fingers have been dragged through it. He's not happy to be here. Guilt gnaws away at me. I ruthlessly cut it out. I need Alex to help me find the truth.

He's decked out in a formal black suit and tie. He sees my appraisal. 'I'm expected at a work party organised by a super-important client. I've said I'll be late, but I can't be too late. So I haven't got much time.'

I can't help suspecting he wants to get away from me as soon as, that he's doing this out of misguided loyalty to his former girlfriend. You know, Sir Walter Raleigh laying his cloak down for Queen Bess. As we climb the stairs, I remember how things went from great to disastrous with us.

It was one of those Saturday nights when the tube was heaving and there were so many people spilling out onto the streets of London, I wondered how on earth there was enough space for us to all live in this awesome city. I was surprised at the numbers because it was so cold. The type of weather that chains and locks around your bones. Alex had managed to snag much sought-after tickets to the latest must-see, five-star musical in town. Despite the performance being spectacular, getting to my feet for the thunderous standing ovation wasn't really my thing. I wanted to remain hidden in my seat. Alex was having none of it – he'd hauled me up, tugged his arm round my waist and pulled me into the heat of his side. His joy was so infectious I couldn't help grinning like there was no tomorrow and clapping along. After that we'd hit a bar and knocked back too many margaritas. Unsteady on our feet, we'd weaved our way to his place. I couldn't believe that this gorgeous guy who loved cracking jokes, who wasn't interested in digging into my head, who adored living for the moment was mine. All for me.

As soon as we got into his flat we didn't hang around; we hit the sack and had sex. The first time we made love, a couple of weeks back, I'd surprised myself by not being nervous and being upfront with him about the marks on my body. I hadn't been upfront with him about anything else. Nor did I let on that it was my first time having sex. Does that matter in this day and age? Is the word virginity still in the modern dictionary?

Alex, darling Alex, hadn't said a word. Instead he'd peeled my clothes off and… it still brings a rush of tears to my eyes now… he'd kissed every scar he could find. Quick, soft kisses as if he were leaving behind a seed of love. Our loving was fierce and sweet. After, I lay curled in Alex's arms.

I hadn't used my scarf the first night we went to bed with each other, praying that I wouldn't need it. And it had worked. For the first time in a long time, I'd woken to a new day feeling fresh, ready and most importantly, still in bed. The second and the third times were the same. I was silly, of course, I should've known better – my life has never been that easy.

That night the dreams were back. Bad. Gleaming razor-sharp blades transforming into ice-pick pointed needles, shifting shapes, twisting colours, running, running, running. I'd jack-knifed awake, leaking sweat, with Alex's startled face hovering over me.

'Are you OK?' A stupid question for him to ask because it was clear I wasn't.

I could've lied to him – looking back, maybe that's what I should've done – but his reactions to my scars had lulled me into thinking I could tell him the rest. I'd given him a small kiss and got out of the bed and hunted for my bag. I'd faced him holding my one true friend, my scarf. He'd sat up and I couldn't blame him for the wary expression he shot at me.

He tried to lighten the mood with, 'Just so you know, I've never done bondage before.'

'It's nothing like that.' I could only be dead serious. No one, not even my parents, knew about this. 'I have to tie my leg to your bed.'

'Excuse me?' All joking had fled.

'I sleepwalk sometimes. Have crushing dreams. This' – I held the scarf up – 'usually stops me from wandering about in my sleep, but not all the time.'

The look he sent me: disbelief turning into confusion, finally shutting down. I'd known I'd lost him.

He'd got up and wouldn't come near me. I stubbornly refused to explain anymore. If he couldn't accept me what the hell was I doing in a chilly room that had promised so much unconditional care and love?

'I'll go and sleep on the sofa. You' – he waved at me, his gesture including the scarf – 'have the bed.'

Bitterness overwhelmed me. Why had I opened my heart to this type of rejection again? I'd cried that night. Really cried, holding my scarf shoved in my mouth to muffle the sound. I wasn't surprised when he told me with utter politeness the following morning that he wasn't sure we should see each other anymore.

I was alone again.

Once we're in my room, Alex must sense where my thoughts are because he scowls as we sit on the bed. His eyes drop for a second before he brings them up again. 'I'm really sorry about that night—'

'Look, Alex, I've got enough crap going on here without you dragging me down a very rocky memory lane.'

'My brother, he's a lot older than me.' He launches into his story anyway. 'He was in the army. He came back from the Iraq War a different guy. Nightmares, screaming in the night…' He presses his fingers over his lips, his cheekbones straining against the skin.

'Alex, you don't have to—'

It pours out. 'That's why I behaved like an idiot that night. I didn't want to go through that again. My parents got my brother the treatment he needed but the road to it was pure hell.' He looks deep into my eyes. 'I didn't want a girlfriend with that kind of trauma. I know it's selfish but seeing my brother like that, day in, day out, left me feeling like I was dying inside. Joel was the one who taught me how to ride a bike, gave me my first taste of alcohol behind my parents' backs, took me on my first holiday abroad.' He raises his head. Staggering pain dulls the colour of his face. 'I know he was ashamed for me to see him like that when he came back. He prided himself on playing the big brother.' A vehement heat enters his tone. 'I could never feel ashamed of him. But at the same time, it was an experience I don't want to ever go through again.'

I'm stunned and feel so sad for him. I'd thought that Alex was so different, but the reality is he's just like me. We project one thing to the world but inside there's hurt, there's pain, there's memories chasing us that will never go away. Still, I feel guilt that my demons have dredged up his own.

I stand up, pushing my own wants aside. 'Alex, you don't have to stay.'

'Don't be daft.' He grasps my hand and pulls me back onto the bed. 'I don't want you to be offended, but it's my considered opinion that you need professional help.' That pisses me off, so I try to butt in but he won't allow me. 'I'm not saying what you've told me isn't the truth, your truth. My first concern is your well-being—'

I'm fuming. 'Well-being? Why don't you say what you mean? She's off her trolley, not the full ticket, bonkers, touched in the head—'

He grabs my arms and draws me nearer. 'I know all those words, Lisa. People said them about my brother. They weren't true. What was true was he needed treatment. Help. The right kind of help.' His voice lowers. 'That's what you need too. The right help.'

I pull my arms away. Shake my head with grim misery. 'Don't you get it, Alex? This house' – I spread my arms wide – 'this is my treatment. I can take as many meds as I can for as long as I can, sit in untold, frigid rooms with untold concerned shrinks, but you know what? This house will continue to haunt me to my dying day. I refuse to live like that anymore.' I need to stop, so I do before emotion tips me into a place I don't want Alex to see.

I'm calmer, at least on the outside, when I speak again. 'I can't go on like this.' I stand again and let my gaze roam around the room. 'Will you help me find more of the writing on the wall?'

I let out a long sigh of relief as he gets up and begins to tear down the next set of lining paper near the first lot of writing I discovered. I start helping him. We carefully peel down two rolls. A growl of frustration leaves me; there's no writing there. Bollocks!

Alex turns to me. 'What if there isn't any more? I said that the last time I was here.'

My head moves in denial. 'It's here. I know it's here. The house is talking to me through these walls.'

Alex can't help giving me the arched-eyebrow, that's-just-mad look.

'Tell you what,' he suggests. 'Why don't I start over there, near the window, and you continue here?'

That's what we do for the next few minutes until he excitedly calls, 'I've got something.'

I rush over. Can't believe it. I was beginning to doubt there was any more. Together we peel the lining paper down to the skirting board. My breath holds in my throat as it always does when I gaze at the writing on the wall. The handwriting isn't as bold, the marks of ink weaker, in places wavy, as if the person writing it was trembling.

I'm too eager to wait. 'What does it say?'

Alex doesn't answer as he reads. Then turns to me. 'This time there's a date. 1998—'

'That's the year I turned five. My fifth birthday.' I'm excited. My first real link to the author of the farewell letter.

'What's your birthday got to do with this?'

'That was the year, I think, that whatever happened to me in this house happened.' My wide eyes plead with him. 'Do you believe me now?'

Alex makes no comment. Instead he focuses on the writing. 'It's our old friend, Doctor Death, Solanov, again. The lines taken from his work say: "If you fall in love with a beautiful woman, you're digging your own grave and the graves of the others who you love".'

I'm unimpressed. 'He didn't like women very much, then.'

'Maybe he loved one too much and it all went pear-shaped. A lot of men will know that feeling.'

Alex doesn't give me a chance to ask if his cryptic comment refers to me.

He starts to translate.

Twenty-two

Before: 1998

In a daze he rushed along the street, and when he reached the house he expected to see lights on everywhere and to hear the noises he always associated with his family even when they were asleep. But of course there weren't any lights. No noises. There was never going to be any again.

He opened the door. Didn't go in. Stood on the threshold dreading going inside. By rights the racing rate of his heart should push him into a heart attack. Sweet Jesus, he wished it would do it. Do it! Make him not have to deal with what he knows he must.

He stepped into the house. Closed the door with a quiet *click*. Put his keys down on the table in the hallway and looked around at the scene.

The worst was over now. Actually, it wasn't the worst; that was still to come. He was going to have to start lying now. Lying all the time and forever more. And acting. Carrying on just like before. What man could possibly keep that up? But he knew he had no choice. He owed people. He owed his family. He owed her in particular. He was going to have to do it whatever it took.

Because he was to blame.

He flicked a light on in the cupboard under the stairs. Everything he needed was there. Green rubble bags that didn't burst open when they were full, mops, cloths, brushes, brooms, detergents, bleach and steel wool. He was going to have to do a fingertip search of the whole house to make sure he found all the evidence of what had happened and eliminate the lot.

The simplest thing to do would be to use petrol, splash its noxious liquid everywhere – on furniture, clothes, books, photos, toys – and burn the place down. But that wasn't an option; the only way ahead was lying and acting because he owed people and he was to blame.

Blame. His legs gave way, tumbling him into the wall. Bile snaked up his throat and he repeatedly vomited onto the floor. He couldn't go on like this. Tears flashed into his eyes, trailed down his cheeks.

Or perhaps there was another option.

He went back to the cupboard under the stairs. Found the coiled rope. He picked it up and stared at it before putting it back. It would come to the rope one day. But for now there was lying and acting to be mastered first.

He started in the dining room. Total chaos. The table was at an angle where it had been pushed aside. Chairs were overturned. Food was scattered on the floor, trodden into the rugs and smeared down the walls. Broken plates and cutlery had ended up in the strangest places, as if they'd been arranged there deliberately. There was an upright glass, still full of orangeade, on a top shelf. And toys of course. They were everywhere.

He stood for a moment with his green rubble bag hanging open in his hands and let it slip through his fingers. He couldn't do this now and there was no hurry anyway. No one was coming; it could wait until tomorrow. He had as long as he needed.

He walked back through the abnormal silence to the morning room and sat down on the piano stall. The piano was open and it was obvious someone had been playing it earlier because there was a house rule about keeping it closed when it wasn't being used. It must have been his son. His adored son was a promising piano player.

Lying. Acting.

Without thinking, he touched the keys and played Rachmaninov's 'Prelude in C Sharp Minor', and it was as if his son sat beside him. It soothed his tormented soul. Why did this piece always end up on English people's list of favourite works? Only a Russian could understand these notes and what they meant. English people didn't know anything about music. It was true he wasn't actually Russian, having been born in England, but his father was. The blood and heritage of Mother Russia ran through his veins too. They understood. They understood what blood and death meant; their history was soaked in it.

His phone began to ring. As the notes died away, he pulled it from his pocket and answered.

'I'm sorry, not now. Something terrible has happened but I can't talk about it at the moment. I'll call you sometime.'

Lying and acting already. But he didn't need to.

Her voice was both alluring and mocking. 'Yes, I know something terrible has happened and you know who's to blame for it, don't you?' She waited a few moments before delivering her killer blow. 'You are.'

Twenty-three

Mine and Alex's breathing crackles in the room, rushed and ragged, stung by the impact of what he's just finished reading.

We look sideways at each other. It's me that starts. 'So taking his own life has been something he's thought about before.'

Alex slowly nods. Blows out a long path of unsteady air. 'That wasn't easy reading. I nearly stopped part way through.'

I turn back to the writing, frowning, hiding the hope in my heart. But I dare to say it. 'The food, broken plates—'

'Glasses on the floor,' Alex takes up. 'Do you think that's your birthday party?' He assesses me closely. I can still hear the doubt in his tone.

There's an ache deep inside that so wants this to be true. But… 'I don't know.' My features scrunch up as I think hard.

'No way do I want to burst your bubble but food and smashed plates and glasses could be anything.'

Alex is right. I start pacing, my arms wrapped with hard tension across my lurching middle. I'm frustrated. Wishing the writing ignited a memory. It didn't. Nothing from that time is real. The only reality plays out in my howling nightmares.

He softly offers: 'Do you want my opinion?'

I keep pacing as I nod.

'OK, this is how I see it from what I read.' He turns to face me fully. 'The year is 1998. So the date corresponds to when you reached five years of age, and say you had a birthday party.' He waits for confirmation from me, which I give.

'When he comes back the house is a mess, like a tornado has been through the place. He keeps blaming himself to the point of thinking about suicide.'

I wince. That word is so vicious.

Alex continues, 'This looks like a classic scene after a breakup. They had a row beforehand that got physical. The house ends up in chaos. After he leaves for work, she packs her and the kids' stuff. They leave. In retrospect he blames himself. Wished the row had never happened.'

'But what about the lying? The acting? Why use those particular words?' I unfold my arms and stalk over to him. 'Odd choice of words to use for a row.'

Alex's fingers rush through his hair. 'When I trained to be a lawyer I did a stint in a chamber specialising in divorce cases. This one particular client was trying to stop his wife divorcing him, insisting she had only recently left him. That meant that his wife had to wait years before starting divorce proceedings. It turns out he'd been *lying* and *acting* to all his family, friends and us; she'd left him a year and half ago. He'd been pretending to everyone that things were normal, that she was still living in their family home.'

Alex gives a who-knows shrug. 'I suspect that's what our man here meant. He was going to have to act and lie to everyone that everything was OK. Do you know why our client did it?' He didn't wait for my answer. 'He was too embarrassed, scared of people finding out that his marriage was over.'

I still won't let it go. 'What about the woman he wrote about at the end? The one who calls him? He seems surprised that this mystery woman already knew what happened in the house, whatever that may be.'

'Who knows what was going on in his home?'

I scoff. 'Whoever this woman is, she hardly sympathises with him. In fact, she comes across as a really nasty bitch.'

'Maybe it was a friend of his wife's? Someone from her family?'

I have a sudden urge to cup my palms round Alex's so-kind face. He's the type of guy I would've loved to spend the rest of my days with. Leaning my head against his shoulder for comfort and strength.

Now I may be about to spoil the ease between us.

'I need to find out everything I can about this man—'

His brow hitches up. 'And you want me to help you.'

'You're a lawyer, so you have access to all sorts of stuff. You can find documents related to this house.' I'm not on my knees begging but that's what it feels like.

The silence is intense as Alex thinks on what I've asked him. 'Alright.' A smile bursts out of me as Alex continues. 'Don't forget what our deal is. If this has nothing to do with you, you must leave this house.'

'Aye aye, captain.' I salute him, standing to attention. Then I remember something else. My gaze roams across the walls. 'What you read tonight sounds like the end of a story. I think there's more writing here. A middle part to this story.' I turn to Alex hopefully. 'Will you…?'

'I can't.' He checks his watch. 'I'm already late for my firm's function. It isn't going to go down well with the boss if I'm a no-show.'

The room seems to disappear as we look deeply at each other. I know what's going to happen next. So does he. We kiss. No pressure, no tongues, a simple, sweet touching of the lips that's over in seconds. Neither of us explores what it means. Some things are best left gift-wrapped and never opened.

He heads for the door without really meeting my direct gaze. I lead him back downstairs. At the door I ask him a question:

'The other day Patsy was going to tell me something important, then she saw her cat in my arms…'

'You want me to ask her?'

'That would be so good of you.'

He opens the door and tells me, 'In the meantime, don't search for more writing. Let me try and find out what I can. You, on the other hand, get some rest. Build your strength back. I'll be in touch.'

Then he is gone. As soon as I'm back in the room the writing on the wall beckons me. There's that pull again. An uncontrollable need to lay my palms flat against it and lean in. The bond is so strong it borders on frightening, something almost beyond my control. I hastily step back.

I'll put the lining paper back up in the morning.

'Get some rest' was Alex's advice.

I can't do that. I know I'm getting close to the truth.

I lie in bed. I hear the house calling me again.

For once in my life I'm glad I will myself not to sleep.

**

Just after midnight, Martha and Jack arrive back, laughing and talking. He sounds boozy, a bit worse for wear.

The stairs creak at 1am. My landlord and lady are heading upstairs. God knows what they've been doing downstairs all this time. Having naughty sex across the dining room table? No. I can't imagine Martha letting him muck up her glam look. For that matter, I can't see Jack getting into anything that means the disintegration of his man bun. Their bedroom door closes.

The house is silent at 2am. I'm ready.

I leave the room. Travel on light feet in the dark. I head for my crappy lease-rules loo downstairs. I do what I need to do and pull the old-style chain. The outhouse – let's not pretend it's anything else – practically shakes with the gurgling whoosh of water. The noise of the tank takes over with what sounds like the chatter of a thousand bubbles. I've long past the stage of resentment at being denied access to the grand bathroom upstairs. It is their house; they're entitled to their privacy. The strange thing is I've come to enjoy this, the most inhospitable room in the house. There's something elegant, model-like, about the long, curved pipe that leads to the tank. I love the sturdiness of the walls. The window that gives a peep into the forbidden garden.

And that's why I'm really here now. The garden.

I'm dressed like a robber in the night in old black trousers and a pullover. I have my hair in a cap and I'm armed with my phone with the torch facility ready to go. The window's permanently locked which explains the fragrant odour but I already know that any generic window key will open it. And I've got one from a store. The only slight problem is the size of the window, but that's one advantage of being slight: you can squeeze through things.

I climb up onto the toilet seat. Unlock the window. Push it outwards. It fights back. I'm not giving up. Finally, with a drawn-out, squeaky groan, it opens. I push some more, then it sticks at an angle. I can't risk using more force in case the whole frame crashes on to the open ground outside. I turn myself sideways and try to wriggle through. Getting out is fairly easy but there's a drop with nothing for me to hold on to. Using the toilet wall as a springboard, I push my feet hard against it. I'm through and land in a tangle on a rotten wood-decking contraption that gives way when I land on it. Presumably that's another of Jack's half-finished and uncared for bodged jobs.

I hurry away from the house and hide behind one of those mini greenhouses that you buy in garden centres and put up yourself. The plastic is torn and flapping. There's nothing inside. I wait for a minute or two in case Jack has heard the noise although what my excuse for coming out of the window is going to be, I don't know. But he doesn't come. I make my way down the garden. Switch on my phone's light.

The garden is dense. What shocks me is that it's uncared for, unloved.

'He's a touch possessive of the garden. Grows all sorts out there.' That was Martha's explanation as to why Jack had grabbed my arm when I'd tried to go out there. She's right, there's lots growing in the garden, but Jack's so-called green fingers aren't taking care of anything out here. Large fruit trees with weedy apples and pears. Bushes that might have a fine display of flowers if they were pruned, watered and fertilised. Brown water-starved patches of grass, overgrown paths, a derelict washing machine and a rusty bike with one wheel missing. This garden looks like it's cursed. Only the fences on either side look like they're being kept in order. I suppose I should be grateful there are no long mounds of earth with crosses on them either.

Is that what I'm looking for? A grave? The writing on the wall and the farewell letter written by a man now buried in the garden? Even that sounds a bit too Hollywood movie to me. Nevertheless, Jack is hiding something out here. This house is in my blood; I'm compelled to find out everything I can about it.

I go deeper and deeper. There's plenty more junk lying around and more thickets of dense vegetation. Then it changes. It's as if I've stumbled into a completely different garden. Little patches of earth that are watered, weeded, well tilled and have canes supporting happy, healthy and tall plants. My torchlight against the leaves makes them a stunning green. They're tucked away in this jungle but must be open to sunlight through the day. Nearby are the tools of the trade of a dedicated gardener. Hoes, rakes and shears. There's a tap with a hosepipe wrapped around it. Unlike the handle and lock on the toilet window the metal tap looks greased and shiny. There are also metal spikes in the ground by the fence with little red lights flashing on them.

Wow! I have to take it back about Jack; he knows how to cultivate a garden.

I stare with wonder, can't really believe this. Why would Jack hide this captivating oasis away from the world? It doesn't make any sense. I go deeper and these little groups of plants become more frequent. I take the leaves of one between my fingers. I'm no garden or plant expert but they look familiar. My brain goes into overdrive as I try and try to remember where... Abruptly my hand on the leaf jumps back with the sensation of being scalded. I know what they are. I've found the garden's dirty little green secret.

Cannabis.

Twenty-four

J ack and Martha are running their own mini cannabis farm out of sight in this quiet suburb. Now I see that the man I saw Jack with in the garden the day I found Bette in my room must've been either a drug addict or a buyer. I can't believe this is Martha's doing. She wouldn't get her finely manicured nails scratched and dirty tending to these illegal plants, so it must be Jack. Does his wife know about it? Have I solved the puzzle of why these two want me out? Or raised a new one of why they allowed me to rent a room in the first place?

I can't shop Jack to the cops; if I do that I might not be able to live here anymore. Then I'm back to square one, not understanding why this house means so much to me.

There's not much else to see on Farmer Jack's smallholding so I make my way back up the garden. Little red lights, like eyes watching my every move, flicker as I go. I turn off my phone as I get closer to the house. Ferret around for something to stand on so I can climb back through the window. You'd think in this junkyard that would be easy but it's not.

A shocking white light blinds me. Instinctively, I cover my eyes. Now there's bursts of powerful lights on the house shining outwards, hanging in the trees, on the tall poles. The whole garden is more a floodlit football pitch for an evening game in the winter.

As I rapidly blink to get my vision back to normal, I hear locks turning on the back door and bolts being pulled back. It's too late for me to run and hide. The door swings open and Jack appears. He's rumpled from been woken up. He's wearing a pair of unlaced workman's boots and a pair of scruffy boxer shorts, and has naked, hairy legs. He's got a white T-shirt on and over that a puffy sleeveless green gilet of the sort that horsey people use. In his jacket pocket the top of a long knife is clearly visible and he's swinging a baseball bat in his hands. He stands for a moment, framed in the doorway with the stance of a man determined to defend his property or a criminal with badness in his heart. I don't know. I do know I'm shivering with fear.

He's shaking his head with an evil grin of recognition. 'It's you, is it? I might have guessed.'

He comes towards me. I'm petrified now. He's going to beat me, isn't he? Batter me black and blue until I agree to keep his nasty secret. I think of him bashing the life out of the mouse until its blood and skin are splattered across the floorboards of my room. And now he's looking at me like a dumb animal. I'm walking backwards, my hands raised in surrender, stumbling and tripping as I go. I think of screaming but I know that will just be a signal for him to lay into me with the bat. I think of shouting out for Martha but I already know how much she's willing to overlook and I can't be sure beating me won't be another thing she chooses to ignore.

He's right in front of me now with his well-lit face and its malicious grin. He prods me in the chest. I stumble back.

He sneers, 'Who are you working for, eh? Is it the cops? Collecting a tenner a week in a pub from some bored member of the drugs squad? For services rendered? Is that it? No, I don't think so, they've got rules about working with flaky people like you… I don't think it's the cops…'

His prod this time feels more like an attempt to stab. I tumble backwards into a thick bush but bounce back slightly and recover my footing. I turn to run but I already know that the fencing is like Fort Knox and I'll never get out alive.

He takes up where he left off. 'Or is it one of my customers who's decided to cut out the middle man and blow a hole in my fence when my product is ripe and harvest it himself… and you're here to keep him posted on developments? Yeah… I reckon that's it. I'll tell you what; you tell me who this scumbag is and I'll take care of things from there. If you're a good girl, I might even be willing to let you pay the rent back, pack your bags and piss off tonight. But you are going to tell me who it is, I promise you that.'

I get nasty too. 'One of your unsatisfied customers belt you across the face, did they?' The bruise on his face I first saw after finding Bette has faded but I can still see it in the glaring light.

Strangely, he says nothing, his expression one of brief embarrassment. The little red lights become an extension of Jack's eyes, flickering as I retreat down the garden. That's when I figure out they are his eyes. They're infrared beams. I tripped them; that's how he knew I was in his illicit garden.

Now he's mocking my accent. 'Oh Jack, I'll take you and Martha to court with one of my super-duper lawyer friends I went to public school with. You wouldn't like that would you?' And then he adds in his own voice, 'You posh bitch.'

His piss-take speech is the trigger that reminds me why I'm here, in this house. Nothing and no one, or weed plants, is going to make me leave. Determination stiffening my spine, I stand my ground. Let him push me over and over; I'll get back up every time.

He sees my resolve in the way I defiantly lift my chin and backs off slightly in surprise.

I tell him, 'I don't give a stuff about your poxy little drugs operation. I'm not informing the police and I don't work for drug dealers. I don't need the money because I'm way, way better than that. I'm not some junkie with debts to pay. You're way out of line.'

Now I figure out what he was accusing me of when he discovered I have a house. Asking me what I was really doing in the house. He thought I was a mole to take down or muscle in on his drugs operation. If this wasn't such a horrible situation I'd laugh my head clean off.

He steps into my space as he rests the bat on his shoulder. Pushes his face into mine. His bedtime breath coats my skin. 'Out to catch some night air, were you? Is that it? Or are you just the curious type? Because you know what happened to the cat that got curious… don't you?'

My face invades his space now. Our eyes inches apart. I hiss, 'Well, you'd know all about dead cats after what you did to Bette.'

His eyes blink quickly and his voice is less angry; in fact, it sounds almost weary. The lethal bat droops slightly. 'Please, not with the cat thing again. Why would I have killed her bloody cat?'

He's lost some of his mojo, so I use my fingers to push him back a touch. 'So, Bette climbed up on the roof, stuck her tail in my window and then poisoned herself? Some kind of suicide as art statement, was it?' Now it's my turn to mock. 'I should've kept her body and sent it in for next year's Turner Prize.'

He genuinely doesn't seem to understand. 'I never touched her cat. Why would I do that? I like her cats; it's the only thing I do like about her. I'd feed them bits of liver when I was watering the plants. You're mad.'

Either he's telling the truth or he's wasted as a failed handyman cum small-time cannabis cultivator because he should be strutting his stuff on the West End stage.

I tell him, 'Right. I'm going back in the house now. I don't give a monkey's about what you get up to in this garden.'

His body language changes. 'If you need any gear, I'm your man. I've got all sorts of modern delights up my enterprising sleeve.'

The bloody cheek! I brush past him. I can feel his hot gaze on me but he doesn't follow. I stride back to the house but I stop as I go. Because in an upstairs window, a shadowy figure stands in the half-light with her arms folded. Martha looks down at me for a moment and then turns away.

***

It's Martha's perfume that alerts me she's waiting for me. It's heavier than her usual delicate, citrus choice, an overpowering scent like a fistful of lilies crushed by the squeeze of a hand. I move my head back to get away from it, but it won't leave me alone. I am scared.

I don't want to admit it, but how else can I explain the ice-cold adrenaline rushing through my blood? This woman has the power to tear apart everything. Absolutely everything.

I take the final step. Raise my gaze. And there she is, at the foot of the stairs that lead to my room.

Martha's shiny-red dressing gown makes her pop in the soft glow of the wall light. For the first time I really see it: the sexiness she wears like a double skin. Her head angles at just the right degree to catch the light, perfectly highlighting her strong bone structure – cheekbones, jawline, even the bridge of her nose. The swell of artificial filler has made me dismiss the plumpness of her lips; her mouth is different now, lips slightly apart as she breathes in fragile jets of air. The glow of her green eyes sucks me in. A slice of one of her legs peeps out from her dressing gown. The silver pendant on the black velvet choker snug around her elegant neck winks at me. I had got it so wrong thinking Martha was a stunner only in her youth; she is still a stunner now. Maybe it was Jack who was captivated by her, not the other way around?

'Lisa,' she calls me. There's no smile with her words, which makes me edgy and nervy. 'I need to talk to you.'

My heart kicks up a beat. I forget all about Jack and his cannabis kingdom because I know what's coming. I swallow the lump in my dry throat and walk over to her with as much confidence as I can muster.

'Can it wait till the morning?'

I could slap myself because my question sounds so defensive. Implies I have something to hide.

She still doesn't smile as her gaze runs over me, assessing me as if she's checking me out for the first time. Well, that's how it looks to me.

'I heard something today that I simply must speak to you about.' Her words are easy. There's no tension in them. But I know what's coming.

I manage to keep my tone equally as easy. 'Whatever you've heard, I'm sure we can work it out.'

Wrong thing to say again! I'm implying that I've done something wrong.

Martha wets her full lips.

I know what's coming.

'Jack's informed me that you already have a home.' Martha carries on, her beauty marred by a puzzled frown. 'I don't understand why you didn't tell us this when you came to view the room.'

Self-assurance flows from me. I have got my story all ready to go. 'The truth is that I've had a few financial knock-backs lately and got myself into a bit of a hole. The money I get from renting my house for six months will sort me out. In the meantime, I needed to find somewhere else to live.' I can already read the question on her face, so add, 'I could've gone back to my mum and dad's...' I do a fake shudder. 'My parents are lovely but would've treated me like their little girl again. Plus, this is my problem and I'm going to be the one to sort it out.'

Martha is silent, the confusion still stamped across her features. 'I'm going to be upfront and honest with you. When Jack told me, I felt a bit funny. Started thinking, have I got a liar living under my roof?'

'That was not my intention and I apologise for that.' Martha does look like she's got a serial killer in her house. I suppose I would react similarly too. 'The truth is, I felt embarrassed. No one wants to admit they can't manage their cash.'

Martha's poise changes; her leg retreats behind her dressing gown as she stares right into my eyes. Her green gaze can be quite unnerving. 'You are telling me the whole truth? Are there any other lies?'

Lies. My heart's back to pounding. Is she trying to tell me something? Putting me in the heat of the spotlight so I confess why I'm really in her house? *Stop it*, my soft inner voice scolds me. How the hell can she know?

I keep my stare strong and steady. 'I can assure you that I'm keeping nothing else under my hat. I'm really tired, Martha, I'm going to head off for some shut-eye.'

She surprises me by leaning forward and patting me on my arm. 'I don't want there to be any awkwardness between us.'

'Neither do I.'

'Good.' The other woman finally smiles. It's sweet and strangely calming. 'Have a good night.'

And it's as she goes to lean back from me that the pendant on her choker swings by my eyes. It's so quick that I can't be sure, but I swear there's engraved writing on the pendant, and something else. A name.

Bette.

***

I gag and struggle to hold back the bile as I shove the chain with fumbling fingers against the door. Did I see what I think I saw? Bette's name tag on Martha's choker? Or were my tired eyes deceiving me? The movement was so quick, the lighting so dim. There was definitely writing on it; of that I am sure. But Bette's name? I squeeze my eyes shut as I try to re-picture the scene. Martha's long, fine neck. The tops of her rounded breasts as she breathed and her slightly opening dressing gown. Her heavy scent becoming a mask over my face. The pendant swings by my gaze... I see a 'b'. Was it real or is my mind now making this up?

My eyes flash back open. The enormity of what I might have just discovered hits like the bricks of the house falling on me. There's only one way that Martha could have got the cat's tag: she was the one who killed it. It wasn't Jack, it was his wife. And the mouse? My mind skids back... Jack's denial that he hadn't put the mouse stuck on a trap in my room had been furious. What if he's telling the truth? There had been that moment when I'd reached downstairs and I'd heard a door shut upstairs, giving him the opportunity he needed to hurry to my room and put it there. But what if it had been Martha? Standing behind the door of her bedroom, the disgusting mouse and trap dangling from her fine, soft hand, listening for me to go downstairs. Then she opens the door, tiptoes upstairs and does her vile deed. And the pigeons and flies? It was Martha, not Jack, who brought the subject up with me, insisting she saw a fly in the house. I hadn't seen any flies other than in my room. And she'd been all ready with her excuse that pigeons getting stuck in the chimneys are a common occurrence in this house. I imagine her laughing inside her head as she told me, relishing every last moment of our discussion.

And the cat? Did she really kill Bette? My tummy turns over. How else can I explain the possibility that she's wearing the poor animal's tag? Did she lure that innocent cat in and poison it with chemicals or rotten food?

I'm finding it hard to take any of this in. My God, to walk around wearing the tag of an animal she's killed is sick, really sick. Pure evil.

That's if she did it.

I can't believe this. I don't want it to be Martha. She was so patient and caring when I was awake-sleeping. She helped me with gentleness to my feet, guided me with the love of a mother for her distressed child back to my room. Even stayed with me until I felt more myself again. And what about the time I heard Jack hitting her? No, I convince myself again. This is Jack, not Martha. Maybe he forced her to wear the cat's tag? He's been abusing her, physically hurting her, goodness knows for how long. Isn't that what they say? That abused women will stay with their abuser because they're too terrified to leave, have had their self-esteem literally punched out of them?

But what had I really seen and heard that day when I came into the house and was shaken to the core by the flesh-on-flesh sound of a blow? The closed door of the lounge meant I hadn't actually seen anything. There had been the raised voices. No. It was a single, raised voice. Now I remember, I wasn't able to tell if it was a man or a woman because it was so ravaged with rage. And Martha's not the one with a bruise the colour of ugly on her face. It's Jack. I think back to us a while ago in his pungent cannabis den in the garden and how embarrassed he'd been when I mentioned the mark. What if it wasn't embarrassment but shame? Humiliation that his wife's knocking him around?

I see another possibility right in front of me, as if it's the writing on the wall: what if it's Martha who wants me to pack up and go? I shake my head; it doesn't make any sense. Jack wanting me to go I can understand. I knocked back his advances, he's ticked off, can't deal with the fact a woman doesn't want him in her knickers, so he wants me out. I get that.

But Martha? What have I ever done to her? Is it because she doesn't want the competition of a younger woman inside her home? Not that there's any type of competition going on here. Hadn't Martha admitted she hadn't factored in the effect of having a younger woman near her husband every day?

'Did you sleep with him?'

Those were her exact words.

My brain's foggy. I can't figure out what's going on. I put the chair under the door and drag the desk there too. I'm spooked. Scared witless.

Is Jack the danger in this house? Or is it Martha?

Or am I seeing things that aren't really there?

Twenty-five

Mum looks on with disbelief as I step out of my car the next afternoon. She's flustered, checking the time on her watch.

'What are you doing here? You said you were coming this evening. Don't you recall that your father's out this afternoon?' Then her mind works overtime as she visibly frets. 'Darling, is there something wrong?'

I've skipped work for the rest of the day – the excuse of a dental appointment doing the trick – and driven down to Surrey. I kiss Mum on the cheek, offering her immediate reassurance. The scent of cloves clings to her; she's been drinking her special gin and tonic, where she sticks three cloves into a slice of lime.

'Something unavoidable has come up this evening and I didn't want to reschedule my visit here,' I rattle off. 'So here I am.' I take one of her hands in mine. 'If I'm honest, Mum, I didn't like the way things ended yesterday. You were so upset.'

She gives me one of those generous smiles I sometimes feel she only reserves for me. Except this time it wobbles at the corners and doesn't produce that added light in her eyes.

She takes my arm and leads me inside. 'I was feeling slightly under the weather. It's this menopause thingy. Mother Nature certainly has some shit in store for us females.'

'Mum!' I'm shocked. I've never heard a swear word pass her lips ever.

There's no apology. 'Well, what would you call periods and the menopause? Shit seems to be the only word to describe it.'

I made the right decision to come while Dad's not here. When he's not around she's different. I get these flashes of what she must've been like as a young woman. But I'm not here for a cosy chat. Mum is the weak link in whatever happened in my past, the one who will talk under extreme coaxing if Dad isn't here. I don't like pulling this kind of dishonest trickery, but what choice do I have?

The house smells of gin and polish. She's very house proud and no doubt has been partaking in her favourite beverage while cleaning up.

'I'll get you a glass of crushed-ice pineapple.' She smiles quickly. 'I know you like your pineapple.'

I want to tell her that I don't drink it so much these days, being a devoted bottled water girl, but I don't. I need her to feel as comfortable as possible. Plus, I've only managed an on-the-go latte from Starbucks today, so something to wet my lips will be gratefully received.

While she goes into the kitchen, I make my way into the front room. I know at once something has changed. Nothing in this house ever changes, so when it does, I notice at once. On the wall, the photo of young Dad and the two other medical students jokingly wearing surgical masks has disappeared. It's been replaced by another of our family on holiday in France.

I stand and stare at it as she joins me. 'Lovely photo, Mum.'

'Oh, that photo. Yes, it's a nice one, isn't it? It was taken in…' – she looks at the frame – '2001. Near Bordeaux. We rented a place near there. I remember you loved it.'

Mum's recounting a treasured memory, so why is her hand shaking around the glass? She wears the expression of a sheepdog that's lost its shepherd, the shepherd being my dad who takes the lead in all my questions about the past.

Mum hastily hands me my drink without making eye contact. 'I'll go and call your father. Perhaps he can come straight back.'

'That's OK. He doesn't have to be here. I'm allowed to see my mum on her own; it's not against the law.'

She looks anxious, fluffing her fingers through her hair. 'But I know your father's looking forward to seeing you. He'll be disappointed.'

'Well, you can tell him I'm fine when he comes in.'

I take a seat on the sofa, compelling her to do the same on the armchair opposite me. She holds her hands locked between her knees, making her pose look like some type of medieval torture.

On the drive down, I considered laying a trap for Mum by luring her into a false sense of security, wittering on about trivia and then pouncing when she's unprepared. But now I'm here I can't be bothered with those kinds of games.

'2001? That would be three years after the accident on the farm, then?'

She reaches for her half-finished G&T on the coffee table. 'That's right, dear. We rented a little place near the beach, I remember…'

But I cut her short. 'I'm not interested in France, Mum. Not at all; I just want to know what happened on my fifth birthday, down on the farm.'

Her hands wrap tight around the glass, her voice a hush. 'You know what happened. You had an accident. It was very distressing but thank God you got better; that's all that matters.'

I expect her to avoid my eyes but she doesn't. She fixes them on me with a steely stare. Whatever it is that happened, she wants to stick with their story and go down with the ship if necessary. In a way I admire her determination. But that's no good to me.

'Since you brought this word into play earlier, shall we cut the shit? There was never any accident on any farm.' My words become strident. 'Why don't you tell me what really happened? Why am I not allowed to know?'

Mum knocks back the remainder of her drink and carefully puts down the glass. 'We've been through this a thousand times, Lisa. I don't know why you don't believe us.' There's anger, but also fear, in what she says next. 'Why are you tormenting yourself like this? Why are you tormenting all of us? Do you really understand the pain this is causing everyone?'

I plonk my glass down too and inch to the edge of the sofa. 'Because it's not true, that's why.'

'Do you know what it was like when we got the call you were in the hospital having your stomach pumped?' Her voice doesn't tremble; it's sure of itself. 'I felt like I was dying. And when I saw you on the bed it was like someone had punched a hand into my chest with the force of a dagger, wanting to rip my heart out.'

She squeezes her eyes shut in tremendous pain. This is the first time she's ever really spoken to me about what happened. Really spoken to me. The other times have all been wrapped up in 'How are you doing?', 'Are you eating?', 'Let me give you a hug.' The emotional impact of my actions she's kept locked quietly away.

It's in this moment that I see. Out of all of us in the family, Mum has always been the person to keep her feelings carefully hidden, as if to say that's what mums do. Mums keep everyone together, must never fall apart. The real backbone of the family.

'Don't you get it?' I cry. 'We're a family that speaks, eats, loves, but discuss our emotions? Never—'

'Are you saying what happened with the overdose was our fault?' Now she does sound like someone's ripping her heart out.

'No.' I take a breath. Calm it down. I open my mouth, close it again. This is so hard to say. This isn't Doctor Wilson or Alex I'm talking to, this is my mum. The woman who took me into her arms during my years of screaming nightmares and awake-sleeping in this house. The person who massaged my scars when the skin grew tight. She deserves words that are frank and true – to a point – but don't pierce her. I don't want my mum to be broken.

I start. 'I haven't felt like "me" for many years. And that's because I don't know who "me" is. In the night, things, images, come to me that tell me there's a missing chunk of my life. I know it's got something to do with my fifth birthday.'

'Is that why you've come down when your father's not here?' That voice of hers is now the pure legal secretary she was when she met Dad. 'Because you're hoping to browbeat me into telling you whatever lies you want to hear? Is that it? That's not worthy of you, Lisa. I'm disappointed. I'd have hoped you were better than that.'

I won't let up. 'Does Doctor Wilson know what happened to me on my fifth birthday? You said yourself he helped during the accident when I was five.'

'As your father and I clarified at the time, I misspoke.'

'Then why is the photo of Dad and Doctor Wilson missing from the wall? And before you ask how I know it's Doctor Wilson, he has one in his office where they're not mucking around with surgical masks on their faces. He displays it on his desk the way someone does of a photo of their much-loved family.'

She looks at the ceiling, as if seeking God for divine strength. 'You're going to remain here, young lady, until your father gets home. Then, we as a family are going to decide together what help you need to get. Obviously going to Doctor Wilson hasn't done the trick—'

I'm on my feet. 'I'm going to find out Mum. I'm already well down the road. I know full well there was no accident in Sussex. I know where the...' I bite back my words. I don't want her to know I'm living in the house. 'I'm well down the road to slotting all the pieces of the puzzle together.'

In a way, I admire my mum. She's being loyal to someone or something. I suspect she even thinks she's being loyal to me by hiding what really happened but she's not. I can't understand why she can't see that. Or maybe she's been living with this lie for so long, she's ended up believing it herself, like cheating spouses who've told so many lies they don't even know what the truth is themselves anymore.

Mum's face looks haunted. I'm sure she wants to tell me. But she can't.

'I'll tell you what you're well down the road towards, Lisa. You're heading for a complete breakdown. It's not me thinking that, although I'm your mother, and I can feel it. But both your father and Doctor Wilson are medical men and they can see all the symptoms. They're trying to help but you won't let them. Why can't you come back here, where we can help you, keep you safe and make you better? Why are you so determined to drive yourself off a cliff? Don't you know what's at the bottom of it?'

I'm sick of this. 'I don't care what's over the cliff as long I land on the truth.'

I head for the door with Mum and the tang of cloves and gin following close behind. I wrench the door open and step outside.

'Lisa! We're only trying to help you!' Her eyes carry the signs of heavy-hearted despair.

I go off like a firework. 'You're not helping me. Can't you see that? You're driving me mad. You're killing me, your own daughter. You're slowly killing me!'

As I accelerate away, I can see in the rear-view mirror Mum standing in the driveway. She seems so alone. I don't know what she does next because I stop looking. I harden my heart.

She's made her choice and I've made mine.

Twenty-six

As I'm sipping water from my bottle in the car at the traffic lights, my mobile pings.

I check out the text.

Alex.

Meet me at Aunty Pats'.

I drive over to see him at Patsy's straight away. I barely get my bearings straight as Alex ushers me quickly into her house. I feel strange. I can't explain it. It's as if I'm not there. I'm floating; my feet don't seem to be touching the ground. There's a low buzzing noise, as if all those death flies who invaded my room are deep inside my ears. I know I'm stressed out from the visit to Mum but I shouldn't feel like this.

Alex's mouth is moving as if he's underwater; I don't hear a word of what he's saying. His mouth keeps twisting into odd shapes, growing large, taking over his face. An immense wave of tiredness washes over me and stays. My legs aren't working. I tip over into the hallway wall, gasping for breath. What's happening to me?

The alarmed expression on Alex's face says the same.

'Lisa? What's wrong?' His mouth is back to the shape and size it should be. His comforting hand touches my rigid arm.

'I'm OK. I'm alright.'

Of course I'm not, but the last thing I need is him giving me a you-need-to-get-help speech, a duplicate of mum's earlier on. Maybe I should get a T-shirt printed with the slogan 'SOS. I Need Help'.

Somehow, I manage to get my act together and stand straight. I hesitate for a second to ensure I won't make a fool of myself by falling. Move away from the wall. Abruptly, an alertness blooms inside me. I feel incredible, on top of the world, can't get enough of the air around me. The colours on Patsy's hallway wallpaper are vivid and strong, jumping out, begging to be caressed. I don't understand any of this; one minute I feel like a drunk and the next, turbo-charged.

I brush it off, saying, 'I've had a long drive back from my parents and just feel wiped out is all.'

Alex's concerned look becomes penetrating. 'Lisa, maybe you should go home – your real home – and crash for a couple of hours.'

'I need to know what you've found out.'

He's not happy with my response and takes me into the lounge. I halt when I see Patsy sitting in an old armchair, cradling Davis protectively in her arms. Protection against me, the neighbourhood cat butcher. Her stare is red-hot, slicing into me with an accusation about something I haven't done. I want to tell her about Martha and Bette's tag. Best not, especially as I'm not sure that's what I saw. Anyway, the last thing I need is a re-run of the whole incident; I feel crap enough as it is.

'Hello, Patsy,' I greet her awkwardly. How else am I meant to do it? She thinks I offed her cat.

She's still wearing a woolly hat. Royal blue this time, with a bright-red knitted flower. Patsy makes a big drama of snubbing me and switching her harsh gaze to Alex. 'Can you tell her that only my friends call me Patsy? I'm Mrs Hawkens to her. Not that I'm going to allow her to speak to me.' She ends on a huff, which makes Davis purr in discomfort. She scratches behind his ear, settling him, whispering, 'Don't you worry, darling. I won't let her get you like she got our much-loved, much-mourned Bette.'

I know I'm feeling weird but this is really weird. Being in the home of someone who refuses to acknowledge me. I look sideways as if it's Alex who needs medical treatment.

He has the grace to look embarrassed. 'I've told Aunty Patsy that you didn't hurt Bette…' The older woman snorts. 'That you could never do such a thing.' Another snort, louder this time. 'After I've spoken with you, she may decide to tell you something she knows that may or may not help you.'

I jump in, straight at my neighbour: 'Was it what you were going to tell me the other day when I came over with...?' My voice dribbles away when I catch on that the end of the sentence is about Bette. *Don't go there.*

Patsy flinches, no doubt seeing her poor cat wrapped in my scarf. 'Can you remind this person not to address any words at me?'

I can't help it; this situation is beginning to hack me off. Why doesn't she simply tell me what I want to know? Enough with the cat and mouse games. Cat and mouse? Bloody hell, I've had enough of them to last me a lifetime. This overwhelming urge comes over me to go over there, grab her by her woolly hat and shake and shake her until she tells me what she knows. My hands cave into furious fists by my sides.

Calm the hell down. Where is this need to punch someone's lights out coming from? I might have my problems but one of them is not being violent to old ladies. Violent to anyone for that matter.

One, two, buckle my shoe.
Three, four...
That's better. Feels easier now.

I address Alex. 'Please tell Mrs Hawkens I will be eternally grateful for anything she can tell me.'

Patsy, clutching Davis, gets up. 'Alex, when you've finished talking to this person come and get me in the garden. I'll then decide whether to tell her what I know.'

Patsy holds her nose in the air as she passes by me. I'm surprised she doesn't make the sign of the cross to ward off my evil presence.

'You look like you could do with something to eat,' Alex tells me.

I don't remember eating this morning. I should be hungry; I'm not. I'm running on an unnatural mix of bone weariness and energy. At the back of my mind I pop in a reminder.

Note to self: not eating is a trigger sign for you. Get something down you soon.

'Alex, tell me what you found out.' The hope is apparent in my voice. Please let what he has discovered help me.

We take a seat on the sagging sofa that has a crochet throw on the back. Its flowers match the ones in Patsy's hats. Ah, Patsy's a knitter. There's no evidence of wool or needles in the room. I imagine her sitting by the roaring fire in winter in her armchair, cats contently curled in the warmth by her feet, needles clacking away. Did young me sit by the fire in the twin of this room, next door?

Alex plonks his rucksack onto his lap and settles in. I sit anxiously on the edge of the seat. He takes out his phone, fiddles with it and then scoots over to show me what's on the screen. I don't immediately understand what I'm looking at.

He sees my frown and fills me in. 'This is a photo of an electoral register for the house at the start of the millennium, the year 2000.' Usually I'd huff that's he talking to me like a kid; I know what year the millennium was. But I'm not offended; I want him to spell it out.

'How did you find this?'

He gives me a crooked smile. 'Let's just say we lawyers have our ways.' He turns back to the phone. 'Up until 2000 the name on the electoral roll was John Peters and his wife.'

John Peters. I dig deep in my memory. There's nothing. The name doesn't spark anything in me. I don't even know any Johns.

Alex brings up another photo. 'Now this is a copy of the census of 2001. It was an important one because it marked two hundred years since the first census in 1801.'

On any other day I might have been up for a history lesson. My irritation obviously shows on my face because he raises his brows as if in apology and carries on.

He points. 'This shows the names of the household members. The only name written on it is Martha Palmer.'

'That's Martha…' I straighten with tension. 'What happened to John Peters and his family?'

'They've obviously gone. Remember in the second part of his writing, where he talked about his wife taking the children, leaving him?'

I'm impatient. 'Where would they go?' Suddenly, I'm on my feet marching towards the door.

Alex hastily lets go of the phone and strides purposely behind me. His hand snakes out and draws me back before I can enter the hall. 'Where are you going?'

The hyped alertness is back, with determination this time. The words grit through my teeth. 'I'm going to ask Patsy point blank what she knows about the family who were next door—'

'No,' he snaps. He takes in air before adding, calmer and quieter, 'You leave charming Aunty Patsy to me. If you go out to her now she'll likely chuck Davis at you.' He assesses me closely, leaving me feeling uncomfortably naked and bare. 'You seem a touch jumpy. Not yourself.' He doesn't need to add 'again'.

I don't need to see my face to know it changes to something ugly. 'How do you want me to feel, Alex? Of course I feel like I'm falling apart at the seams. How would you feel' – my finger stabs him in the chest – 'if you thought your whole life was a lie? If you'd just been to see your mother and knew she was holding something major back from you?'

The air pumping from my lungs is ragged, a muscle in my cheek ticking and ticking.

His hand loosens around me. 'Let's sit back down because I found out some other interesting stuff.'

I let him lead me back. The silence between us as he retrieves his phone is prickly.

'This is the land registry.' He shows me another form. 'As you can see, the house is now in the name of a company called MP. I'm assuming that means Martha Palmer, your current landlady, in the same year, 2001.'

'So she's owned that house for sixteen years?'

He hesitates, putting the phone down. 'It would appear so. The census of 2011 shows that by that year, her husband, Jack, was living there as well. The strange thing is that it also shows that the previous owner of the house, John Peters, was living there too.'

I'm stumped. 'I don't get it.'

Alex shrugs. 'Neither do I.' Alex lets out a long sigh. 'Maybe his family leaving was the reason the house was sold in 2001. John Peters and his wife got a divorce and went their separate ways.'

I'm trying desperately to analyse it all. Intent on getting it to make sense.

I say slowly, more for my benefit than his, 'John Peters owns a house with his wife and children. He then sells the house to Martha. Then, years later, Jack is now living with her in the house. And also John Peters. Why would he go back there?'

'If there's one thing I've learned in the legal profession it's that people can live the strangest lives. Maybe he went back because he knew he could rent a room from Martha? If she was trying to cover up his being there why put his name on the census?'

'I'll tell you why,' says another voice, joining us in the room.

We look over to find Patsy standing in the doorway, minus cat. 'I was still on speaking terms with the Devil and his disciple next door, back then. I bumped into him with the census ready to mail at the post office one day. Told me that Lady Muck was too busy to complete it, so she palms the job off on him. He must've been the one to put John's name on it. Maybe he didn't realise he shouldn't have. Let's face it, my big toe has got more sense than that boy.'

'Did you know this John Peters and his family?'

She squints, no doubt getting ready for her I'm-not-talking-to-you spiel. My temperature starts rising.

But she surprises me. 'I did. Lovely family. He adored his wife and kids.'

'Why did they move away?'

She shakes her head with sadness. 'I wish I knew.' Her tone changes to slightly peeved again. 'You asked me if I knew who the man was in that room before you. It was John. The reason I didn't tell you before was I wasn't sure. What I will tell you is I rarely saw him. He hardly ever came out. The glimpses I got into their front room… I never saw him there either. Or in the garden, except that one time. I sometimes think he lived day in, day out, year in, year out in that room, all on his own. No company. No one to speak to.'

Davis' meow draws her attention. 'Ooo, it's his dinner time.'

She hurries off, but I know she's escaping really. Recanting the past had brought tears to her eyes. Or was she holding back another secret, like why was she scared of Jack the day of Bette's death when he mentioned the cops?

'There's one more thing you need to know about John Peters.'

Alex's grave statement makes me turn around. 'What?' I walk up close to him.

'His family's original name wasn't Peters but Petrov. It's a very common Russian surname related to the name Peter. So, his family maybe wanted to appear more English when they immigrated here, so changed it to Peters.'

Finally! A light-bulb moment. 'Are you saying…?'

'That the man who wrote the suicide letter and on the wall is likely John Peters, who at one time owned the house. Patsy has just confirmed that.'

I grab Alex's hand and drag him towards the hall. He's flustered. 'What are you doing?'

I look at him in astonished disbelief. 'We're going to my room, of course. To find the remainder of the writing so you can translate for me.'

He snatches his hand briskly away and looks really, really annoyed. 'You need to calm down.'

Doesn't he get it? We need to solve this puzzle. I'm becoming frantic, not understanding why he's not moving. My bearings are off again; now my head feels like it's tipping off my shoulders.

'Don't tell me to sodding well calm down.' My shout bounces about us. I'm seething. 'Women are tired of men telling them to calm down. You might be frightened of your emotions. I am not. All I need to know is: are you prepared to help me?'

He folds his arms, as stubborn as I am. 'I can help you, believe you me, but only after you get some food down you and sleep and—'

'You know what, Alex? I don't need you. Stay the bloody heck away from me from now on.'

I'm out of there before he can say another word.

This can't wait a moment longer. I will find the missing part of John Peter's story if I have to tear my room apart.

***

John Peters. John Peters. John Peters.

The name bounces from one corner of my brain to another as I enter the house with manic determination. Who the bloody hell needs Alex; I'll discover the rest of John's writing myself. Haven't I been searching for years on my own? I refuse to consider this might be a fool's errand, that there's no more writing on the wall. There's a missing part – parts? – of the story, I know there is.

The strange sensation has gone, leaving me feeling almost in control. Almost. There's a fatigue hovering over me that won't piss off. I hold on to the bannister as I take the stairs. I've lucked out because there's no sign of the landlords.

I've spoken too soon because I run into Jack as I turn into the first-floor landing. He looks a mess, clothes dirty, probably been doing his dodgy handiwork about the house. But that man bun of his is done up like he's the belle of the ball.

'I need to have a word with you,' he says, stepping closer. He stinks of turps.

'Sorry, it will have to be later, I'm in a hurry.'

I brush past him and ignore his cry of 'Lisa!' I'm not in the mood for whatever he has up his filthy sleeve. Mercifully, he doesn't follow as I head eagerly to the stairs leading to my room.

John Peters. John Peters. John Peters.

The name gets louder; my feet pick up their pace. I reach the landing. Face my door. The anticipation is so high about what I may find, I worry my grip on control may slip away again. I get my breathing in order.

One, two, buckle my shoe.

I'm ready. I hope that John is too.

I reach the door. Open it.

I rock back on my heels in stupefied shock. Disbelief. Outraged horror.

My room is painted completely black.

Twenty-seven

The walls, floor, ceiling, skylight, the window frame…

No! No! No! The walls. I lose awareness of what I'm doing, of moving. The next thing I know, my curved fingers are madly clawing for the paper on the walls. Except they hit cold, hard brick. There's no paper. The lining paper has gone. This can't be real. Isn't really happening. I'm in the midst of another crazy dream or I'm awake-sleeping. My eyelids slam down as I try to calm my racing breathing.

One, two, buckle…

The rhyme falters. I try again.

One, two, buckle…

My eyes snap open. Oh God, this is real. My trembling hand covers my quivering mouth as I spin helplessly around. The wall by the window is black. The wall near the bed is black. By the door… black. Black. Black. A shiny-gloss endless ebony black.

John's writing is gone. Gone.

Such overwhelming grief shatters me I almost crumble to the hideously painted black floor.

Moaning, I slap both hands into the wall nearest me, trying to rub the paint away. Rub. Rub. Rub. It won't come off. It's stuck fast. In a daze I stare at my palms, as if I expect to see them covered in blood.

Rage, as dark as the room, consumes me. If that weed-growing bastard thinks he's going to get away with this, he's living on another planet. I storm from the room, march downstairs and find Jack whistling in the kitchen, making a mug of tea.

'How dare you,' I throw at him with all the force of my anger.

He's wearing that sickening, sly smile of his. 'I did try to tell you before you went marching up with your prim nose in the air that the room's been decorated.'

'Decorated?' I'm yelling and intend to continue in that manner. 'Who gave you the right to go into *my* room and change anything? You don't have the right.'

He's dead serious now. 'Right? First off, it's *our* room in *our* house. Second, if you read your lease properly it says, as clear as the nose on my face, that the landlord can make any cosmetic changes they like.'

He had me there. I'm furious with myself. 'I want you to somehow get that paint off. I don't care how you do it, just do it.'

He picks up his mug and sips. 'No can do, sweetheart.' He has the audacity to grin. 'Thought you'd be pleased that I've fixed the skylight. Although I told Martha we should leave it for a few days, but the missus says to get it out of the way.'

Suddenly I'm still. So very still. 'Martha told you to do this?'

He takes a big gulp of his tea as he narrows his gaze at me. 'What's your problem? The skylight's been fixed. It's what you've been pestering me about since you got here, isn't it?' He tips his chin arrogantly up. 'You know what you can do if you don't like it?'

I nearly snarl, catch it back. Don't give the moron the satisfaction.

I decide to kill him with kindness. With the utmost pleasure and brightness, I tell him, 'I'll be here for the full six months. I'm sure you'll get used to it.'

I turn on my heels and leave. As I climb the stairs there's a name in my head. It isn't John Peters, it's Martha Palmer.

There's only one reason she'd order her husband to paint my room black – to drive me out. The mouse, the death flies, Bette… it's all been Martha. Good grief, she's wearing that poor cat's name tag around her throat like a medal of honour. Isn't that what serial killers do? Take trophies of their kills? She's the one calling the shots in this house. I should applaud her really for her stellar act that sucked me in, playing the poor put-upon wife. She's done a pitch-perfect rendition of 'We girls gotta stick together'.

I sense something cold and calculating about Martha that leaves me in dread.

***

I keep to my room that evening. Don't eat. Don't drink. No Amy, either. The black walls seem to have made my room shrink. Usually I adore the colour black. It has a range that not many people understand. This black that surrounds me smothers. It's as bottomless as my despair.

'Did Martha do this to you too, John?' I ask the room as I lie on the bed. 'Is that why you took your life? Because she was trying to drive you away?'

No. Whatever made John say farewell to the world I really believe had nothing to do with Martha, the cat-killing freak. His writing laid bare something much deeper, more hurtful, that hurtled him over the edge. What was it?

Now I may never know because his writing, his story, is gone.

Twenty-eight

The violent hammering on the front door the next morning drags me from my sleep. Desperately I look over at the walls. Groan. Still funeral black. The walls seem to have inched further in, turning a once spare room into a tunnel to hell. Is that how John Peters got to feel about this room? A hell on earth?

I reach for my water bottle, desperate to wet my unnaturally dry mouth. With lacklustre movements of my hand, I unscrew the lid. Tip it towards my lips.

The enraged shout I hear bellowing downstairs stops me drinking.

'Where's my daughter? What have you done with her?'

It's my dad. It takes a few moments before I can process what's happening. What the hell is he doing here? And how did he find me?

Heaving myself out of bed, I hear Jack respond. 'I don't know what you're talking about, mate. Now clear off, there's a good boy, you're on private property. Oi, where do you think you're going?'

It sounds like there's a struggle on the doorstep. My distorted mind makes the dark walls close in even more as I stagger towards the door. I'm unsteady on my feet, shaking my head, trying to clear my mind. If Dad sees me like this there's no accounting for what he'll say. I climb down the stairs, feeling more like I'm sliding. At the bottom I rock back on my heels and stop. Count and breathe:

One, two, buckle my shoe.
Three, four, knock at the door.

The noises from downstairs grow louder.

No more time to count and breathe; I need to get downstairs. Now. When I reach the hallway, I stop in the heart of the house on the rug, alarmed by the scene playing out before me. Dad is trying to barge his way past my landlord, but Jack is having none of it, using big hands to push him farther backwards.

When Dad sees me over Jack's shoulder, he shouts, 'Get your things together. You're leaving this place. We're taking you home.'

I'm too stunned to say anything.

Martha appears and sashays past me to stand behind her husband. 'Who the hell are you?'

'I'm Lisa's father and if you don't let me take my daughter away, I'll call the police.'

Martha looks him up and down. Her voice is calm. 'If you don't get off my doorstep, *I'll* call the police.'

Once again, Dad attempts to push his way past Jack, and once again he fails.

He's frantic. 'I'm not going anywhere without my daughter.'

Martha turns, giving me a curious look. 'Do you know this man?'

I'm embarrassed, in the same way you're embarrassed by your parents when you're a teenager. 'He's my dad.'

'Well, you'd better go outside and sort this out. And can I remind you,' she pointedly adds, 'that your parents are allowed to visit, but only with prior agreement from me and Jack.'

Head hanging, I walk past Jack and out of the house. The door's pulled back, but not all the way; I'm sure Jack and Martha are eavesdropping with delight behind it.

I cry out as Dad seizes me by the arm and drags me down the drive to where his car is parked. In the passenger seat is Mum, her face the picture of parental distress.

'What the hell is going on, girl?' Dad's still yelling, his fingers digging into me. My dad is never, ever violent. 'Have these people hurt you? What are you doing here?'

I'm lost for words. I'd considered various possibilities that might occur when I came to the house with the mason's mark but never that my parents might track me down here.

I try to sound calm and outraged at their intervention but I'm aware it's not coming off. 'I've rented a room here, that's all. It's more convenient for work. Now please, go away.'

'Don't lie!'

I feel a sting across my cheek. For a moment, I'm unsure what's happened until I realise he's just slapped me. I've never been struck by either of my parents before and I can't believe it. His face is contorted with fear and hatred and I'm genuinely afraid of him for the first time in my life. At the same time, there's a cry of distress from the car and the passenger door flies open and Mum rushes over and tries to separate us.

She's clearly been crying. 'Edward! Edward, what are you doing? Don't hit her.'

Dad takes a couple of steps back. He looks as shattered as I felt lying on the bed.

'I'm sorry, Lisa. You know I'd never hurt you.' His voice becomes a controlled quiet that sounds harder than any shout. 'Get in the car. I'll go and collect your things.' He's already turning.

'Don't you dare.'

I set off after him but Mum grabs my arm and holds me back. We struggle briefly but she's surprisingly strong and I'm surprisingly frail. I can't get away.

She twists me roughly to face her. 'Lisa, darling, what's going on? What are you doing in this house? Why aren't you living in your own home anymore?'

I'm about to tell her the story about moving closer to work but I haven't got the heart because she's so upset.

'Lisa, you're not well. You look terrible, my beautiful angel. You have to come home with us now.'

My dad thrusts the door of the house back. I'm surprised that Martha and Jack make no attempt to stop him. No words are exchanged. Perhaps they saw him hit me and don't want to interfere. Or perhaps they've just realised this is the perfect opportunity to get rid of me without resorting to the courts. What a stroke of luck for them.

Dad takes the stairs two at a time and he dashes up to my room.

'Lisa? Are you listening?' Mum gets my attention again. 'You don't look like you've been eating, sleeping.' She sounds tearful, urgent. She wraps her arms around me.

I lean into her, suddenly drained to the core. So tired. The kind of weariness that makes me want to lie down in a park somewhere and go to sleep.

Sleep. Sleep. Sleep.

It seems so much easier to say I'll go with them. To say goodbye to this house and its secrets that will probably be bad for me anyway. To abandon this hunt that is slowly destroying me.

The cat killer and the cannabis grower now stand outside the house with blank expressions, watching me and Mum. Dad storms out, carrying a sports bag that's bulging with my things. I'm shivering although it isn't cold. Dad throws the bag into the boot of the car and then takes me by the arm. I allow him to ease me into the back seat. When he gets into the driver's seat, for a few moments he tilts his head back in what looks like relief. The key turns in the ignition and we set off.

For a moment, I share my dad's relief. But then I look out of the rear window of the car. Not at Martha and Jack, still standing outside, but up at the house. The large windows that hide their secrets from me and the outside world. The brickwork that seems to grow darker, more forbidding, every time I view it. The mason's mark remains the same. My touchstone to find the past.

In some deep recess of my memory, and my soul, I'm that five-year-old child again being driven away from this house. What am I doing? I can't go, not now. I have to stay and see this through, no matter how weary, crushed and frightened I am.

If I don't, I won't be able to go on. That road leads to vodka and pills and…

I struggle with the door handle. Mum screams and grabs hold of me to stop me climbing out of the moving car. Dad's shouting over his shoulder but I can't hear what's he's saying. The car judders and veers off the drive before we reach the avenue.

I jump out, away from my mum's loving embrace, and head back towards the house. I fall into a patch of stones and grass. It's damp and cold, and I slither towards the front door like a pilgrim seeking salvation. Mum's sobbing won't stop.

I look up. Dad stands over me. He makes no attempt to drag me away. Instead places my belongings on the ground beside me.

His voice is calm and collected. 'Very well, Lisa. Have it your way. We've got other options to save you and don't you forget that.' He turns to go but then he adds, 'We're only doing this because we love you. You know that, don't you?'

I want to speak, to reassure him, but my mouth won't move. His feet crunch on gravel as he walks back to the car. The door slams, displaying his true emotions. My beloved parents drive away. And I hurt. Hurt that I'm causing them so much gut-wrenching pain. But they could stop all of this if they told me the truth.

It's perfectly quiet now. The birds are singing. Truth is I could lie here forever, staring up at the blazing blue sky, inhaling the carefree summer air. I want to get up but don't feel like I can. I don't know how long I lie there. Probably only a minute or two before a figure stands over me. It's Martha. There's no sign of Jack.

She gives me a grin of recognition. 'You're a fighter, Lisa, I'll give you that. You're just fighting for the wrong things. You should have gone with your parents. If they'd let me know they were coming instead of turning up carrying on like football hooligans, I would have helped them.'

'Is that why you…?' I hold back on confronting her about painting the room black. It might provoke her into escalating her malicious deeds against me.

Martha tilts her head in a way that makes the sun no friend to her face, exposing the lines and creases beneath the layers and layers of make-up. 'Why I what?'

'Why you let them in?' The lie comes quickly.

She offers me a hand to help me up but I don't take it. I struggle to my feet on my own. Martha shrugs and goes back into the house. When she's gone, I pick up the bag with my unsteady fingers and walk the short distance back to the house with my eyes fixed on my special key in the mason's mark.

My mind's fixated on something else though.

There's only one way my parents could've found out I am living in the house.

***

It should be warm, but the summer breeze feels like shards of ice digging away at my skin as I stride with manic purpose towards Doctor Wilson's studio the next day. I'm determined to have it out with him. He shopped me to my parents. Told them where I am staying. So much for sacred doctor-patient confidentiality. I revealed my deepest secret to him and he… How could he do that to me?

At least I had a good night's sleep. Nightmare free, no awake-sleeping. Maybe I'm getting better and haven't realised. Yeah, and the Beatles will be getting back together. I've taken a few pills to steady my nerves. I walk, my legs feeling like they belong to another person, through the upmarket streets of Hampstead in my own bubble. My mind won't rest about what Doctor Wilson has done.

A high-pitched giggle from a child skipping along beside her mother, who's pushing a stroller, turns my head. And that's when I see her. Coming out of Hampstead tube is a woman dressed in a tailored black suit, unbelievably thin heels and an elegant black striped straw boater hat tipped at a jaunty angle. She carries a classy handbag, gliding with the grace of a model heading to New York Fashion Week's catwalk. At first I think, *wow, that woman is the spit of Martha*. But she holds herself differently from the Martha I know.

She has the same stamp of elegance as my landlady, however this woman breeds arrogance. Her head's up; she cuts her eye at passers-by as if they're not worthy to be walking the streets of North London with her. I drop into a shop doorway and pretend to look into a window as this vision of don't-touch-me-chic floats by.

My breath roughly stills on my tongue. It really is Martha.

Quite why I am so shocked to see her here, I'm not sure. There's no law that says my landlady can't be in this part of London or looking more like a model than ever. But it isn't that. I'm not used to seeing her looking like she owns the place. Usually she doesn't even look like the woman who owns her own house, never mind Hampstead.

I step out and watch her walking away. There's no reason I shouldn't call out and say hello; I don't have a problem with her. Instead, I observe her turning left onto a side street, one I have come to know well in the last few weeks. The small street is a shop-free zone. Is she visiting?

Then I wonder…

I pick up my pace. Follow her. Martha turns into another side street and it's the same one I came down a few minutes ago. I discreetly observe her scanning the houses and cottages. Looking… for what? Her designer bag is stiff by her side as she finds the building she's been searching for. Martha goes up to the door. I have to be careful now. I duck down and scamper along behind the crowded parked cars until I'm about twenty yards away from where Martha is looking with contempt at a brass plate over a buzzer. No doubt about it now. She is indeed paying a visit.

To Doctor Wilson.

She jabs the buzzer. No answer. Martha hits it impatiently again and leaves her finger there for about five seconds to make her arrival extra clear. The door slowly opens. I can't see who's there but I assume it must be the good doctor. She tilts her head back and talks as if to a servant, and a few words are said back, but I can't hear what they are. Then the door swings open wide. Martha steps inside. The door closes behind her.

I stand up and shake my head in disbelief. It's not that I can't believe she's seeing a shrink. Who isn't? What are the chances of her therapist being the same one that I see? Too much of a coincidence? And what about the fee? Doctor Wilson doesn't come cheap. A grand just to give Wilson a ring, never mind actually climb up onto his couch. Where's she getting that kind of cash? Handyman Jack is neither handy or much of a man; he never seems to have any work on, and the house is falling to bits for want of ready cash to fix it. Plus, Martha has told me that one of the reasons I'm in the house is because Jack needs the extra money.

I'm so lost in thought that I almost don't notice Doctor Wilson's door swing open again a couple of minutes later and the unlikely couple emerge onto the street. I duck down behind the bonnet again. The two of them walk past where I'm hiding.

As they go by, his words are clear to me.

'You should have rung first. I don't like being put on the spot like this.' His voice has the backbone of steel. Surely a psychiatrist wouldn't use such a harsh tone with a patient?

Her voice is equally hard. 'No. I'll bet you don't.'

Their irate voices become tangled, fade as they drift out of earshot. My knuckles are tight in hands I hadn't realised are balled into fists. Since yesterday, I've been raging that Doctor Wilson had told my parents about me being in the house. Now I'm scared stiff he might say something to my landlady, inadvertently or otherwise. That the tenant in her spare room deliberately targeted her house.

I go back to *maybe she's a patient? Maybe she's a patient?* It goes round and round my mind, a chant I'm willing to be the truth. The alternative... I can't deal with that. Can't deal with Martha trying to throw me out. What if she calls Jack and I get back to find my belongings piled up on the pavement? I've come this far. I won't – can't – let anything stand in the way of me finding out the truth.

Urgency surrounds me. An overwhelming need to get back to the house and... What? Barricade myself in the room? Carry on as if I haven't seen Martha with the good doctor? Yes. That's what I'll do. Pretend. I've mastered the art of pretence.

I rush down the road, my steps grinding against the hard ground, to keep sight of them, although to what end, I don't know. It crosses my mind to accidently bump into them and let them see I know what's going on. *That's plain stupid! You mustn't let them know.*

I catch a glimpse of them turning onto the road that leads down to the high street. When I reach it myself, they've gone. The adrenaline charging through my veins sets my body to shaking. Where have they gone? I peer into the first pub I come to. No sign of them. A café specialising in coffee – not there either. Absently, I pop a pill to iron out my hyperactive nerves.

Think. Think. Think.

I backtrack. Check the coffee house again. Ah, there they are. Snug in their own world at a table in the back. They'll spot me if I go in. From the window I watch. You can tell lots about a person just by looking at them.

He's speaking in stops and starts, avoiding her eyes. There's a sideways twist to her expertly painted lips that suggests anger. She's out of her chair with such force it makes me jump back.

Doctor Wilson looks embarrassed by what she tells him next, but says nothing and uses his hands to indicate that she should sit back down. Instead, she snatches her bag from the table. Leans down towards his face. Her words are only for his ears. Her mouth moves so quickly her lips take on the appearance of red worms wriggling on her face.

Hastily, I move to stand half-turned, gazing into the beauty parlour next door. *Click click click*. It's the sound of Martha marching towards the door. A delicate, citrus scent reaches my nose – Martha's back on the street. I turn completely away. She mustn't see me. When I look back, they're face to face on the street.

I think I hear Doctor Wilson say, 'She was meant to be your best friend…'

A lorry drives by and I can't hear the rest.

Click click click; she's walking away.

He shouts after her, 'Don't threaten me, Martha. I'm not going to be intimidated. My conscience is clear!'

'You're not going to be intimidated?' Martha must be facing him again. I imagine her poised with that staged Hollywood glamour she had that night she came to my room after she and Jack tried to chuck me out. 'You pathetic little man! I'll break you like a twig!'

She's on the move again. He doesn't call her back. There's the sound of an approaching car. It stops. A door briskly closes. The engine growls as the car heads off. I'm assuming she hailed a cab.

Doctor Wilson starts moving away. I dare to turn around. His shoulders are hunched, and yes, they're trembling. Is he weeping? I don't follow him this time.

What have I just witnessed and heard? A doctor and patient who have become too close? A man who has just revealed my closest secret? Or two friends falling out? Standing in the street won't help me find out. There's only one thing to do when I get back to the house: wait.

Let Martha make the first move.

Twenty-nine

It's as if Doctor Wilson is expecting me. We have no pre-arranged session in his diary for today, so when I buzz his studio I expect it will be his medical secretary who will bar my entry with the advice to make an appointment.

Surprisingly, it's the man himself who opens the door, just like he did for Martha. 'Lisa, did we have an appointment?'

He doesn't appear fazed by my appearance. I suppose in his profession he's had all sorts in all conditions turning up on his doorstep.

I'm ushered inside and we're soon both sat in his consultancy room. I take the chair on offer, not the couch.

As he reaches for his notebook, I tell him, 'I'd rather what I have to say stays between us, not recorded in your book in black and white.'

Doctor Wilson's hand hovers over his trusted tool of the trade. 'This is a professional visit?'

I stretch my fingers against my thighs in pure anxiety.

'How do you know Martha Palmer?' I immediately go in for the kill. He needs to understand from the word go that I'm the one running this session.

He doesn't disappoint. 'Who?'

So, we're playing *that* game, are we? He can't hide the sudden colourless quality of the skin round his mouth or the rapid blinks of his usually detached eyes. For the first time, I see the toll listening to and living others' problems has taken on him. It's a strange thing. I'd expected to become more stiff with tension, but instead a measure of calming control cloaks me, like the good doctor is on his couch and I'm the one taking notes.

My gaze is steady. 'I saw you with her—'

'Have you been spying on me?' He's blatantly annoyed now. 'Why was she here?'

He recovers his control, blank expression back in place, relaxing back into his chair. 'I understand you went to see your mother and made some very serious allegations against her and your father.'

'If I recall, you were the one who advised me to speak to them. To ask them about what really happened the day of the accident.'

'And what did she say?'

He's not using his notebook, his prop for controlling our discussion, but that doesn't stop him thinking he's the one in control here. The one sitting at the high table asking the questions.

He's so wrong. 'You didn't answer my question about Martha.'

Doctor Wilson gives himself time to think. 'If you must know she's a long-standing patient of mine. I'll be breaching confidentiality if I tell you more than that.' He drums a fingertip against his thigh as his gaze narrows. 'Martha seems important to you. How do you know her?'

I nearly laugh then. The gall of this man is unbelievable. 'I know what you did. What you told my parents—'

'That you are living in a place they know nothing about? Yes, I told them.' No apologies are offered. His neck stretches as if to see me better. His gaze becomes soft. 'I wouldn't normally behave in such a way. Remember, your father is my friend who I've known for many years. Lisa, how would I feel if something happened to you and I never informed them where you now live? They believe you're living in your home.'

I can't fault him on his loyalty. I've struggled with loyalty to my parents for so many years, knowing that I'm keeping the truth about the years I've spent looking for the house, my past, from them. Knowing I won't take their word about what happened in my childhood.

Doctor Wilson cuts over my thoughts. 'Your father was, understandably, very upset when I told him you were living somewhere else. Did they find you at your new address?'

My head lowers. 'It was ugly, really ugly. Our dirty washing aired in public for all the world to gawk at. Mum will have hated that. They treated me as if I was a child again. You know, ordered me to my room without any supper until I'd mended my defiant, naughty ways.'

'How did that make you feel?'

My head jerks up, my gaze dead centre with his. *No, doctor, I'm not letting you ambush me.*

'John Peters. What can you tell me about him?' I throw it out there. I don't expect him to know anything about Martha's former tenant, but hey, you don't get if you don't ask.

The concern is back on his face. 'John who? I can say, hand on heart, that I am not treating anyone called John Peters.'

There's no sign he's not telling the truth. I'm not giving up.

'What did you tell Martha?'

His mouth works, no sound coming out. Then: 'I don't understand. What could I have told Martha Palmer?' His brows shift together.

'She called you pathetic.' I purposefully say the final word with as much disdain as I can muster; I want a reaction from this man. Nothing happens. Emotions are frozen cold in him. 'Said she'd break you like a twig.'

It's as if I haven't spoken. 'I ask you again: why are you obsessed with Martha?'

I don't answer; instead I drill my hardening stare into him, desperately trying to find ways to see if he's lying. In his eyes, the set of his body, the poise and posture of his hands. I see nothing, except a man concerned with my well-being. Do I believe him though? His business is emotion. Getting people to deal with the vast range – betrayal, rage, stress, love, the rest – is the bread and butter of his job. He'd be the master of knowing when to hide it in a situation such as this.

Then I realise: 'We're agreed that you told my parents where I'm living?'

'I have no reason to lie to you.'

'How did you know where the house is?'

His head rears back slightly. 'What? But you told me, Lisa. You gave me the address.'

I rewind back to when I revealed my secret in this very room. Did I tell him?

'You don't believe me?' He confronts me with my doubting thoughts.

'Believe you?' I could laugh or cry; either would work. 'Believing in those closest to me seems to be at the heart of my problems, don't you think?'

He moves, ever so slightly, forward. 'No, I don't. I believe the person you don't believe in is yourself. Your distorted dreams are a product of you not being able to grapple with the truth of what really happened to you on your fifth birthday. This John Peters and your fixation on Martha I believe to be part of your unstable condition. And do you know what else I believe?'

The weight of his soft voice pins me to the chair even though I'm desperate to rush to my feet and get out of there. I don't speak. Can't snap my gaze from his.

'The only way you will find peace with the past is with long-term care. The type that I cannot give.'

That makes me move with a quickness that has the chair rocking back on its legs. The image of what he's suggesting leaves me chilled, raging in turmoil, hardly able to stand straight.

He remains seated, his tone even calmer than before. 'You're going to break, Lisa; any day now. I've seen the type of breakdown you're heading for many times. One day you'll find you just can't get out of bed. Or you'll be going about your everyday business and suddenly fall apart. You'll shatter into a thousand pieces, wondering if you'll ever be able to put yourself back together. You need to get help now before it's too late. I can recommend—'

I don't give him the chance to say more. The images he's painted are a horror story I can't go back to. Is he right? Am I having a breakdown?

***

I hungrily reach for the bottle of water on the bedside cabinet. As the coolness soothes my dry throat, I know I should eat. How can I when I'm devastated? My heaving thoughts and the flashing images in my head twist into the tightest knots.

Martha murdering the cat.

Martha wearing Bette's name tag with her best fifties-style cocktail dress.

Martha with Doctor Wilson.

Doctor Wilson telling my parents my deepest secret.

Cannabis plants.

Bette.

Martha.

Doctor Wilson.

Dad.

Bette.

Black. Black. Black.

Leave me alone. Leave. Me. Alone.

I squeeze my hands over my head, trying to get rid of tortured images of the puzzle. I feel like sobbing my guts out. But what good would that do? Leave me in a desperate heap, feeling more sorry for myself. And I'm sick of the pity. Of the low self-esteem. Not feeling worthy of this world.

I slug more water back. It tastes slightly stale but I've already got a house rule now not to touch anything in this place that I can't vouch for. If Martha's willing to poison a cat you can be sure she'd be willing to poison me too. Perhaps that's a bit paranoid. But there can be no doubt that nothing would delight her more than for me to be carted out of this house in a wooden box. No doubt the same way John Peters went, despite me finding no record of it.

As I place the water bottle back, that strange ultra-alert sensation is inside me again. I experience excitement. No, elation. I sit up with the feeling of being born again. Coming into a world that's only filled with beauty. That's when I hear them. The voices.

They don't sound like Jack and Martha, I don't think. I listen more closely. The voices are distinct. It's a woman and children.

Am I dreaming? Awake-sleeping? I know I'm not. To make sure, I put the bedside lamp on. Yes, the room is all bright. I touch the surface of the cabinet table. It's hard, immovable beneath my hand.

This is all real, but I can still hear the voices coming from the dining room as if they were in this bedroom with me. Then there's something else. The blackness of the walls become the queen of colours, exuding power and mystery. How didn't I see this before? Its awesomeness. Its absolute right to be in this room. The walls move in and out with rhythmic elegance as if they're breathing. I get out of bed and lay a hand on the in-and-out, in-and-out wall. It's solid but wraps itself around my hand like soft plastic. How does it do that?

I was warned. I was warned that if I carried on down this path, I would go crazy, and now it's finally happening. Voices in the dining room and breathing walls? I've gone over the edge and I don't know if I can find my way back to a world where there are no voices in the dining room and walls that remain still. My breath balloons in my chest as the black changes colour to imperial purple, glittering like diamonds. I should be scared out of my wits; instead I'm fascinated.

I moved into this house hoping it would talk to me. Now, it is. It's come alive. I'm just not sure what it's saying.

I open the door to my room, step onto the landing and put the light on. That will alert Jack and Martha that I'm moving around but I don't care. Outside, everything seems to be out of proportion and distorted. The long length of the staircase belongs in a palace or an ocean liner. It twists and turns and narrows and widens, like the stairs from one of those creepy black and white German horror films. The walls are breathing in and out and there are all kinds of soft noises. That's the house saying something I can't hear. But above it all, I can hear the voices in the dining room and I have to go down and see who it is and what they're saying.

Gripping the bannister tightly, I make my way down the stairs one foot at a time to avoid tumbling down these crazy steps. I carry on down the next flight until I'm in the heart of the house, the hallway. The door to the dining room is closed but I can clearly see movement behind it. Wow, what a thrill! I laugh out loud. I've got superpowers.

My attention jerks behind me to the soft patter of footsteps. I look up and Martha's coming down. Well, not so much coming down as floating down. Really floating. Is she really there? Those big green eyes watch me closely. They're trying to say something. Telling me to do something. But I can't see what it is.

Why can't this house, these people in the dining room, and Martha's eyes speak clearly and tell me what's going on?

Her voice is soft and sounds like a mother's. 'Are you alright, Lisa?'

'Yes, of course. I'm fine.'

I resent her interruption. I want to go into the dining room and see who's there.

'Are you sure? You seem a bit disturbed. Would you like me to call a doctor?'

Jack's grumpy voice shoots down from the floor above. 'What's going on?'

Martha looks up. It strikes me as curious that she seems perfectly at home with all the bizarreness going on around me, while at the same time looking exactly like the usual everyday Martha.

'It's Lisa.'

'What's the matter with her? Is she murdering cats again?'

Martha peers at me innocently. 'Don't be rude, darling. I found her sleepwalking awhile back. I don't think this is the same thing. She appears to be having some kind of funny turn and won't let go of my arm.'

Jack's fed up. 'Haven't we got her folks' number as next of kin? Call them and get her shipped out. We can't put up with her crap anymore. She's a nutter.'

Martha looks at me again and says gently, 'Shall we do that, Lisa? Call your dad and mum for you?'

I sound like a child about to blow a tantrum. 'No, I want to know who's in the dining room.'

'There's no one in the dining room.'

'There is, there is! I can hear them!'

I notice Martha is right. I am gripping her arm. With her free hand she takes mine. 'Alright, let's go and see who's in the dining room.' We walk down the hallway. Martha lets go of my hand and opens the door. 'You see? There's no one here.'

But she's wrong. There are people here. Except they're not quite people. Three chairs are scampering around while a tall cabinet is overseeing them and telling them to behave. I'm transfixed. I can't take my eyes off them. How could I have ever thought the dining room was the most forgettable room in this house?

Martha repeats, 'No one here.'

There's a knock on the front door. I'm mesmerised by the cabinet walking past us. It goes to the front door and answers. There's a woman on the doorstep. I can't see her but somehow I sense it's a woman. Then the cabinet and the woman go in the front room. They're talking; I can't hear what they're saying. That seems to be how this works. But I can hear what happens next. There's screaming from the front room, a wounded animal howling in agony. The chairs stop scampering around in the dining room and huddle together in fear.

I don't like this anymore. I'm terrified. My clothes are soaked in sweat. *Please stop screaming. Stop. Stop bloody screaming.* She won't.

'Lisa? Lisa? You need to snap out of this.' It's Martha, who has no business being here.

I loosen my skin-tight grip on her arm and dash into the dining room. Curl up in a ball in the corner. Plaster my hands over my ears. The screaming won't stop. Won't stop. Won't stop. I'm shaking and sweating like a pig and that won't stop either. My throat is desert-dry, craving water. And the screaming goes on and on.

Jack's there now. 'What the hell is this about?'

Martha tells him, 'I don't know. She's having some kind of episode.'

Jack is curt. 'Well, call an ambulance.'

Martha is curt back. 'No, she doesn't need an ambulance. Go and get some tranquilisers from your medicine chest. We'll give her those.'

'Tranquilisers?'

Martha is angry and grabs his T-shirt below the neck, pulling him viciously close to her. 'Yes, tranquilisers. You're a fucking drug dealer, aren't you? You must have some downers in your fucking collection somewhere.'

The screaming finally fades away and I can catch my breath again. I'm choking tears.

Jack disappears. The next thing I know, Martha's crouched beside me, holding a glass of water with two tablets in her palm.

'Take these; you'll feel better.'

'No.'

'It will help.'

'No, I know what you're doing; you're trying to poison me.'

Martha tries to force the pills into my mouth but I spit them on the floorboards and knock the glass out of her hand. 'Poison me like you did to Bette.' I sob, 'Poor Bette.'

She puts her arm around me. 'I'm trying to help.'

I turn my eyes on her. 'You want to help? Tell me what happened in this house. That's how you can help.'

She goes pale. 'I don't know what you're talking about.'

'Yes, you do,' I harshly accuse.

Martha looks at me in disbelief. I can hear her mind turning over in her head. Then her arms are around me, helping me to my feet.

'Come on, my girl, let's get you to your room.'

The last thing I remember is Bette's tag swinging like an executioner's blade around her throat.

Thirty

I'm shattered, the embodiment of a zombie as I lie on my back on the bed the following morning. Well, I think it's morning; I can't be sure. I don't remember sleeping. Recall coming back to my room. I don't need the unkind reflection of a mirror to tell me what I must look like. Puffed-up bags under my bloodshot eyes, dull, lifeless skin. My limbs ache. I have scratches and bruises in strange places and my mouth is parched. It feels like the morning after a hen night that got out of hand or a half marathon that should have been cancelled because of the heat.

Flashes of yesterday come back to me. Voices. Chairs. The dining room cabinet. All moving. The screaming? The same screaming that haunts my nightmares. It splinters inside my head right now. I squeeze my eyes tight, trying to drown out the terrible, inhuman sound.

Get out of my head. Out of my head. Out. Out. Out.

When it leaves I want to curl up into a ball, a spiral getting smaller and smaller until I disappear. What the hell is happening to me? Did any of yesterday happen? Was I awake-sleeping again?

Then I remember: Martha and Jack were there too. Weren't they? There's only one way of finding out. I don't want to seek them out, but what choice do I have?

When I get to the kitchen, I take a pint glass from a cupboard and fill it full of water from the tap and bring it to my lips. Then I remember I only drink the bottled water in my room. Never anything from this kitchen in case Martha does to me what she did to Bette.

As I dash the water into the sink, the back door opens and Jack appears. When he sees me, he looks wary and puts two flowerpots down on the flagstone floor. My hand shakes as I place the glass on the draining board. He carefully locks the back door. He openly gazes at me with deep suspicion mixed with distaste.

'Are you alright?' He sounds more like a cop interviewing a suspect than a concerned landlord.

I resist the urge to wrap my arms protectively around my lurching tummy. 'Yes, I'm fine.'

'What was going on with you yesterday?' He sounds reluctantly sympathetic.

At least I now know that it all really happened.

I'm not sure what to say because I don't really know. 'I suppose I was a touch stressed out. You know, having a bad day.'

'A bad day?' His brows flip up along with his tone. 'It didn't…'

But he doesn't finish. Martha's appeared and she cuts him short. 'Don't harass the girl, she's not well.'

Jack gives me a dirty look. Maybe that's what he has to do when his wife's about: be hostile to me. 'That's certainly one explanation. I can think of others.'

Martha's not interested in his explanations. 'Why don't you go and prune the grass or something?'

Jack's been told and he doesn't look in the mood to give her any backchat and now I understand why. I know who gives the orders in this house. He slopes off, eyeing me while avoiding Martha. The back door bangs behind him.

I scowl hard as I stare at Martha; it comes back to me that during yesterday's terrifying incident I accused her of something. What was it? No matter how hard I rack my brain I can't remember.

She's concerned but in the way a strict teacher would be. 'What was going on with you last night, Lisa? Wandering around the house in a stupor, saying all kinds of crazy things, making all kinds of wild accusations? Acting up like a teenager, drunk as a dockyard sailor? Is that it? Are you a drinker? Or have you got mental health issues?'

Amid this blizzard of questions, another memory from yesterday comes back to me: Bette's name tag swinging on the choker she was wearing. When I search her slim neck, of course it's gone. If it was ever there at all.

'I don't have a drink or drug problem, Martha.' Then something occurs to me. My gaze becomes penetrating. 'Did you try to give me downers?'

A scowl darkens her face. 'Downers? I wouldn't know where to get them. No, I asked Jack to get you some paracetamol.'

'But you called Jack a drug dealer.'

A thin wan smile crosses her face. I think I can see Bette's name tag around her throat again but of course I can't. 'You were really out of your mind yesterday. The brain can be such a delicate thing. I'm not a psychiatrist, my dear, but that rather sounds like paranoia to me. You should really see a doctor.'

Like our mutual friend, Doctor Wilson, I nearly blurt out.

'You know what else, Martha?' I persist. 'You were swearing at Jack like a trucker. Dropping the F-bomb like it had just entered the English language. The Martha I know wouldn't do that.'

Martha shakes her head. 'Look, Lisa, we're not prejudiced against people with issues. It's a very common thing in our troubled times. But you can't seriously expect Jack and I to shoulder the responsibility for them. You understand that, don't you? You see what I'm saying? Is it really fair to burden us with your problems when you clearly need professional help? The best place for you is in your own home.' She reaches for my arm, I suppose to express some kind of physical comfort. I flinch away.

Martha's mouth twists as she sees my reaction. 'Go home, Lisa; call a doctor and get better in an environment that you feel safe and comfortable in.'

I look her square in the eye. 'Are you saying it's not safe for me here?'

I don't give her the chance to respond as I turn my back and walk away. There's no remnant left of the Martha who helped me that night she discovered me awake-sleeping. I know this much: the real Martha is the arrogant, cutting woman I saw with Doctor Wilson. The woman who walks with her chin up, sneering down at the world. I saw her in the coffee house on the high street, talking to Doctor Wilson like he was muck under her shoe.

All I can do is watch my back and try to stay one step ahead of any future horrors she may have in store for me. Let her do her worst; nothing will make me leave this house.

Upstairs, I close my door, get ready to go out. I take out one of the water bottles I've hidden in the wardrobe. Drink long and deeply, trying to clear my mind.

***

It's like a monster now exists inside me. That intense, walk-on-water, beautiful-world feeling I had yesterday has now flipped to its dark side. Now I'm no longer on cloud nine but filled with anxiety and depression.

I'm on the high street and walking but it feels like I'm on a treadmill because I don't seem to be getting anywhere. How can that be? I can feel them, my feet, in the motion of walking – one in front of the other – but when I look around I'm still near the tube station. Panic is rising and rising. My nerve endings are tiny dots of electricity shocking my skin. The bright colours on the street have melted away, replaced by one colour alone – shadow. Shadows that waver and move, sway. I sense people watching me; my lips are moving. Am I speaking? The high street is an ugly place I need to urgently escape from, but my feet refuse to help me get away. Maybe someone like me deserves to be in a bad place like this?

I'm out of control. *Please help me. Someone please help me.* Doctor Wilson is right. I'm breaking apart.

A hand touches my shoulder. I don't start or jump out of my skin – what a silly phrase! – but I stop pacing. See, I know that hand. It once brought me comfort, made me feel safe. Made me forget all my troubles for a while.

I turn and face Alex. Unlike my surroundings he pops with bright colours.

He looks shocked. I don't blame him. I must appear like the wreck of the century: a haunting scarecrow with short hair and bulging, big eyes.

'Lisa, I want you to listen to me.' His words are slow, as if I'm an idiot. 'I'm going to take you to a café across the road. I'm going to order you a double espresso. You will drink it. Then you need to tell me what's the matter.'

I don't respond, allowing him to guide me to the café and a table near the back. Soon I'm drinking the coffee and its full-force caffeine kicks in, shifting me slightly out of this world I can't control.

'What's going on?' His face is so full of concern I want to put my head on the table and weep.

'I don't know. I didn't sleep very well last night.' I correct myself. 'My mind was on the go.' I don't tell him about the strange incident yesterday. 'I'm so tired. So tired.'

He places his palm over my limp hand. 'Why don't you come back to mine and put your head down—'

'No. I can't do that. I have to get back to the house.' I try to get up. The pressure of his hand keeps me in place.

His expression is intense. 'Have you been taking drugs?'

I know what drugs he means: the type you buy on street corners, not courteously of a prescription from a doctor's surgery.

'I'm not into that kind of crap.' I drag my bag into my lap. Fish out my pills, my face going hot with humiliation that he's going to discover another one of my shameful secrets.

I hold the pill bottle up like a hand grenade. 'You want the truth, so here you go,' I spit out. 'These are anti-depressants. I've been taking them since…' My lips slam together; I don't want him to know about the incident cum suicide attempt. 'For a while now. I take them on a need-to basis.'

'Are they meant to make your eyes dilate like they are now?'

I want to roar back at him, but my voice is as small as I feel inside. 'How the hell am I meant to know?' My tone turns tart with sarcasm. 'Before I take them I don't have a conversation with them, asking them to tell me the ins and outs of how they work.'

Why am I being so vicious to Alex? He only wants to help me.

His hand slips away, his stare frank. 'When I saw you outside the station you were pacing and muttering over and over again, "Where are they? Where are they?"'

'Do you think I'm losing my mind?' Alex, of all people I know, will tell me the truth.

He leans closer. 'I think you need to go back to your doctor and get him to either change your level of meds or change the type you're on.'

'Could you love a woman like me? Really love?' I don't know where it comes from; it certainly wasn't what I intended to place on the table between us.

'Do you want me to be honest?' He doesn't hesitate.

I nod and pray. The last thing I need is rejection.

'I can't think of love at the moment. It's trivial compared to what's happening to you. What I do feel for you is fear. I'm terrified you're being dragged into a bottomless hole you won't ever get out of. And I feel guilty—'

'Why?' It rings out as a small cry.

His hands come up; a gesture of hopelessness. 'If I hadn't given you the information about this John Peters maybe, just maybe, you might have packed your things and left that shitshow of a house. It's not safe for you there.'

'I know I probably appear like something out of *The Rocky Horror Show*' – we allow ourselves small smiles at that – 'but without you I'd never have got anywhere near the truth. And I'm getting closer, believe me.'

His lips purse and a frown stains his forehead. I know that expression; he's deciding whether to tell me something or not.

In anticipation I lean closer. 'If you've found out anything else, *anything*, don't hold out on me.'

'OK. I've found out more.'

'What?'

'I'll tell you, but only after you've come back to mine and got some shut-eye.'

Thirty-one

I'd never figured Alex for the emotional blackmail type, but here I am walking into the place he rents. It's the garden flat in a Victorian terrace, a hop, skip and jump away from Camden Market. I've been here once before, on a night that had begun with promise and ended so badly.

He leads me straight to his bedroom. Everything has a place; books on shelves, a rug by the bed, a bed smoothly made, a closed wardrobe with no clothes on hangers on its doors. What captures my attention is what's on the wall.

I'm drawn towards them as if in a dream. 'How did you do this?'

Pinned to the wall are two poster-sized copies of the writing on the wall from my room, translated into English.

Alex looks embarrassed, slightly sheepish. 'One of the secretaries in the office is a tech whizz. She rustled them up in no time.'

My heart lurches. It feels so good to see the writing again. My lifeline. What I mentally hang on to in those increasingly frequent moments of doubt.

'They painted my room black,' I finally confess to Alex.

'What?' He comes to stand beside me, ignoring the writing, keeping his gaze firmly fixed on me.

'Jack said that Martha told him to do it. I'd been badgering him to fix the skylight, which he did. But he painted the room black too. *She* told him to do it.' In a quieter voice I add, 'Martha murdered your Aunt Patsy's cat too.'

Alex looks wild, like he wants to punch someone's lights out. 'Lisa, you can't go back to that house. These people are dangerous.'

I growl back, 'Don't you get it? I'm never going to be normal—'

'Who the heck is normal?' He's mad now and not afraid to show it. 'What does normal actually mean? It's a bloody myth, that's what it is. You know what my grandmother said to me once? "You young people think you're meant to be happy all the time." She was right. Life is full of ups and downs. The sooner we get used to that, the sooner we can rest easy in the skin of the life we're in.'

I stare at him sadly, the fire in me gone. 'My only up has been finding you. Other than that, it's been down, down, down.' Grief cracks my voice. 'I can't live like that anymore. Only the secrets in that house can lift me up.'

I wobble on my feet. Alex catches me.

'Sleep now, talk later.'

The smoothly made bed sucks me in. I feel the mattress sag and then the warmth of Alex's body as it curls around me. Almost in a panic, as if I'm frightened he might disappear, I twist into him, tuck my head into his chest and hold on to him with a strength that says I don't want to ever let go.

He soothes me with a kiss on the top of my head. 'Don't think, honey, just sleep.'

I don't think of my scarf, just sleep. My body relaxes. The fuzzy fog thins in my mind.

Sleep.

Sleep.

Sle…

***

I wake in a dark room. Anxiety and panic kick in. I don't know where I am. Then I remember. The warmth of Alex's body is missing.

It's his soothing voice that makes me ease back. 'You finally back in the land of the living?'

He's sitting, with his legs stretched out, in a modern-style chair that reminds me of a tulip starting to close.

'Can you put up the blinds, please?'

As he does this I get out of bed. Stand. Test a step to ensure I'm steady. I walk over to the writing on the wall. Sit in front of it and cross my legs. Alex does the same. I can't help noticing he's wearing his trademark odd socks: one red with flying pigs, the other white with penguins on.

I don't feel brilliant, but better, more myself. 'Please tell me what you found out.'

'I started looking into John Peters. Digging up information about him. He was a highly regarded trauma surgeon.'

'What does that mean?' My back stiffens with anticipation.

He leans his elbows on his knees and rests his chin in the cups of his hands, his gaze shining with alertness. 'One of my firm's clients was one. She saw her job more as a critical specialist, someone who needed to be quick on their feet, assess a situation and then be able to treat a patient who had multiple types of injuries. Terrible physical assaults, car crash victims, that kind of stuff.'

He leans back. 'John Peters taught at one of the large teaching hospitals. The strange thing is, after he moved back into the house as Martha Palmer's lodger, he quit his job.'

'Why would he do that?'

He shrugs. 'I wish I had a crystal ball. Maybe the job took its toll. He must've seen stuff the average person wouldn't want to witness in a million years.' He squints. 'Is any of this jogging your memory?'

If only Alex had been there at the house last night when the door to my memory crashed open. I don't care what anyone else's opinion is – I know that's what happened. If I'd been in possession of this information then, maybe I would've seen John Peters too, started to piece together who he was. How he's connected to me. The sensation brewing within me must be what is meant by 'so frustrated I could scream'.

I don't scream. 'What else did you find out?'

'His wife is called Alice. She was a stay-at-home mum. In the first section of writing' – he points to it on the wall – 'he describes his wife as being beautiful and fragile. I couldn't find out anything else about her.'

'What about his son and daughters?'

Alex sighs. I feel bad for him; I've brought a load of trouble to his door. 'I could probably find out more about them. You know, names, what schools they went to—'

'Why are you saying probably?' There's also a reluctance embedded in his tone.

He uses his hands against the floor to swivel to face me fully. 'The thing is, Lisa, I don't think you're well. Your behaviour since you turned up at Aunty Patsy's and then on the high street has been erratic. You were pacing and talking to yourself outside the tube for heaven's sake.'

I'm angry with him and let him know it. 'Who do you think you are?' I scramble to my feet. 'The conduct police? The only thing wrong with me is the people who claim to love me the most are hiding my past from me. They're the ones who need medical treatment.'

'The bad guys aren't your parents but your landlords. Martha and Jack painted your room black, for heaven's sake.' He looks like he wants to do serious damage to someone. 'Killed Aunty Pats' cat and, I suspect, did a wagonload of other stuff you haven't told me.' I can't keep the guilt from my eyes. 'I know that your parents tried to take you home.'

That surprises me. 'How do you know that?'

'Aunty Pats saw it all go down from the comfort of her perch behind the net curtains in her front room.' He's pleading now. 'Don't go back there. This has gone from weird and creepy to bloody dangerous.'

I'm defiant. 'Let them do their worst. The only way I'm leaving that house is with the truth walking along right beside me.'

I'm raving, can't stop. In fact, don't want to stop. Everyone's against me and now Alex, my beloved Alex, is too. I should've known better. Isn't this what happens to me all the time? I make a commitment to another human being and they let me bloody down. Tears stain my face. I ignore them just as I ignore Alex as he rushes to his feet, somehow sensing I'm leaving. The strained expression on his face tells me he doesn't want me to go.

I swipe up my bag, wrench open the door. Then his calm words stop me.

'You remind me of my brother. For so long he refused to accept our help, help from those outside our family who could assist him. Make him better. It got to the stage where it was almost too late. If you carry on like this, Lisa, I worry it will be too late for you with no way back.'

The terror of his prediction hits me hard. I see me guzzling down vodka, gulping down pills like a kid with no rules at her fifth birthday party. See me in a hospital room, white from the walls to the floor. Hear the sound of my mum's sobs, those of a ghost who can't find eternal rest. I see Doctor Wilson, emphatic in his diagnosis that I'm falling apart. Martha with Bette's name tag on, displayed like her most prized possession. I see young me in the back of a car staring back at a house with a key in a circle as its mason's mark gets smaller and smaller.

I close the door.

Thirty-two

The cooling air outside sends me off balance again. A tipsy-drunk sensation. I'm disorientated, not sure where to find transport back home. Is that what the house has become? My home? No, home is a place where you feel safe and secure, not afraid to put your head down at night. Certainly not somewhere where the walls of your room are coated in the glossiest black. Unless you're a goth.

I stop at the first bus stop I come to. The bus comes along a few minutes later and once I'm on board I figure out it's going to the wrong destination and the wrong way. Once I get off, I walk and walk from nowhere to nowhere. As I drag my feet along, passers-by look at me. Some are kind enough to ask me if I'm alright. Why do English people ask you if you're alright when you're clearly not?

I turn a corner and recognise where I am. Camden High Street. I spot the yellow light of a cab office. A woman behind a metal grill, munching a burger, asks me where I want to go. After I've told her she tells me to sit down and someone will be along in five minutes.

A portly middle-aged driver comes in, dangling car keys, and smiles at me. He leads me outside and I get into the back seat but tumble on my side when the car pulls away. The driver looks over his shoulder at me.

He's concerned. 'Are you alright?'

'No. I mean yes.'

'You're not pissed?'

If only alcohol was my problem, that would be easier to solve. 'No, I'm not drunk.'

He's probably worried I'm going to be sick in his car. He turns on the cheer, with a constant stream of banter, when it's clear I won't be messing up his car: how awful the traffic is, what bastards cyclists are, how violent London is becoming and how he's fed up with customers who run off without paying when they reach their destination.

I want him to shut up but that seems so unkind to such a friendly man so I say nothing. I begin to recognise streets out of the window and I feel an immense sense of relief. He turns down the avenue and we come to a halt.

I tell him, 'It's a bit further on, by the white van.'

We pull up outside the house with the mason's mark. The driver turns around. 'That's ten pounds fifty. Call it a tenner.'

I find my purse. Hell! I've only got five pounds and loose change. I should've taken an Uber where the fare is docked from my credit card.

'You've got no money.' It's not a question but a statement.

'Yes, I have.'

With an irate twist of his mouth he holds his hand out expectantly.

'But it's not on me. Wait here a minute, I'll go inside and get it.'

He rolls his eyes. 'Oh no, not another one…'

I scramble out of the car. Have I got money upstairs? But in the end, it doesn't matter. When I take my first few faltering steps, he drives away without his money.

It takes an age for me to walk up the drive. I stand in front of the house and stare at it, in particular at the mason's mark on the wall that led me here in the first place. So many secrets in this house. So much to answer for. But if I'm mentally blasted and blown, I might not find out what they are and I'm running out of time. It only needs a little more work and I'll be there. I'm convinced of that. I can't afford the luxury of going to pieces. This is my last chance to find the truth and nothing's going to stop me.

When I walk through the front door, I think Martha and Jack are out. It's quiet. I call their names to make sure before heading for the kitchen. The fridge is divided into mine and their sections. My section is empty; after Bette who knows what Martha might do to my food. I steal some of theirs. I don't want to eat – even thinking of it makes feel sick – but I make a gigantic ham sandwich, pour mayonnaise on it and find pickles and other bits and pieces to spice it up. I sit in the dining room where the chairs and cabinets were running around during my episode and force-feed the snack down my throat. It makes me light-headed but I come to my senses a little. I haven't been eating, and that hasn't done me any good. I pinch one of Jack's beers and that helps too.

Then I realise. Jack and Martha aren't here. I can seize my chance. Or maybe they are lurking around, but I'm going to seize it anyway.

Carrying Jack's beer, I walk into the living room and stand in a corner trying to soak up the vibrations or whatever you want to call it, I don't care. I shut my eyes tightly and try to feel the past. I open my eyes. I remember 'the cabinet' coming in here with the 'woman at the door'. It's mad; of course it is. But it's true at the same time. This *is* where the woman was screaming on my fifth birthday. I'm sure of it. I walk out of the living room and try the door to the morning room. But it's locked. I consider kicking it in, but I'm not even sure I've got the strength to do that.

I go up to the middle floor and begin trying doors. The room that serves as Jack's den is open and I go in. Even before I cross the threshold to find the shambles inside, I know there's nothing in here for me. Their bedroom next door is locked. Martha has her own, private room and, surprisingly, it's not locked.

The curtains are drawn. It's an Aladdin's cave of clothes, wigs, perfumes, make-up and photos of a young Martha looking impossibly glamorous and attended to by adoring men. She exudes power in these photos. Hypnotic and mesmerising, even in a simple snapshot, never mind the carefully composed ones. I don't know why but I look under her bed and immediately wish I hadn't. I know it's not real but the eyes of a dead mouse are staring at me. And I hear screams. Was a woman screaming in here? Children screaming? A man?

Suddenly the room reeks like a sewer. I feel an invisible stranglehold on my neck. I'm suffocating. Can't pull in breath. My vision's wavering. Fading. It's not real. None of it's real. I haul myself to my full height and get out of the room. On the landing I lean against the wall, panting heavily as a chill envelopes me. What happened in there? Is Martha's private kingdom connected to my past? Maybe I should go back... I approach the door again, this time with trepidation. Reach for the handle... My trembling hand flies back. I'm scared to go back in. So scared.

I have an idea. I hurry down to the dining room. I try to re-enact the chairs scampering around from the night before. Then I imagine the knock at the front door and the cabinet going to answer it. I hear the screaming from the living room and I hurry back upstairs and will myself into Martha's room. I cringe, am terrified again. I close my eyes.

Remember. Remember. Remember.

Mouse eyes. Woman. Woman at the door. Children. Man. Screaming. I'm almost physically sick this time when I rush out of the room and slam the door. Something evil happened in that room. Something terrible. I can't work it out but I know something happened in there. Something terrible that laid my life to waste before it had even really begun. I sit on the stairs that lead up to my room and try to think things through. But I'm out of ammo.

I hear a key in the front door. Firm footsteps in the hallway. The scent of Martha's spiced apple fragrance drifts up as the low screeches and groans of old wood signal her coming up the stairs. I stiffen like a thief caught in the act.

Martha's wearing a pair of jeans; it's the first time I've seen her in them. Black, probably designer, slim-fit to show off every line, curve and muscle. I can't see if she's wearing Bette's tag because of her high-necked blouse. I wonder if she knows I know?

'I hope you've had a chance to see a doctor about...' Her low statement doesn't finish. She doesn't need to; we both know what she's talking about.

'What I've had time to do is think about the scene I saw downstairs. In the dining room.' Her green eyes shutter slightly as I speak. 'The front door.'

'I worry about your sanity,' she says with pity.

I'm wrung out; nevertheless I manage to pull some strength from somewhere and stand on the step looking down at her.

'During whatever happened yesterday,' I tell her with feeling, 'nothing seemed real, except one thing.'

She's curious. 'What are you talking about?'

'I remember now. There was a person at the front door. Do you know who that was?'

Martha tries the whole pity routine again, but it won't wash this time. 'You're seeing things. Need help.'

I shake my head against her accusations. 'It was you. I saw you at the front door, Martha.'

***

I tie my leg with three knots that night because I'm worried what will happen if I awake-sleep and leave the room. Where I might end up. The black paint makes the walls and floor blend into each other. I'm in a cloud of dark. Feel like I'm levitating on the bed in the night. I want to sleep but I'm frightened of shutting my eyes. Of the screams in my nightmares that I'm sure will become my own.

Martha's not only trying to drive me out; somehow she's connected to my past. Connected to my nightmares of what happened in this house.

There's nothing to fear. The chain's on; the chair's secure against the door. I close my eyes. Do my breathing exercises to a new set of words:

'It was you. I saw you at the front door Martha.'

'It was you. I saw you at the front door Martha.'

Thirty-three

I awake to the sound of vehicles pulling up urgently into the drive outside. The morning light streams strong through the skylight. I wonder who can be visiting the house. The only visitors my landlords have had since I arrived were Mum and Dad trying to force me to come home. Perhaps in other circumstances I would get up and look to see who it is. But these aren't other circumstances and I couldn't care less. A car door bangs. There's a scattering of voices. I recognise one: Dad.

God give me strength.

Can I even be bothered? I'm exhausted, spent, finished. I turn over in an effort to get some more fractured sleep. But I'm interrupted by a knock at my door.

'Wakey-wakey; you've got visitors.' It's Jack.

'Tell them to go away.' *And you can sod off too.*

But he won't so I'm forced to untie my leg, get up and open the door.

He looks serious. And oddly troubled. 'You'd better come down before they come and get you. I'd take your bag if I was you.'

Why do I need my bag? I'm seized with fear. My Dad's brought the police. I anxiously try and remember whether I've done anything illegal in the past couple of days when things have fallen apart but I can't think straight. If I have, I'll need Alex to support me but I don't want to ring him because he might think this is the final piece of evidence that I need serious professional help.

I put on some clothes, not caring that Jack might get an eyeful. I take his advice and sling my day rucksack over one shoulder. I'm unsteady on my feet so he offers me his arm as a means of support.

I should tell him to stuff his support but instead I take it gratefully. Jack playing the gentleman is something I can't turn down.

He escorts me out of the room and I shuffle along like a prisoner in leg irons. Then it occurs to me: it can't be the police because Jack would be shaking like a marijuana leaf in a strong wind, worried his secret garden will be found out. It's someone else. It's my dad and someone else.

'Who is it?'

'You'll see.'

When we get to the hallway, my dad is standing there. Martha is reading some paperwork. And next to her is Doctor Wilson. Martha shrugs her shoulders and hands the papers back to my therapist who slides them into a Manila folder. My mind thinks furiously. Why is there paperwork? What's written on it? Then it dawns on me with a crushing dread. I realise what all this is about.

I don't remember moving. I lash out at Doctor Wilson, trying to kick him, but Jack holds me back.

I'm surprised at how loud my outrage is. 'I'm not going anywhere and you can't make me.'

My dad has his dad voice on. 'Now look, Lisa, it's just for a few days until you're better.' He turns to Wilson. 'It's a very good place, isn't it?'

I wrench out of Jack's hold. Fold my arms. 'You're wasting your time. I'm not going anywhere.'

Dad's voice softens in an attempt to persuade me. 'Well, I'm afraid you've got no choice in the matter. Now, come on, no time to lose.'

'I'm not going. You can't make me.'

It's Martha who explains. 'He's right, you really don't have a choice. They're sectioning you. Doctor Wilson here has signed the paperwork. I've just read it on your behalf.'

I turn on her, my eyes blazing with hatred. 'I know you're part of this. I saw you at the door.'

'Of course you saw me at the door,' she flings back. 'This is my bloody house.'

Activity outside the front door catches my eye. On the drive are two cars and a private ambulance. Loitering near the ambulance are two guys in green paramedic gear.

I explode. Anger has resurrected me back to life. 'You're committing your own daughter? Is that right? On the word of Doctor Frankenstein here?'

My dad does his best. 'We've all seen evidence of your condition, my dear, and I understand your landlords have too. It's nothing to be ashamed of; you're just not well, that's all.' He looks out of the door. 'Gentlemen, can I have your assistance please?'

The two goons in green come in. I struggle but it's an unequal fight. Jack helps them out. Fair play to him. He doesn't seem very enthusiastic about it. One of the paramedics takes me by my bony wrists while the other grabs my ankles and I'm carried out and gently placed in the back of the ambulance. There are straps inside of it but mercifully they don't use them.

Doctor Wilson, the bastard, makes his escape in his car while my dad shouts to the ambulance driver: 'I'll follow in my car.'

The doors are closed. I can't go. They're taking me away from the house. Away. I'm frantic that I can't raise my head to see the house disappearing. Can't see my talisman of the truth: the mason's mark with my special key inside.

'Would you like something to settle you down?' one of the men supervising me asks.

'Sod off.'

He takes it in good part. I suppose he's trained to.

The ambulance rumbles and rolls for a long time but I don't know how long. When it comes to a halt, the doors open and I'm in the countryside. We've stopped outside what looks like a country hotel but it's obvious where we really are. There are medical staff wandering round and patients sitting in the sun. I decide to be a cooperative prisoner for now because that will give me more opportunity to escape later, although how is not easy to see. They won't have brought me to a place you can just walk out of. They're not stupid. But who has really brought me here?

I keep the fury alive inside me. It's giving me the energy to think. Clearly this was my dad's idea. He wants me out of that house for good to prevent me from finding out what happened there. But why?

Is he just concerned for my health? Trying to save me from the awful truth? I hate the final question; I don't want it to be true. I force myself to think it.

Or is he implicated in it?

There's no sign of Mum so I'm guessing her conscience wouldn't allow her to get involved in this intervention. Her conscience isn't even well developed enough to tell her daughter what she knows. Doctor Wilson is Dad's helpful sidekick. Is he doing this as a despicable favour to an old friend? Or is he implicated too? His attitude towards me changed when I told him I was living in the spare room in the house.

I'm registered at reception and led to my 'room', which is little better than a highly decorated prison cell. A smiley nurse tells me that I can treat the place as a hotel and come and go as I please. Utter lies. There's an electronic lock on the door and one look at the window shows me that while there are no bars on it there might as well be. The glass looks as if it's shatterproof and the locks are so secure a burglar at the top of his game couldn't pick them.

'This is a great place to rest,' Dad rattles off, hands behind his back; he's barely able to look at me. 'You've got your own telly with lots of satellite chann—'

'Why are you doing this to me?' I slash over his stupid words. Who gives a bloody damn about how many channels the TV has access to. 'Stop talking as if this is a five-star holiday resort.'

He still won't meet my eyes. But then guilty people find that hard to do.

'I want to leave here. Now.'

It's as if I haven't spoken. Am I invisible now too? 'You're going to stay here until you get better.'

'Look at me,' I roar, as if I'm the parent talking to the child.

I wished I hadn't asked because the expression he gives me is of a man who's been stricken with the news that he's dying. 'I love you. Everything I have ever done for you has been with the caring hands of love.'

He heads for the door, leaving me stunned. I don't disbelieve his aching words. Don't disbelieve his truth. But it's my truth he refuses to tell me about. He would rather lock me away than help me. How can he do that? He's forfeited any right to be called my dad.

When he's gone, 'the warders', as I like to think of them, have their first go at trying to drug me up. It's sedatives probably, so I only half resist. I drink the cloudy drink but keep the pills under my tongue to spit out when they've gone. I don't blame the staff. To be honest, in normal circumstances, I wouldn't blame my dad or Doctor Wilson either. I know how erratic my behaviour has been since I discovered the location of the house. Or even before that. But I'm not here on account of any erratic behaviour. I'm here because they want to stop me getting to the truth. When the nurse has gone, I feel sleepy and lie down. I'm actually feeling quite happy. The conspirators wouldn't have gone to this length if they weren't seriously worried I was getting near the truth.

Then something hits me that I should've seen before. It takes my breath away. The first time Dad and Mum tried to get me out of the house.

How did my dad know where my room was in Martha and Jack's house?

***

A sharp knock on the door wakes me. My mouth tastes sour and furry. Whatever was in the cloudy drink has done its work. I suspect the job of the tablet I pretended to take was to dull my senses, sending me into a cooperative, zombie-like stupor. Thank God I didn't take it.

No medication can obliterate the one question still doing the rounds in my frazzled mind. How did Dad know where my room was? I've played it out over and over from all different angles. Martha told him? Jack pointed the way? I told him? No. No. Surely I would remember if I did that, wouldn't I?

As I swing my legs over the side of the bed, a woman in her early thirties wheels a food and tea trolley in. I guess straight off that she's no nurse; she isn't wearing a uniform. She's decked out in black jeans and a T-shirt that's baggy against her body. Her limp, brown hair is pulled back into a facelift-tight ponytail. When she gets close there's the smell of nicotine wafting from her.

'What do you fancy from the trolley?' She sounds bored.

This being an upmarket kind of a place, the trolley is full of tasty treats. Exotic fruits, fancy sandwiches with a variety of teas, herbals included of course. There's a flash-looking menu too.

I'm not in the mood. 'I'm OK, thank you.' My voice sounds rusty to my ears.

She gives me a speculative look from under lowered lashes. 'You new?'

'Came in earlier today.'

'Been in here nearly three months now. They tell me I'm getting better.' She shrugs. 'I suppose I don't want to chuck myself off buildings no more.'

I swallow nervously. As much as I sympathise with her plight, I won't be stopping here long enough to make friends. She starts wheeling the trolley back towards the door when an idea comes to me.

'Have you got a mobile?'

Her hands tighten against the trolley handle as she half turns to me. Her eyes widen as she weighs up my request. 'I don't think you're allowed mobiles on this part of the unit.'

I get to my feet. I'm surprisingly grounded. 'I only want to check on my cat. You know, make sure my friend is feeding him. My poor Henry, he'll die without me and then I don't know what I'll do. There'll be no point in living anymore.'

Maybe I shouldn't have said the last part since this woman obviously has a problem living, but pets always tug at people's hearts.

She folds her arms. 'What do I get out of this?'

I'm not sure what to say, so she continues, 'You got any perfume? Haven't had a decent smelly since I got here. The soap here leaves you whiffing like a car engine.'

Sod's law! I don't have any of that. But I can't let my chance of getting out of here waltz out of the door with the tea trolley.

'I only just got here, as you know, but I can get some perfume for you. You name it, I can get it,' I coax.

She mulls over what I've said. 'How you gonna do that then?'

I tap the side of my nose with a finger. She likes that. 'You leave the how to me. Can I use your phone?'

'I'll have to get it from my room on the other end of the unit.'

I take up guard duty position near her trolley. 'I'll take care of this while you take care of me.'

She's gone and back in three minutes flat, but when she hands the phone over she holds on tight when I try to take it.

'It's got to be Eternity.' At first, I'm a bit out to sea about what she's talking about, then the penny drops. 'None of that Chanel shit.'

She lets the phone go. 'Make it quick. They find out, there's going to be major-league trouble.'

My fingers fumble as I tap the number into the phone. I'm conscious of her watching my every move.

The call goes to voicemail. Damn!

I leave a message in a voice that sounds like I'm chatting away to him.

'Alex! Hello, darling. Listen, I've had to come into hospital for a few days and there's no one to look after Henry… No, nothing serious, just routine… Look, could you pop next door and make sure my little darling's not too upset?'

I give Alex a list of fictional Henry's dietary requirements and try to sound like a mad cat woman while I'm doing it. Finally, I get to the point of the call. I pick up the menu from the tea trolley.

'Oh, it's a wonderful hospital. I need some Eternity spray, darling. It's…' I give him the name and postcode from the details on the menu before adding in my most carefree voice, '*Au secours, Alex! Au secours! Maintenant! Au secours!*'

Alex speaks Russian and deciphered the handwriting on the wall. I only hope he can pick up on my schoolgirl French and that my fellow patient can't. I hand the phone back to my new buddy who's smiling like it's her birthday.

'I'm not mad, you know,' she announces starkly. 'My baby died last year and I took a turn for the worse. When I wore Eternity it made him smile.'

I suck in a stunned breath. She doesn't wait around for a 'sorry', a friendly smile or a rub on the back. Just wheels her tea trolley out of the room.

I lie back and try to relax. I don't touch the sandwich because I think they might have poisoned it.

Thirty-four

I'm in that groggy world of half asleep, part conscious, when the door to my room starts opening. My heart lurches with hope now Alex has finally arrived. What a star he's turned out to be even when I've, to my shame, kicked him to the kerb. To finally be liberated from this room. To feel the sun on my skin, the wind in my hair, the taste of freedom, all those things I've taken for granted my whole life.

My heart drops to the hollow of my belly when I realise it's not Alex. Behind the tall nurse is a woman visitor. When my eyes focus, I figure out why I couldn't tell who it was immediately. It's the last person I am expecting. Mum.

The nurse's voice is soft and firm as he explains to her, 'As you can see, Lisa's very tired so if you can limit your visit to about fifteen minutes, we'd be very grateful.'

Mum doesn't answer. She doesn't even seem to hear. Looking pale and shell-shocked, she appears more like a patient than I do. What catches my gaze most about her lost look is her hair. She's never said it but I know Mum prides herself on how well and effortlessly her styled hair always turns out. Glossy, alive, each strand knowing its place and order. Now it's limp, tangled, and, I suspect, unwashed. When the nurse leaves, Mum searches the room before her eyes finally end up on me.

'So, here you are.' Her voice is as lifeless as her hair. Her fingers knot together, pressing against her middle as if desperate to hold inner turmoil in.

'Yes, here I am.' I refuse to get up. Bitter sarcasm coats my words. 'Big round of applause to Dad and his very good friend Doctor Wilson. What a dynamic team they make. I suppose you're going to tell me you had no idea what they were up to? Save your breath. I'm not interested.'

Mum sits in the armchair, back straight. 'No, I had no idea what they were up to. Your father mentioned it at lunchtime, almost as an afterthought.' Her tired eyes drop to her clasped hands. 'He thinks it's for the best.'

I lie back on my pillow. My lightning-fast response brims with anger. 'And what do you think? Do you think locking me up in here is for the best? Does this cell look like the best to you?'

Mum closes her eyes for a few moments. 'Listen, Lisa, I want you to know that everything we've ever done for you is what we thought was for the best.'

Best. I am starting to loathe that word. Doesn't it mean excellent, outstanding, supreme? Is that what this looks like to her? Then I remind myself, it's one of those cover words that middle-class families like mine hide behind so they don't have to deal with emotion.

Mum stares out through the reinforced window at the landscaping outside. I can't put my finger on it but there's something about her manner that's a little unnerving.

I wring my lips together. 'Well, that's good to know. Thanks for dropping by.'

She won't look away from the ordered gardens. 'But I don't feel like that anymore.'

What? Did I just hear her say…? She has my full, astonished attention.

'Maybe, when you were a little girl, it was. But not now.' Her voice brings a new hush to a room that understands quiet so well. 'You have to understand, when you go down the road we went down in those days, after a while it becomes impossible to turn it off again. One untruth leads to another and you're stuck with it.' Her tone hardens on 'stuck'. 'You can't just turn everything on its head in a day. You understand that, don't you?'

What does she mean? Untruths? Does she mean…?

Now she looks at me. Her skin tightens with strain, but my God her eyes are on fire with determination. 'The thing is, you were right. There was no accident in Sussex. There never was.'

Does she expect me to be impressed or jump up, punch my fists in the air and shout 'Yippee'? I already know there was no accident in Sussex; I'm well past that stage.

'You've left that a little late, unfortunately. Still, thanks anyway.' My mouth tastes sour.

Mum doesn't appear to be listening to me and hasn't noticed the sarcasm dripping off my tongue. Or perhaps she has and doesn't give a shit.

She has this far away quality to her words as she carries on. 'We took you to a hospital for a while, a private one. We were only supposed to be looking after you for a while—'

I slam the bedclothes back and am up and out of the bed and crouched urgently down by her chair. 'What do you mean, look after me?'

Mum won't look down at me as her fingernails dig into the padded arms of the chair. It's like the garden is a court of law and she's testifying, after swearing on the Bible. I want to twist her face to me. Make her see *me*. But I leave her soaked in the past because the gates of the truth are finally opening.

'But one month led to another.' Her measured tone is slipping, shaky. The words fall out of her quivering mouth like hot stones she can't expel quickly enough. 'Finally, it seemed simpler for all concerned if we adopted you. Once we'd done that, we had to come up with a story to cover up what had happened and so we told you about the accident. We meant to tell you the truth later, when you were old enough to understand, but we never did. That was unforgivable and I'm really sorry.'

I've been waiting for this for so long. Now it's here I'm not ready. Not quite sure how to react. 'So, what really happened?'

Her eyes squeeze tight as she fights with her demons. 'I don't know. Your father does and I think Doctor Wilson does too. But I don't.'

'What do you mean you don't know?' I'm leaning over her now in outrage, my short, wild breath lashing her.

Her eyes flash open with such twisted sorrow I stumble back. 'I. Don't. Know.' Her torment echoes round and round the room.

Then an awful stillness almost suffocates me from head to toe as my brain rewinds. Mum's words slowly make their way from my ears to my heart. 'Adopted? I'm adopted?' I sound like I'm practising a foreign language.

The woman whose heart beats in the chair near me isn't really my mum? Someone has swung a sledgehammer into my chest because the pain is like nothing I've ever experienced before.

'You're not our natural child. We adopted you. I've loved you with my whole heart since the first time I saw you.'

She rocks on the chair, tears streaming down her face. I can't speak. Can't cry. Only blinding fury has a place inside me. Not at the people I have called mother and father, but at me. Why did it never occur to me to think that might be part of the puzzle?

Since the day you came into our lives. Hadn't Mum said that to me when she and Dad had visited me at my house? Hadn't I questioned it then? Why didn't I take it all the way and figure it out or press them further? And where's my birth certificate? Why did I never think to ask that question? All the records I checked and I never thought of that?

I have so many questions but they are jumbled up in my mind. I can't see a straight path through them. My mother tries to help. Except she's not my mum, of course. 'I don't know where your real parents are. Or if you have brothers or sisters. Your father knows more; he'll probably be able to tell you.'

Mum flinches as my fingers dig desperately into her trembling knee. 'Does he know what happened in that house? On my fifth birthday?'

'There's no point in pretending anymore.' She's drowned in a daze; I'm not sure if she even sees me anymore.

I feel utterly lost. Furiously angry, but not sure who at anymore. Straightened out but totally confused while at the same time I feel like I'm looking at a world that makes sense for the first time. But then again, it doesn't. I still don't know what happened in the house. I have to know that.

I think I know the answer to this question but I've been tripped up by assuming things before. 'Who is he?'

The woman who calls me daughter is in her own private nightmare. 'You understand why we did this, don't you?'

She's pleading, begging, no doubt holding her arms out for forgiveness. Well, she'll be holding them out for a very long time.

'Who is he? My real father?'

My mum – who isn't my mum; God, this is so messed up – pushes out of the chair. It rocks back on its legs as I tumble back onto my bum. She's at the door, but I catch her before she can leave. I spin her to face me.

I growl, 'Who is my dad?'

Mum tries to shake free. 'Lisa, let me go.'

'Not until you answer me.'

We start to struggle. God forgive me but I slam her into the wall. Winded, she uses her palms against my chest to heave me back. I won't be budged, not now. Other hands grab my shoulder and waist and rip me away.

'Let me go. Let me go.'

They won't.

Mum escapes through the doorway. No. No. I can't let her go. She's gone as I scream, 'Who is my real father?'

And my real mother? Who hugged and held me before Barbara Kendal did?

***

I've slept again. I'm dejected; beat down by the exploding dirty bomb Mum detonated in this room. Adopted. One word that has changed my life forever. Where do I come from? Who gave birth to me? I have my suspicions, of course, but my journey has taken so many turns I'm not taking anything for granted. At least Mum told me the truth. I should be grateful for that. Mum? Do I keep calling her that?

I hear voices outside my room. The cast of the sky outside has the shadow of the beginnings of the evening. The door opens and a doctor steps inside and closes the door.

'Lisa?'

My heart sinks. I was hoping it was going to be Alex.

'Look, we want you to get better as quickly as possible,' he continues, 'but if we're going to do that we need your help and that of your family. Do you understand?'

'Of course.'

'And that means we all have rules we need to stick to.' My spirits plunge further; he's tumbled about the phone.

'I did advise your father that it's unhelpful for you to see visitors for a few days,' he carries on, 'apart from him and your mother. Unfortunately, he's neglected to tell your brother and he seems to be a very confident young man who won't take no for an answer. In the circumstances, I'm willing to allow him to make a brief visit but I'm afraid it needs to be supervised, and I'd be grateful if you could explain to him that in future we expect our rules to be observed.'

Brother? I've just lost a mother and gained a brother?

Before I can figure out what the heck is going on the doctor opens the door and escorts Alex in. Oh, that brother. I resist the urge to triumphantly grin.

Alex wears his unhappy face. He sits on the armchair near the bed while the doctor stands back with his arms folded.

Alex turns to him. 'Can we have some privacy please?'

'That's not possible, I'm afraid. Lisa is very unwell.'

Alex is cold and curt. 'I'm a lawyer. I'm familiar with human rights legislation as it affects families and privacy. Are you?'

The doctor's nostrils flare as he seethes. He stalls before displaying the fingers and thumb of one hand, in the air. 'Five minutes only.'

He goes but I suspect he's got his ear pressed against the door.

I give Alex a knowing smile. 'I thought you were in commercial law and looked after dodgy deals with Eastern Europe, not human rights legislation.'

Alex shrugs. 'He doesn't know that.' He takes my hand. 'What's happened, Lisa?'

'They…' I realise I'm about to go off on a rant about a conspiracy involving my parents, Wilson and Martha to get me locked up in a lunatic asylum but I realise how that might sound, so I change tack. 'I've been sectioned.'

Alex purses his lips. 'I see. And what do you think about that?'

I nearly shout but manage to force my voice down. 'Are you serious? Can't you see what's going on here?'

He's searching for words. 'Well, be honest. Given what's happened, perhaps it's for the best.'

Best! Someone needs to ban that word.

I snatch my hand away and flop back. I'm not ready to share Mum's bombshell news with him. 'Not you as well? Are you in on it too? With those other creeps?'

He remains calm. 'I'm not in on anything. I just want you to be safe and right now, this looks like the safest place for you to be.'

Fury laces my every word as I sit back up. 'They want me out of the house because I'm closing in on the truth. Can't you see that?'

He sounds like a lawyer now. 'Who wants you out of the house?'

'My dad knew where my room was.'

He's confused. 'I don't get what you mean.'

'Admittedly I was preoccupied, but I don't recall Martha and Jack telling or showing him where it was. I might be wrong, but he confidently took the stairs to my room.'

'What are you saying?'

My head shakes and throbs. 'I don't know. What I do know is the puzzle pieces are starting to show themselves and the house is the only thing that will help me put them together. Look, I don't need a legal consultation at one hundred quid an hour. If you can't help, you might as well use the door.'

He looks around the room. Sighs and catches my eye. 'Yes, you're probably right; they want you out of the house. But I'm going to be honest with you; I want you out of that house too. I've been plain and upfront about that. It's dangerous. Terrible things have happened in there and they might happen again. Meanwhile, while you're in here, they're not going to happen. That's why I think you should lie back and relax. Forget the house for a while. It'll still be there when you come out.'

'No chance. I'm going back with or without your help.'

His hand fiddles in his pocket and he takes out the Eternity perfume bottle and thrusts it at me. 'Asking me to buy perfume? If that isn't a sign you're not well, I don't know what is.'

'It's a gift for someone who did me a good turn in here.' I remember the woman's heartbreaking story. 'It will do wonders for her, more than any medication will.'

He looks pensive. 'Remember when I met you on the high street and you were acting weird?'

I reluctantly nod.

'What exactly were you seeing?'

I don't want to go back there but somehow manage to make myself describe all the images that were in my mind – the shadows, shapes, the darkness and the flipside of beauty and the world being the most amazing place to be. I take him through what I saw in the dining room.

He now appears shaken up. 'Listen, I've been asking around. What you describe sounds like the classic symptoms of a mind hallucinating. An acid trip.'

'Wh... what? Acid?' To say I'm stunned is the understatement of the year.

'Did you take it deliberately to expand your consciousness and work things out that way? An extremely dangerous thing to do, I might add.'

I'm beyond affronted. 'I bloody well did not. I'm not a junkie if this is where this is going.'

He's matter-of-fact. 'There's another possibility. Jack or Martha or both might have spiked your food to send you over the edge and get you put in here. Do you think that's a possibility?'

I'm horrified and alarmed at what he's suggesting. 'No, I don't. I don't touch anything in that house.'

He nods. 'Anything at all?'

I rack my brains. 'I've got water in my room.'

I suddenly come to life. My mind flashes back to Martha standing at the bottom of the stairs that lead to my room after my confrontation with Jack in the garden. Is that what she'd been doing? Coming back from my room after drugging my bottles of water? I see myself drinking it just before I saw Alex at Patsy's, when I got back to my room preceding the incident in the dining room… and each time it was followed by the scary, strange feeling.

'Do you think Martha could have fiddled with it? Spiked it with LSD? Jack's a drug dealer—'

'He's a what?' explodes from Alex.

I wave his question away; we can sort through that one later.

'Jack would be able to quickly get his hands on some.' If Martha and Jack were present I'd slowly squeeze their necks at the same time. How could they do that to me? Or maybe Martha asked him to get it and didn't let on what she was planning to do? 'She sent me tripping—'

'No, it's only a possibility,' Alex quickly butts in. 'But the thing is, people who are willing to do something like that are going to stop at nothing. You see? You can't go back to that house. You don't know what they might do next time.'

I throw the covers back as a statement of intent. 'I don't care. I'm going back. Now help me out.'

He looks pained. 'You know, Lisa, when I was at law school, we had a young student. Brilliant boy, top of the class, going to be a big star at the Old Bailey, the lot. The thing is, he liked to dabble in stuff. Nothing too serious but he was convinced that he could open doors with hallucinogenic drugs. He said objects came to life and started talking to him.'

Just like the chairs and cabinet in the dining room did to me.

Alex resumes: 'You know, answers to the universe and all that. Well, he was wrong, he couldn't. It's a long story but he's been in and out of places like this ever since. He works in a charity shop now, two days a week. You were on the edge already, before all this; now you're hanging off it. If they pull any more stunts in that house, you'll fall off and you might never come back. Now, can't you see? You can't go back there.'

Of course, he's right. But what he doesn't understand is that I've been living in my own private hell since the age of five. And I'll be living in it forever more if I don't get the truth. In and out of places like this or working in charity shops. It makes no difference to me. But at least if I go back to the house, I've got a chance of breaking out and being free. Or maybe not. But I have to try.

I come up with a way to satisfy his conscience and his concern for my welfare. 'If I go back home to *my* house and promise to stay there, will you help me get out of here?'

He brightens slightly. 'Really?'

'Sure. I'll do it but you have to help me get out.'

He waits for a long time before getting up. 'OK. Let me go and demand to see the paperwork for your case. There's bound to be a mistake in it, there always is. And if there isn't, I'll front it out and pretend there is one.'

He goes to the door. As he does so, something occurs to me. 'Alex?'

'Yes?'

'What did you mean something terrible happened in that house?'

He averts his eyes. 'Oh nothing. I was thinking of your possible acid trips and Bette, that's all.'

Thirty-five

Thirty minutes later, there's a veritable posse in my room. A man in a suit is clutching paperwork. A secretary, a doctor and a nurse are standing by. Alex is standing near my bed with a copy of the paperwork in his hand. He's circled the important bits in rings of red ink.

The man in the suit is furious. 'Your brother here seems to think we're holding you against your will. I've explained to him that despite any discrepancies he claims to have found in the documents, you're here as a voluntary patient anyway. Would you be kind enough to explain that to him?'

I take great pleasure in telling him, 'No, it's not. I'm very much here against my will. I'm a prisoner.'

The man in the suit says nothing. Alex tells him, 'Even if she were here voluntarily, no assessment has taken place, which means you have no right to take her belongings away or deny her access to her mobile phone and no right to section her.'

Alex turns the screws again. 'I'll have an injunction on you in the morning. And who knows how a story about how this hospital is riding roughshod over the law will have ended up in the newspapers. I'm sure you'll agree that for a hospital with such a well-deserved reputation for excellence, that would have very unfortunate consequences.'

The man in the suit hesitates. Then he walks out without a word followed by everyone else. Alex and I are left alone.

But they've left the door open for us.

***

'Do you really think Martha spiked my water?'

We're sitting in his car on a lay-by near the M25. We've driven about thirty miles and there's another fifteen or so until we get back to my house.

He looks out of the window. 'Well, there are three possibilities. One is you took it yourself but that would be so crazy, I can't believe that would have happened. Or your mental state meant you ended up having hallucinations that resembled exactly those that you get after taking LSD. Or Martha spiked the water. That's the only other explanation.'

'Yeah. That must be it.'

'Do you think Jack's in on it?'

Cars accelerate by at such a speed that litter and plastic cups blow across the lay-by. The sound of their engines hum low in the distance, builds up until they zoom by and then the noise fades away again. They have sidelights on for the early evening gloom. It feels like we're at the end of the world.

'I don't know,' I admit. 'I can't help thinking he's too stupid to be a conspirator. Plus, he more or less told me he only wanted me gone because he thought I was an undercover cop or working for a rival dealer.' I make a nasty sound at the back of my throat. 'It wouldn't surprise me if Martha planted the whole idea in his head. She's the one pulling the strings. Martha somehow knows what I've been up to from the start. Martha wears Bette's name tag around her neck.'

Alex recoils with disgust. 'You have got to be joking.'

'I know she wants me gone, but there has got be something seriously wrong with the woman.'

Alex scowls, cocking his head to the side. 'What difference does it make to her? She can't be involved in your fifth birthday; she wasn't there. What's her stake in this unfortunate business?'

'She was at the front door the day of my birthday. I know she was.'

Alex grins, but he's not happy. 'You trust your acid trip over the census and the electoral roll?'

I'm left with no choice but to say, 'Yes. I do.'

'It makes no sense at all.'

No. But it will do.

'So, you think they're all in it together then? Martha, your father and Doctor Wilson?'

'What other explanation is there?' The pain in my head has multiplied. 'I get the connection between my dad and Doctor Wilson. They're old mates and they're working in tandem. But I don't know why. Wilson claims Martha's a patient of his. A bit too much of a coincidence for my liking. Look, I really need to get home.'

'Do you though? The thing is, it'll be five minutes before Wilson and your dad find out I've sprung you from the hospital. They're probably hard at work getting a new order ready to have you put away again. Why don't you come back to my place and lay low for a couple of days? They won't find you there.'

He's so hopeful that I lack the heart to say no. 'I'll think about it. I need to go home. But can you do something first?'

He's suspicious again. 'What?'

'Just hold me. Please hold me.'

His arms embrace me in an instant. Sobs, so terrifyingly loud and shuddering that I'm sure my body will snap in two, erupt from me. The horror of what my dad did to me, what he allowed Doctor Wilson to do, is the worst type of terror I've ever felt. Far worse than the nightmares, the awake-sleep, the screams, the knives, the gigantic needles. The worst type of betrayal. No, what's worse is that they never told me I wasn't really theirs. I was part of another family, my blood family, at one time. Why didn't they tell me?

I still can't tell Alex. 'It was horrible in there.'

'I know.' He rubs a gentle, soothing palm over my back. 'You know what attracted me to you?'

I can't answer. I'm so choked up that the shake of my head has to be enough.

'Your face.'

'Stop having a laugh. I look like I've just been turfed out of a bird's nest.'

He laughs a little. He pulls back and cups his palms round my face. I can't look at him.

'You try to conceal it but your face is so full of life. You glow with it so much you don't need the artifice of make-up. I saw you the first day I came into your office. You stood out.' He pauses as if he's having difficulty with his next words. 'Some people have this thing about them. Call it an aura, I don't know, but you have it. I don't want to ever see that dim, burn out.'

My face is so hot you could fry eggs on it. I can't believe what he's saying. That there's something special about me. I'm unique.

The only way I can express my eternal gratitude to him is to lift my eyes and kiss him. We get into it big time in the front of his car.

I'm the one to stop it as I pull breathlessly back. Truth is, I can't deal with any more emotion, so I simply say, 'I just want to go home. My real home.'

Alex understands, as I knew he would. He turns the ignition and we drive away from the end of the world. It's an easy drive back to my house. When we get there, Alex gets out and tries to accompany me in but I won't let him.

'It's alright. I've had enough of personal escorts today. I just want to be alone this evening. It's been a rough few days. I'll have a shower and go to bed. I'll call you in the morning.'

He's really worried. I give him a hug and a lingering kiss. 'I don't have enough thanks for you.'

He turns to go. He sounds like an undertaker when he says, 'Call me in the morning.'

I go into the house where it smells stale and musty. I wait for him to pull away before going for a shower. I don't hear his car start. Instead, there's a knock at the door and it's Alex again.

He reaches into his pocket. 'I suppose you better have this.'

He hands me an envelope. I look at it and turn it over. 'What is it?'

'It's the third piece from the writing on the wall. I've translated it for you. I was going to tear it up but I suppose you better have it.'

'How did you get this?'

He does a nervous cough and breaks eye contact with me. 'Turns out Patsy has a key to the house dating back to when the Peters family lived there. You know, a spare set with the neighbour in case they misplaced their own—'

'But when? How?' I splutter.

Another cough. He meets my eyes. 'Before they managed to paint the room black. It was easy really. I waited for them to leave, slipped in and found the remainder of John Peters' story beneath the lining paper behind the wardrobe.'

'You bastard, Alex.' I'm fuming. 'Why didn't you tell me?'

'I tried to after I told you about the electoral roll and census. Because I was insisting that you sleep and rest, you left in a huff.'

I cry, 'But you've seen me since then.'

'I was concerned for your welfare. I had to judge whether to let you see it or not.' His tone is as stark as the expression on his face. 'Read it at your own risk.'

Then he repeats the words he said in the hospital room, this time the truth: 'Something terrible happened in that house.'

Thirty-six

He walks away, leaving me clutching what I know will be the biggest piece of the puzzle to my past. I start to open the envelope but then don't for fear that I will be too disturbed to go back to that house. I shower and get dressed for battle. Combat trousers, a black pullover, pumps and a beret for my hair. I go into the kitchen and find a long knife, which I sharpen up on my utility stone, and slip it into a side pocket in my trousers. Then I call a cab.

Ten minutes later, a cab appears outside. I wonder if I'm leaving my house for the last time. Alex is right. There's no telling what Martha might do but this time I'll be ready for her. I get in and we set off down my road. At the junction to the main road we stop to let traffic go by. I look out of the window and see that Alex has parked up at the end of the road. He's been waiting for me. He shakes his head. He wasn't fooled by me; he knew that I intended to go straight back to the house. I'm desperate for the car to pull away. Because deep down inside, I want to get out of the cab and go and get into Alex's warm car and be driven away from all this. I put my hand on the door handle and I'm on the brink of getting out when the cab pulls away. I'm too late. But I'm glad of it.

As we go, I blow Alex a kiss.

***

I walk up the driveway to the house with the poise and movement of a woman whose middle name is confidence. My mojo is securely and firmly in place. No one can stop me now. The house looks imposing today. Chimneys rearing, windows jutting outwards, the gravel on the driveway sharp and pointy with the intent of hurting. Even my special mason's mark key is half hidden in the shadows. It's a warning not to come within unless you're prepared to be swallowed up.

Do your worst. There's one thing it can't do: spit me out.

I tense. Eyes are on me; I can feel them. It's the low purr of a cat that tells me I'm not being observed from Martha and Jack's house but by someone else. Patsy's shrewd gaze keeps pace with my every step until I'm standing near her. Davis is as comfy as a clam in her arms. Her arthritic fingers smooth through his fur.

She jumps in fiercely with: 'You could do worse than Alex, you know.'

I sigh. This wouldn't be a conversation with Patsy if she weren't jabbing her finger at me in some way.

'I know.' She means well in her gruff way but my focus is elsewhere.

Alex's Aunty Patsy presses closer. 'I saw the ambulance take you away. A right song and dance. I hope you're OK now?'

'Yeah, I'm good to go.' Suddenly my mind shoots back to the day I last saw her with Alex. How upset she got talking about John Peters and his family. How she bowed her head and hurried from the room. I was left then, as I am now, with the impression she hadn't said all she could possibly say. That she was – is – holding back a secret.

I launch into it: 'What type of man was John Peters? He was a surgeon, wasn't he?'

Now she looks as if I've announced her death sentence. In a heartbeat her hand moves from smoothing the cat to clutching him.

Patsy swiftly heads towards her door. 'Well, I do have to go—'

'I lived in that house. Or I certainly used to visit it.' I elongate my chest as I breath out. Saying this aloud is getting easier, sounding more natural.

Patsy abruptly stops. Turns half around, her mouth an 'O'. Then her brows wriggle together as she peers hard at me. 'I remember everyone on this street. I don't recall clapping eyes on you.'

'Will you tell me what you know about John and his family back in ninety-eight?'

'In ninety-eight?' The date is almost a squeal. Her head shakes with such force it's a wonder it stays on her shoulder. 'Don't remember that year. Yes, I was visiting my girl in Canada—'

'Why won't you tell me the truth?'

She swings to face me, her face flushed, expression bleak. 'Because I can't.'

Anticipation thrums through me, my heart kicking up with the power and force of a stoked fire. 'It's just me and you here. No one else needs to know.'

Patsy's skittish gaze kicks up to Martha and Jack's house. That's when I cotton on that something is terrifying this woman.

I whisper, 'What are you afraid of? Are they threatening you?'

My mind winds back to the public confrontation over Bette's death. Jack had angrily challenged her about calling the police and Patsy had sworn blind she hadn't. In that moment she'd been terrified that Jack had thought she had. What is going on here?

Her gaze settles back on me as her tongue nervously runs along her bottom lip. Davis rubs his head against her chest. Finally, she tells me, 'I don't want to end up in the slammer.'

'Prison?' I'm confused, stumped. 'I don't understand.'

She retraces her steps back to me. For an older woman she's lively on her feet. 'It's him. Tells me that if I open my gob about any of her business to do with the past, he'll shop me to the police.'

'Do you mean Jack?'

Patsy rolls her eyes dramatically. 'Well I ain't talking about the Pope,' she snaps. Her face crumbles. 'I only did it for the pain.'

I resist the huge urge to butt in, knowing she's finally opening up to me.

Patsy waves one of her hands at me, her fingers bent. 'The medication my doctor gave me for my arthritis just didn't work sometimes.' Her chest heaves sadly. 'That's why I miss my Bette so much. She knew when the pain was bad and would jump in my lap and lick my hands, as if she could make the pain go away. What eased the pain was that stuff he grows in the garden.'

'You mean the cannabis?'

She nods once. 'When we were still on speaking terms I told him all about my ailment. Told me he had something that could sort me out.' Her face glazes over with pleasure. 'Ooh, it worked a treat. And made me happy too.'

The image of Patsy smoking a spliff in front of her fire settles in my mind.

'Of course, he has me snared in his web because I knew what I was smoking was against the law. When I told him I was taking them to court over the garden he was furious. Said if I breathed a word of what he's growing he'll tell them I was his biggest customer.' Her face drops. 'The shame if my family ever found out.'

'You were only trying to help yourself out. Stop your pain. The cops aren't going to sling you behind bars for that. They're interested in catching the dealers not the users.'

She cuddles Davis closer, sizing me up. Her voice is a hush. 'In 1998, one minute John's family was there, the next they were not. It was so sad that he split up from his adorable wife. Such a lovely lady.'

'Where did they go?' I press.

'The way he told it, she left him for someone else and took the kids with her to Australia. Funny business. But I'll tell you this. I knew those kids and I used to give them cards for their birthdays. Lovely children. But when I asked John for their new address, instead of saying "No" or "I'd prefer it if you didn't have it" or "I don't know it", he always said he would give it to me, but he never did. About a hundred times I asked him. But he never gave it to me. Strange that.'

'What do you mean?'

'It was like he didn't want me to know where they were living. And come to think of it, I never saw any removal vans turn up when his wife and kids left. They were there one day and gone the next.'

***

They were there one day and gone the next.

I hang on to Patsy's haunting words as I push my key into the lock and open the door of the house. I'm afraid the locks might have been changed but if that was Jack's job, he hasn't bothered. I walk into the hallway. The house has no lights on at all but I can see down the hall that the dining room is flooded with candlelight. It looks like a cross between a romantic dinner for two and a funeral parlour. Jack emerges from the cupboard under the stairs with a powerful torch.

He shines the light in my face and bursts out laughing. 'Well, what do you know? Martha! Mad bird's escaped from the funny farm! Hello, darling, welcome back. Could you hold this light for me? Looks like the fuses have tripped. So, have they drugged you up then? You should have come to me; I could've helped out on that front. Ha ha! Listen, babe, I don't mind a little wacky behaviour but not at night-time. Not when I'm trying to get some shut-eye.'

There's no sign of Martha. I walk up to where he's now struggling under the stairs. I take the torch from him and shine it on the fuse box. There's a shower of blue sparks coming from under the stairs.

Jack sighs. 'The electrics in this house are shot to pieces. I'd better get you a couple of candles, Lisa. Don't get spooked in the dark, do you?'

He disappears down the hallway. I walk into the dining room. Martha is sitting in a Victorian chair in the corner. She casts her eyes over me as I walk in and then stands up. She looks bewitching in the candlelight, almost ethereal. 'So, you really are back?'

'That's right.'

'Do you think that's wise? Given your condition?'

Her beautiful face is only inches away from mine. Her eyes are like sparklers in the light. But I don't back down. 'I'm fine.'

'I don't think you are. Doctor Wilson seems to think you're very sick. You're having hallucinations, imagining all kinds of strange things. I expect Doctor Wilson included that in his report.'

I move closer to her so we're nearly touching. 'Yes, well, you'd know all about that, seeing as you're such a good friend of his. Help him with his notes, did you?'

Martha smiles. 'You're a fighter, Lisa, I'll give you that. You're more of a man than most men I've known in my life.'

'Like Doctor Peters, for example. He wasn't much of a man, was he?'

She levels me with a stony stare. 'Doctor who?'

'Alright, girls, knock it off with the necking. It's not that kind of house,' Jack interrupts then titters at his own crap joke.

He's holding a candelabra in one hand and a bunch of candles in the other.

Martha smiles at me and walks off towards the morning room, taking her own candelabra with her. I wonder if she was once an actress.

Jack lights some candles and then puts them in the ornament. 'There you go. Take that upstairs with you for now. The lights will be back on in a minute; just a little bit of rewiring required.'

I walk up the second set of stairs to my room. Jack and Martha have been busy, obviously anticipating I wouldn't be coming back at all. My belongings are in a heap on the bed, no doubt waiting for my dad to collect them from the room he needs no direction in finding.

I shove my belongings to the side so I can sit. I pick up my bag but don't open it. Instead I inhale, a huge breath to give me strength for what I'm going to do next. Finally, I take out the envelope that Alex gave me and pull out the paper inside. I open it up and begin to read. The light flickers and then goes out again.

Deep in the bowels of the house, I can hear Jack shouting and cursing in frustration. I pick up the candelabra, place it close to me and then begin to read Alex's translation of the writing on the wall.

***

How long I stay there, still and cold as frozen blood embedded in snow after reading John Peters' words, I don't know. A single tear meanders down my cheek. I can't read it again. Can't. It makes me want to howl and slam my fists against the black wall.

Thirty-seven

I move to the bottles of water lined up in the back of the wardrobe. Pick up a small one and notice what I should've before – the seal is broken. Only an evil mind could dream up drugging another person. I remember how stale the water had tasted one morning; no doubt the aftertaste of the drug. Alex had warned me that at the first opportunity I get I should empty each one down the sink, the toilet, out the window, wherever, as long as they no longer pose a threat to me.

I pick up a bottle and travel across the room to the window. Push it wide and look across at London. I wonder how many people out there are so desperate for somewhere to live they're considering renting a spare room in someone's home. The home of someone they know nothing about. A stranger who insists on their rules in their home.

I turn my attention back to the bottle, remembering that Alex told me to get rid of it. I unscrew the lid. Tip it over... straight into my mouth.

***

I drink the lot. Every last dreg of the stale-tasting water. I nearly don't. The first thing I do afterwards is sit on the bed and immediately start to regret what I've done. I don't think I can cope with any more, not after what I've just read.

As for Martha... I feel sick even thinking about her, knowing what I do now. Once she found out who I was, that I awake-sleep, have crucifying night terrors, pushing me over the edge was going to be easy. The LSD in the bottle was a nice touch. But she underestimated me. I'm going to use the weapon she used against me against her. If it works.

I know this is crazy. It might be the purest form of idiocy, but the details of what I've read now put into perspective what the acid trip made me see yesterday. It pushed me to see the beginning of what really happened all those years ago. Now I need to have my memory jogged, that's all. The doors of perception… aren't they supposed to be opened when you drop acid? Or is it the gates of hell? Or both at the same time? I might be risking the horrible effects of a bad trip like I experienced when Alex found me on the high street, but I have to try.

I lie back on the bed and wait to find out.

I think I can hear the pitter-patter of drops on the roof. Has the LSD kicked in? But when I get up and look out of the window, I see it's raining and start laughing. Perhaps there wasn't enough gear left in the bottle for it to work, or it degraded or something. But then I realise that the raindrops are a shower of silver glitter – they're little stars falling from the sky – and I know I'm in business. But then it's rain again. Perhaps it's not working but, whatever, I have no time to lose. I hurry to the door. When I open it I get a shock.

Martha is sitting on the landing outside, her back against the wall.

When I recover from the surprise, I'm glad of it. Bring it on.

'Hello, Martha.'

Her fabulous green eyes look like a viper's. 'Hello, Lisa.'

'Martha, I've been meaning to ask you a question.'

'Really?'

'How did you know who I was?'

She looks like an old hag. Or do I just think this woman is an old hag, so now she looks like one?

'You're wrong, I don't know who you are.'

'Doctor Peters' daughter.'

'Oh, I see.' She looks at me for a long time. 'You don't look well. It's probably all that worrying about Doctor Peters, Doctor

Wilson, your father and mother, writing on the wall. It's enough to drive a girl crazy. And you were pretty crazy to start with, weren't you? Let's face it.'

The blood drains from my face, leaving me cold.

'Yes, I heard all about that from Doctor Wilson himself. You'd think after the way I treated him, he'd slam the door in my face when I paid him a visit to find out what you were up to. But no, he couldn't wait to give me all the salacious details. Another one of my ex-lovers who couldn't kick the habit. I broke him the same way I broke Doctor Peters. That's what I do to amuse myself. Break men.' She looks into my eyes. 'And talking of habits, Lisa, you're not on the stuff again like the other night? That's very unwise for a girl in your fragile mental condition.'

She's confessing to something. I try to put a list of questions together to ask her but I can't put them in any sort of order or get them to make any sense. So, I give up and head for the stairs.

She grabs my hand, her nails digging into my palm. 'Careful, you might fall. Let me help.'

Her hot hand slides up my arm as she gets up. I want to break the contact but I can't. 'Where do you want to go? What do you want to know?'

It occurs to me that she might try and kill me on the stairs and I start to struggle. But at the same time, I'm glad she's there because she's right. I've lost all sense of time and space and I really might fall.

I listlessly tell her, 'You're a murderer.'

Her perfect teeth resemble freshly washed gravestones as she tosses her head back and laughs. 'Me? Oh dear, you're not much of a detective, are you? I've never killed anyone.' She holds me close and whispers. 'It was your father, Lisa. He's the killer. Read his suicide notes. You found one of them on that first day. I saw it on your desk when you went skipping off to work.'

Stupid! Stupid! Stupid! Why didn't you put the letter away? Hide it?

Her breath is poisonous against my face. 'Your father admitted it. He was the killer. He murdered your mother and your brother and sister and he tried to kill you too. And why? Because although I was his lover, I wouldn't run away with him and it drove him mad. The same way this has driven you mad. Imagine, killing your own family all because the woman you love won't run off with you?'

I'm terrified. I need all my wits about me but my wits are shot. I need to trust my eyes, ears and all my senses but I can't. They've disappeared into a hall of mirrors where nothing is real. I need to trust this woman who knows what happened that day but she's spinning a web of truths, half-truths and lies to finally finish the job she started when she spiked my water bottle. I'm desperate to go back and pour that water down the sink. Or even further back, to that dismal but joyous day that I first saw the mason's mark on the wall of this house and cried 'I've found it!' Or even back to my fifth birthday when I could have cried 'Someone's going to kill us all! Let's run!'

I want out. But there is no out. This will unroll all the way to the end but I don't know where that will be.

Somehow we're in the hallway, stuck to each other like two lovers. How did we get here? My confused mind tries to process it.

I hear a voice behind me but I don't look round. 'What's the matter with her?'

It's Jack. Martha turns. Her response is blank. 'She's doing acid again. I'm just helping her walk it off and making sure she doesn't do anything stupid. Don't worry; she'll be back in hospital tomorrow.'

Jack doesn't sound convinced. 'Really? Where did she get the acid from then?'

'How the hell would I know? You're the expert.'

Jack says nothing. I'm screaming at him to help, but the sound's locked inside my frantic mind. He comes around in front of us. He lifts my eyelids and examines my pupils and pinches my cheek. He doesn't believe her. He's suspicious. Not only can I see he's suspicious, I can read it in his over-bright eyes.

'She needs a doctor.'

'Good idea. You call one, and call a good lawyer while you're at it. You'll need one when questions start getting asked.' Her voice is nasty, full of taunting disrespect.

'I know a doctor who's discreet.' He peers at me. 'Are you alright?'

Martha steps in. 'She's fine. Why don't you piss off and watch the telly?'

Deep inside, I'm saying, *She's a murderer. She's going to kill me.* Then I realise I've said it out loud.

Martha taps the side of her head with a finger and rolls her eyes to indicate that I'm off it. 'I've told you to go and watch the fucking football,' she viciously orders Jack like she has all the power over him.

He looks at me and then very slowly slinks off to the front room. Martha is suddenly a woman in a hurry. She escorts me into the dining room.

'This is where it happened. Your father told me. You, your mum and your brother and sister were here having a little party for your fifth birthday. Your father was late because he was making love to me in a hotel room.'

Stop! Please make her stop!

She won't.

'While we were lying in bed afterwards, he begged me to run away with him and said he couldn't live without me. Of course, I said no. He had family responsibilities. And anyway, I was your mother's best friend, did you know that?'

Stop it! Stop it!

'Just imagine when your mother was wailing about your father never coming home and suspecting that he was having an affair; it was actually me she was confiding in. She felt I was the only person she could rely on. She even invited me to your fifth birthday party. Just imagine! Her husband's lover who she thought was the only person she could trust, her closest and beloved friend.

'Pathetic, isn't it? She was virtually an honorary man, your mother. So, I couldn't run off with your father. I couldn't do that, even though he adored me like Doctor Wilson and all the rest of them. Of course, I should have let him down gently but I'm a cruel woman who likes breaking men. And when he walked out of that hotel room, a broken man, he had murder in his eyes.'

I look around the dining room. It's silent and motionless. The chairs and the cabinet are still.

Martha's siren call won't let me go. 'And when he came through the front door, he gave you your present and then he reached for the cake knife and he stabbed your mother to death before your eyes and chased the rest of you upstairs, waving his knife. Do you remember?'

I do remember. She's right. In this silent room, I remember. Martha's arm around me reminds me of that other woman who had her arm around me that day. Singing 'One, two, buckle my shoe' as she put my party clothes on. My loving mother who was celebrating my fifth birthday. I remember the children, those faceless children, who were my older brother and sister. I remember the cake knife and I remember being chased down. I remember the blood and the children's screams. I remember the terror. And I remember hiding under the bed. It's all just as Martha says.

Except in one respect.

'No, that's not what happened. You came to the door that day, Martha. A woman screamed and you don't scream, do you? You didn't come here to scream. You came here to say something to my mum on my fifth birthday. I heard a woman screaming.' The awful, terrible truth spills out. 'And after you'd said it, and you'd left, she came in here and tried to kill us. She chased us upstairs and that's when the children were screaming. That was us. Me. And then she killed herself... and then my dad came home later and he screamed too when he saw what had taken place. That's what happened.'

I nod like I'm drunk, about to topple over. 'That's what happened. What did you say to my mum that made her want to kill us all? What things did you say to her? About you and my dad on my fifth birthday? When you came to our house from the hotel where you were having sex with him? Is that what you told her? About that? You knew she was fragile. Did you try and stop her or did you just walk out on your beloved friend, your evil work done?'

Martha says nothing. She doesn't say I'm right. But she doesn't say I'm wrong either. I feel disorientated but it doesn't feel drug induced now. Perhaps there wasn't enough LSD in the water to properly send me flying.

Martha sighs. 'Why don't you ask them?'

'Ask who?'

'Doctor Peters, his pathetic deranged wife or your siblings? Why don't you ask them?'

I look at her, stunned. This woman is insane. 'They're dead, that's why.'

'You're dead too. You've been dead ever since that day. You're a child out of time. It's what your father used to say when I let him stay in that room in his own house: "I should have died with the others and Lisa should have too, then everything would have been settled".'

I don't believe her. No. It's not true.

She grips my waist firmly and marches me out of the dining room. I go willingly down the hallway and up the two flights of stairs to my room. I look on impassively as she pulls the bedside cabinet across the room, climbs on it and throws open the dormer window. She pulls herself up and out onto the ledge outside where Bette died. In my head, I'm somewhere else but I don't know where. I think she's going to kill herself but I don't care. I don't care about death anymore; I've had enough of it. She offers me her hand through the window. She's going to kill the pair of us or maybe just me. But I don't care. I climb out of the window.

'Before he dumped you with Edward and Barbara, your father told you that your mum and siblings had gone to heaven to be with the stars.' She points upwards at the black sky. 'Go on, go and ask them. Go and ask them what happened. Why don't you be the man your father never was? Go and ask them. Don't be weak.

Weakness disgusts me. There's nothing left for you now anyway, except to go and be with them.'

Of course, she's right. I peer over the edge of the ledge and into the darkness. But now I know the truth, I want to live. I don't want the darkness anymore.

I look behind me. I'm thinking of going back in. She won't kill me, I know that. But when I do, I see Jack staring up at me.

He's talking to Martha. 'What the hell are you doing? Get back in here now.'

Martha sneers, 'Fuck off you idiot boy. She thinks she can fly. Do you want me to leave her out here on her own?'

'No, I want you both to come back in here.' He reaches out and grabs my hand and tries to pull me inside.

There's a three-way struggle. But I can't tell who's pulling at who or why. Martha is holding my arm; is she trying to pull me out or push me in? With Jack's hand firmly grasping mine, I try to hold on to Martha's hand in turn. Or am I pushing or pulling her instead?

Our faces are close and I can see there's fear in her beautiful green eyes. Jack gives me a violent tug and in turn Martha falls and slips away down the roof. For a moment her foot catches the ledge and her face is frozen in time for a moment. Then she's gone.

Jack pulls me inside. He's shaking. He jumps up again and looks out of the window. He climbs outside and gingerly makes his way across the roof and looks over the edge. He mutters something savagely under his breath before making his way back up to the window and climbing back in.

He grabs me by the shoulders and shakes me. 'Right.' He draws breath. 'She's dead for certain. We'll have to call the cops. But when they get here, leave me to do the talking. Do you understand?' He shakes me. 'I said do you understand?'

But I say nothing. Because there's nothing left except the truth.

Thirty-eight

I'm shattered. I lie with my head cushioned against Alex's shoulder as we sit inside Patsy's front room. Davis lies on the carpet next to us, as if sensing my distress.

There's a knock at the front door. I immediately tense. Hope it's not the police again. I've already given a statement to them about what happened and don't have the strength to give them more. I'll let Jack do the talking. A tale about his wife jumping from the window. She'd been so troubled lately… Doctor Wilson had arrived at the police station to back this up; his patient Martha Palmer had been a very troubled woman indeed.

Martha's dead. I don't know how I feel. The end of a human life is never something to rejoice about, but she was evil. Evil doesn't have the right to live among us.

'I'll get it,' Patsy calls from the kitchen.

She's been an absolute love, making tea, producing sandwiches and cakes and, more importantly, not throwing questions at me.

Her head peeps around the front room doorway. She's pensive. 'There's a man and woman at the door who say they're your parents.'

An outraged Alex answers for me. 'Tell them to sling their hook. They should be locked up behind bars for what they've put Lisa through.'

Mum and Dad had turned up almost at the same time as the police outside Martha and Jack's house. They had been beside themselves wanting to speak to me. I refused. Now I knew the truth I was frightened what I might say to them.

'It's OK, Alex.' I raise my head and turn to Patsy. 'Tell them to come in.'

I feel stronger now. There's still part of the story missing and I suspect they are the only ones who can fill me in.

Both my parents are a sorry sight. Dad seems to have aged ten years and Mum's head is bowed, her face ravaged; she can't meet my eyes.

Dad coughs. 'Lisa, we understand if you don't want to speak with us. But we would like to be given the opportunity to.'

I can sense Alex is itching to tell them to piss off. I lay a hand on his thigh. 'Can you give us some time, Alex?'

He reluctantly gets up. 'If you need me—'

I smile wearily. 'I know.'

He refuses to look at my parents as he leaves the room. I get up and move to the armchair. Davis accompanies me.

I wave at the sofa. 'Please.' I keep my tone civil and in control.

Dad starts to talk as soon as they are sat. 'Lisa, I—'

'No.' I'm fierce in my need for control. 'I'm not going to yell, scream or shout. I might one day soon. But that's not important to me now. What is important is you telling me exactly what happened on my fifth birthday. I know some of what happened because John Peters wrote his story on the wall of my room.'

'What?' flies like a missile out of Dad.

Mum makes this strange keening sound and starts rocking. I can't deal with her pain now; I only have time for my own.

'I want to start by reading you the final part of his story,' I tell them. From my pocket I take out Alex's translation and in a firm, steady voice, I say: 'His writings always start the same, with a line of poetry from a Russian poet called Etienne Solanov. Each and every line chosen has been such an accurate starting point for each piece of writing. This one is no different. It says: "When I laid the others to rest, I laid myself to rest as well. But there was no rest for me".'

I fight to keep my voice steady as I continue to read...

Thirty-nine

Before: 1998

He was late. Again. When he put the key in the door, he wondered how much of that had been deliberate. How much of it was because he didn't like going home anymore. No matter what his reasons, he felt guilt-ridden. No father should be late to celebrate his child's new milestone in life. His beautiful Marissa was celebrating turning five. Under his arm was a carefully wrapped present and in the other was his medical bag. As soon as he came through the door, he knew something was terribly wrong.

The house was hushed, unnaturally so. It should be filled with loud raise-the-roof laughter and merriment at Marissa's birthday celebrations. Marissa had so wanted a proper party with invitations for her friends, but Alice had decided that she only wanted her family gathered together. A time for them to close the door and shut out the rest of the world. The world could intrude tomorrow; today was for them alone.

He knew his wife and children were there because the front door wasn't double locked as it always was when they went out. Surely, they wouldn't have gone out without telling him? Especially on Marissa's birthday.

'Hello? Where's my birthday girl?' His happy-happy voice sounded strange in the silence of the house.

No answer. His heart started galloping; something was badly wrong here. He urgently strode through to the dining room. His breath slashes against the inside of his throat. He couldn't believe what he was seeing. A scene of utter bedlam. Party cups and plates smashed. Fruit juice and fizzy drinks splashed and in puddles on the floor and across the furniture. Chairs tipped over. Blown-up balloons aimlessly abandoned on the ground. 'Happy 5th birthday' banners half hanging off the walls.

In the midst of the ugly scene, as if in the wrong place, stood the birthday cake. Untouched, resting on the table as if begging to be cut. Alice had ordered it with such care. A large sponge cake in the image of Bob the Builder, from Marissa's favourite TV show.

Then he saw what was on the wall. Red marks, smears, uneven drips and obscene patterns. Blood. He knew blood when he saw it. It had become almost an unwanted best friend during his job as a trauma surgeon. His apprehension twisted into full-blown fear. His daughter's gift slipped from his hand and crashed to the floor. He felt as if he was going to have a heart attack.

Where's my family? Where's my family? What if intruders…?

Sickened to his soul and terrified, he flew into the kitchen. The back door was locked and secured just like the front door. He started panting, shaking all over, trying desperately to figure it out. Alice would defend her children with her life against an attacker. That must have been what had happened.

He ran from the kitchen to the morning room to the lounge. All empty. He stopped in the heart of the house on the red and black rug, looking up the stairs. His bones felt like they were shaking. Whatever had happened here, he knew it awaited him up those stairs. He bent over with a cry. He didn't want to go. Couldn't face it. He didn't feel strong enough for this.

He straightened one vertebra at a time as he sucked back the threatening tears. He saw trauma almost every day; he could deal with this. He had to deal with this. His steps were heavy against the stairs as he clung on for dear life to the bannister. He nearly fell backwards when he saw the arm hanging over the top of the first landing. He wanted to howl. Wouldn't let himself. He saw trauma all of the time. Broken bodies and shattered lives. The only way he could get through his own shattered life – and there was no doubt it was smashed to pieces – was to don the impersonal white coat of the surgeon he was. He made his way to the top and surveyed the scene.

The arm belonged to his beautiful wife, Alice. Her still, pale body was lying across the landing. Across her wrists were two bloody slits where the life had drained out of her. This would have ended her life in short order from blood loss. Both hands were collapsed under the knife protruding for her heart.

He knew at once what he was seeing. The slashes on the wrists and the knife wound were self-inflicted. His adored Alice, who he had married on a perfect, summer's day in June, had taken her own life. Killed herself. It would take the police and their forensics team a few minutes to conclude that.

Despite the unbelievable grief clawing him raw inside, he refused to cry. Not yet. There was more to come. So much more.

Near the entrance to the bathroom lay his son, Leo. Dead. He'd been the victim of a frenzied attack, his body slashed and cut too many times to count. The two fatal knife wounds were to his back.

He walked calmly through the middle floor and found his oldest daughter, Tina, in a bedroom, by the window. The net curtains were blowing in the breeze over her dead body. She looked as if she had been trying to escape to the outside but hadn't made it. Her wounds were the same as Leo's except there was only one fatal blow this time, through the chest.

Still, with a professional eye he allowed himself to make a prognosis of what had happened here. His wife had flipped. She'd murdered her children while the balance of her mind was disturbed before she turned the knife on herself. That was what the coroner was going to say and that was what the papers were going to go to town with.

He jammed his hand over his mouth and began to scream behind it as if his lungs would break. His mind was going, he was sure. His children were dead. Dead. Dead. *Christ Almighty, help me. Leo, Tina and...*

He hand dropped, with the weight of the dead, from him mouth. Where was Marissa? He was a mad man as he ran from the top of the house, but his youngest was nowhere to be seen. There were trails of blood running along carpets that he hadn't noticed earlier but they didn't seem to lead to anywhere. And then he began to think perhaps she had escaped onto the street where a stranger had rescued her and took her to hospital, but she was too shocked to tell anyone what had happened. He wanted to hope that but at the same time he was filled with fear at the prospect that she was safe somewhere. Because he didn't want any witnesses to what his wife had done.

Finally, he found her under the bed he and Alice had made love in until a year ago. Marissa was curled into a ball, her birthday dress soaked with blood and, good God, the soles of both feet slashed over and over again. He imagined the dreadful scene. Marissa running for her life, away from her attacking mother, who wielded her lethal knife to slice into her youngest child's skin. But his birthday girl had been brave, as she'd kept on running until she found a hiding place under the bed. Alice hadn't been able to force her out; the only part of Marissa's body she'd been able to get was under her feet. Once Alice knew the job was done, she'd gone to the landing and taken her own life.

He went down on his knees and pressed his back against the wall. His life was over. Destroyed.

'Daddy?'

His head jerked back to the bed. He scrambled over. Marissa. She stared at him with huge, pain- and tear-filled eyes. His daughter was alive. Laughter rumbled in his chest.

'It's me, baby. Daddy's here. Daddy will make you all better.'

He slithered under the bed on his belly and carefully pulled his gasping daughter towards him. He took her gently into his arms. The only thing left under the bed was a dead mouse with large dead eyes.

Forty

I finish reading. Mum's weeping openly, a forlorn, mournful beat in the room. Dad is frozen, wearing a ghostly expression as if someone is walking on his grave. I suppose someone is. John Peters, my blood father. And the rest of my family, who were slaughtered in the house next door.

'Why didn't you tell me?' I ask quietly. I don't have the time or stamina for anger anymore.

He's grief-stricken. 'How could I tell you that your mother, the woman who carried you for nine months, killed your brother and sister and tried to kill you too? I couldn't tell you that.' His voice is raspy, barely above a whisper. 'Your mum – Barbara – never knew what had happened. I told her we were looking after a friend's child for a while. Then it turned into years. You became ours.'

'Did you help my blood father cover this up?'

Dad takes a while to answer. 'We all met in medical school – your dad, me and Tommy Wilson. We clicked instantly. Other students nicknamed us the Three Medical Musketeers.' A small smile flickers across his lips at the memory.

'That was my dad in the photo you took off the wall. The one with Doctor Wilson?'

I don't need my dad's single nod for confirmation. 'We all chose different disciplines, with John training long and hard to be a trauma surgeon. He was the best there was.' His tone is fiercely proud at my blood father's achievements. 'We remained close, which was why when he called me in such a desperate state I had to help him. When I got to the house…' He shakes his head, his face stark. 'It was the most hellish scene I'd ever witnessed. He gave me the option of not getting involved because if the police

254

found out I could end up in prison. But John hadn't done a thing. It wasn't fair. He was only thinking of your mother's reputation. If it got into the papers she would be destroyed.'

'Tell me about my mum,' I interrupt softly.

'I don't know where they met. She'd had a tough background. Grown up in the care system. I don't know how she got there but she didn't have any family. She was such a beautiful woman, so striking.' He pauses. 'But there was something fragile about her, like it wouldn't take much for her to fall off the edge—'

'Which leads me to why such a beautiful woman, with a loving husband, would kill her children.' God, it hurts to say it aloud.

Dad looks down for a time. Then raises his gaze to me. 'Maybe it wouldn't have happened if it weren't for Martha. Martha Palmer was one of the most bewitching and narcissistic people I have ever known. Tommy went into the field of psychiatry and very stupidly started going out with one of his patients.'

Mum speaks for the first time, her eyes reflecting scorn. 'I met her once at one of Tommy's parties. She did her best to make him jealous by flirting with so many of the men there. She was gorgeous, I'll give her that, but it was clear as the nose on my face she had a heart that was rotten to the core.'

'I heard they split up.' Dad takes up the story. 'Only later did I realise that happened because all of a sudden she was Alice's best friend. Then she made a beeline for John. She must've dazzled him because they ended up having an affair. He was besotted with her, totally under her control.' Just like Jack. 'I told him to end it. It wasn't fair to Alice and the kids. But he didn't. In fact, he was going to leave his family for her.'

I fill in the rest of the story. 'She came to the house on my birthday. Why would she do that?'

Dad says, 'Martha Palmer was a spiteful and evil woman. She couldn't stand the fact that John came home to Alice and his family every night. So, she went to his house. Alice invited her in, innocently, as her best friend, and she told Alice about the affair. And ripped her world apart.'

I hear the screaming in the front room. Rub my temple to make it stop.

He continues. 'She waltzed out after she'd done her evil, leaving Alice with her world crumbling beneath her feet.'

'But to murder her children, Edward, to kill herself.' Mum's shocked voice shudders.

'I know. I know,' Dad whispers. 'Not only was she betrayed by her husband but also by her so-called best friend. That was too big a burden for her to carry. I think she just snapped.'

There's an awful silence. Then I ask, 'How did you help him?'

'I counselled him to go to the police, but he wouldn't. What he wanted me to do was to take you away for a time, which I agreed to do.'

I see young me staring out of the car window, my gaze on the mason's mark on the house, watching it grow smaller until it is gone.

'He gave you one thing that belonged to your mother. Something she wore a lot. We gave it to you on your fifteenth birthday,' Dad says softly.

'My scarf.'

How ironic is that? The scarf that has kept me safe at night belonged to the woman who tried to murder me. My own mother. And I understand something else: Martha must have recognised Alice's scarf, as she was her best friend. That night she saw it when she guided me back to my room after the awake-sleeping. No wonder she'd asked me who it belonged to. And when I told her my mum... I remember how she'd left it on my bed, tangled in knot after knot after knot.

'What happened to their bodies?'

Dad shakes his head again. 'I don't know. In our business we have access to all types of people, including undertakers who have crematoriums. Or he may have buried them. I don't know.'

In that instant I know I will never find the resting place of my family.

'Enough innocent people have been hurt already.' That's what was in the farewell letter. Too many innocent people.

'Why did he come back to stay at the house with Martha and Jack?'

My dad lets out a humourless laugh. 'That she-devil had twisted her claws into him. He couldn't let her go. Tommy told me how she operated. He said her big thing was taking things away from lovers after the relationship ended.' I think of Bette's name tag. 'What she wanted to take away from your father was his home. She will have tormented him for years with other men, and with what happened to his wife, his children. Blamed him. I suspect eventually she would have brought a younger man back, this man being Jack, and banished John to the room at the top of the house.'

'It must have got too much for him because he killed himself recently. I found his suicide note.'

'Good God,' Mum cries, her gaze wild.

'I know,' Dad says.

'What?' My back straightens. 'How do you know?'

'I was there.'

Forty-one

"What are you saying, Edward?' Mum shouts.

'Martha called me. Told me John was behaving erratically.' He turns desperate eyes to her. 'What did you want me to do? Leave Lisa's father with that woman? No.' His voice is hard. 'I went round there and saw him. He reassured me he was alright. I left him to speak to that woman and we ended up arguing downstairs. By the time I came back up he was hanging there.' The horror of it makes him cover his mouth. Sweat is gleaming on his forehead. 'I took John away. Took him to an undertaker I trusted and gave him a decent burial.' There are floods of tears streaming down his face. 'My friend didn't deserve what happened to him. The least I could do was make sure he was laid to rest. Me and Tommy were the only people at his grave.'

'What about Jack?' I want to cry too, but won't allow myself to. I have to hear this story to the end.

'He wasn't there. Off on a work job up north. When he came back we agreed she would tell him that John had left. She would tell Jack never to mention John's name again to her. Pretend he hadn't existed.'

So that's why Jack had insisted there was no previous tenant. He hadn't been involved, simply following Martha's instruction like a puppy does for its owner.

Dad starts to sob horribly. My strong, stoic father who I know has only tried his best for me. I can't do it, sit there and watch him fall apart. I hurry over and take his body, racked with wretched sobs, in my arms.

'It's alright, Dad. It's alright.'

He raises his wet face to look at me. 'When I found out you were living under the same roof as that sick, immoral woman I thought I was losing my mind. I had to get you out of there. Tommy agreed to help me.'

'Trying to drive me mad was not the way to do it, Dad.'

'I know. But I was desperate. Martha told me she found John's suicide letter on your desk in the room.'

'Is that when she figured out I was John's daughter?'

'No. It was only after she found out from her husband that you had your own home that her suspicions were raised. She traced you through the electoral roll.' Just as Alex had done with the house. My enemy used my own trick against me. 'As soon as she connected you to me, she told me to get you out or else... That's why I turned up with your mother to persuade you to leave. I know it was a terrible thing to do to section you the time I came with Tommy, but I'd have done anything – *anything* – to get you away from her. She was going to hurt you. Alice's last child.'

My mum puts her hand on my shoulder and we remain locked together in the shape of the tight-knit family we so want to be.

Eventually I lean back on my heels and pull out John Peters' story again. Funny. He doesn't feel like my dad. He'll always be John Peters to me.

'Now we've spoken I feel strong enough to read the rest of the story to you. It's hard for me to read because it has given me such bad nightmares for such a long time. I don't understand how he could have done this to me.'

Forty-two

Before: 1998

His injured daughter burst into agonising tears, her little chest rasping as she desperately tried to fill her lungs as he laid her with the softest care on the bed. He couldn't bear the pain she was in. All because of him and the reckless choices he'd made. In that moment he made a decision. Right or wrong, it was what he'd decided to do.

He smiled as he ran his hand over her blood-free hair. 'Daddy's a doctor; he knows how to mend little girls who've been in accidents.'

He kissed her softly on the forehead. Then inspected her injuries. The slashes on the arms and legs were savage, but not too deep. The one on her small belly was much deeper, done with the intent to kill. How could Alice have done this? The slashes under his daughter's feet would mend with time. He wasn't sure if they would fade; the skin on the feet could have a mind all of its own. So many nerve endings run to the feet; these wounds must be hurting his darling baby like crazy.

As he turned for the door, Marissa cried out in a weak, terrified voice, 'Don't leave me, Daddy. Please don't leave me.'

He quickly returned and soothed her with another kiss. 'I'll just be gone for a bit. Daddy will make you better.'

***

He came back, with the doctor's bag he kept in the house. He always had an extra set of instruments at home ready to go in case of an emergency. He gave Marissa all the pain medication he had, and it soon became apparent it wasn't enough. As he laboured over his youngest and only living child for the next three hours, she screamed out in pain, even biting down on the towel he gave her. He hated himself. But what could he do? If he took her to the hospital questions would be asked. He couldn't have his beautiful Alice demonised in the press as a mother who murdered her children. God forgive him, but his beloved daughter would have to endure more tremendous pain to save his wife. This was all his fault. He was to blame.

The secrets of this house must remain buried forever.

Forty-three

Now

'I can feel the needle and the awful pain going through me when I dream,' I tell my stunned parents. 'It hurts so much. I could never understand how a knife could turn into a needle. How could he do that to me?'

Dad pulls me close. 'He blamed himself for what happened. I suspect, knowing John, he wanted only his loving hands to heal you.'

'I don't understand why I didn't remember any of this. How could I forget?'

It's Mum who speaks. 'No child wants to remember their mother trying to kill them and killing their brother and sister. What a terrible thing to have to live with.'

Dad adds, 'It was so traumatic your mind couldn't deal with it. Although Barbara didn't know what happened we both decided to invent the farm accident as a way for you to cope. If we gave you a real-life incident to hang on to then maybe you would come to terms with it in time.'

'Except I didn't.'

'Do you feel more at peace now?'

I think on it as I hold a palm against my heart. 'I'm not sure. I do know that finding out the truth is important to me. I don't feel like I'm going mad.'

I fix my gaze only on Dad. 'Will you take me to John Peters' grave?'

***

John
Father
Husband
Friend
Surgeon
Lover of life

Those are the simple words written on my birth father's gravestone in the cemetery in North London. My parents remain in the car giving me some respectful space as I stand by John Peters' grave a week after discovering the tragic secrets of the house. The wind is high, playing wildly across my face as I stand in this sad place. I'm not sure how I feel about him. He was my blood, the man who helped me come into this world. But he was also the man who failed his family by allowing a pretty face to turn his head. I will never be able to forgive him for denying me the opportunity to stand at the gravesides of the rest of my family. Wherever they rest, I wish them peace and love and no more pain.

I haven't brought any flowers. I don't wear mourning black. What I have brought with me, I leave on the grave.

His farewell letter.

***

Inside the car, Mum and Dad give me a collective concerned look.

'I'm OK,' I assure them. 'I feel ready to look forward to the future.'

They share a long look with each other.

'What's going on?'

It's Dad who hesitantly tells me. 'The house was never owned by Martha Palmer. She always thought it was hers, but your father had the final laugh on her. You dad had it registered in the name of a business called MP.'

Alex had told me almost the same thing, except he'd assumed the business belonged to Martha. Martha Palmer. MP.

'What are you trying to tell me?'

Mum says, 'The house belongs to John's next of kin. That person is you. Marissa Peters.'

Forty-four

Four months later

I watch as the removal firm packs up the contents of the house and stores them in the large van outside. I don't want any of it. A local charity shop is taking the lot and is grateful for it. I put the house on the market and now a young family will be moving here in a week's time. I'm glad. I want it to be a family home again, ringing with the very special sound of children laughing and playing.

Jack's long gone. All evidence that the garden was once a cannabis factory has disappeared. I helped him cut and pull out every last green leaf of illegality. I don't know where he is now. Don't want to know.

'Lisa.' Alex is framed in the doorway as he calls my name.

He's been with me every step of the way when I've needed him. As a friend, nothing more. And what a friend! I couldn't have asked for better.

A huge grin transforms my face as I walk towards him. It slides off when I see his grim expression.

'What's the matter?'

Alex pulls me inside and out of the way as one of the removal guys carries a chair outside. He calls to the man: 'Can you tell your people to take a half-hour tea break?'

'We're on the clock,' the man reminds him.

'Any additional costs, please just add it to the bill.'

The man nods as Alex carefully closes the door. He tugs me gently into the heart of the house where the fancy black and red rug remains on the floor.

I look at him, not the rug. 'What's going on?'

He hesitates before starting. 'Have you noticed this rug before?'

I don't feel embarrassed to tell him. 'I'd stand on it. Here in the heart of the house. I can't explain it but it would help me get my bearings straight. Sort of make sure I was grounded.'

Now he looks pained, like he doesn't want to say anything. But he does, and he points. 'Can you see these patterns that are the border?'

I nod, completely perplexed.

'Look at them closely. They're not patterns but writing—'

'Cyrillic writing,' I cut in, my heart banging. I don't feel steady on my feet for the first time in a long time.

'They're names,' he continues in a soft hush. 'Alice, Leo, Tina—'

'Marissa. Me.' My tearful gaze hits Alex. 'Do you think my dad – birth dad – had this custom made?'

'It looks that way.'

We stand there in a respectful, mournful silence as if gazing down at my family's grave.

'All these years I've been to untold therapists who have given me all kinds of diagnoses – obsessive, a bully victim, PTSD, plain loopy – when, all this time, I've suffered with the most human ailment of all: a broken heart.' I breathe in deeply. 'Can you give me a minute?' I ask in a distant voice.

Alex doesn't answer. Instead, a few seconds later, I hear the click of the door closing.

Tears roll from my eyes as I get down on my knees and rub my palms reverently across each name. Then I trace my fingertip across each beautifully embodied letter. It's like I'm back facing the writing on the wall. I feel like I've found my family again. No wonder I was so drawn to this rug. All the time my family were waiting for me in the heart of the house.

I curl into a ball and cry.

Epilogue

It's evening as I stand across the street and look at the house with new eyes. All its secrets are clear to me now. Well, those that relate to me. The family who bought the house have moved in. Faint yellow lights are in a window upstairs and in the lounge below. I see a small child zoom across the window downstairs and then is gone. I imagine the child playing and laughing; that's what the house was made for. Happiness and love, walking arm in arm, sitting at the dining table or the breakfast bar, sleeping at night.

The house is back to standing tall and proud, its walls back to the colour of welcome. The ivy rests, a portrait of peace in harmony with its stone walls. As for the mason's mark, it's not my key anymore, nor will it ever be. It belongs to another person now. Another family.

I take one last look at my spare room at the top. Its window is shut to the world, darkened shadows the colour behind it. I hope the walls are back to white, its floorboards scrubbed clean. A light pops on. A boy's face appears at the window. I hope he's happy there. A slither of apprehension turns in me; let's hope John Peters has left no more calling cards behind.

I turn my back forever and walk quietly away.

***

I move towards the table in the restaurant where he waits for me. I'm wearing a low-cut blouse and short denim skirt that proudly display my scars. No one looks at me, no one stares.

Alex jumps to his feet when I reach the table.

'Good to meet you, Lisa,' he greets me, along with his trademark wide smile.

'It's good to meet you too, Alex.'

We've made the decision to try the dating game again. Go back to square one as if we'd never met each other.

As soon as I sit down, I say, 'There's something you need to know. I have scars on my body. I got them when I was young, in a childhood accident. I sometimes have nightmares, but not so many these days. I like to tie my leg to the bed at night because sometimes I sleepwalk, which I call awake-sleep because I always recall what's happened.'

'There's something you need to know about me,' he counters. 'I like to wear odd socks.'

'I'm a bit obsessed with Amy Winehouse.'

'I love Russian poetry.'

We catch each other's eyes and laugh.

Thank you!

Thank you for reading *SPARE ROOM.* I hope you enjoyed it. We had a total ball writing it!

For News and loads more head off to my website and sign up. https://dredamitchell.com

I adore hearing from readers, so please do get in touch with me if you'd like to.
My website: https://dredamitchell.com
Facebook: Dreda Facebook
Twitter: Dreda Twitter

Reviews: I write for you!
I love to hear what you think about the books.
So please leave a review

All About Dreda
Dreda wrote five books before partnering up with Tony Mason to continue her writing career. Dreda scooped the CWA's John Creasey Dagger Award for best first time crime novel in 2004. Since then she has written eleven crime novels. She grew up on a housing estate in the East End and was a chambermaid and waitress before realising her dream of becoming a teacher. She is a passionate campaigner and speaker on social issues and the arts. Dreda has appeared on television, radio and written in a number of leading newspapers including The Guardian. She was named one of Britain's 50 Remarkable Women by Lady Geek in association with Nokia and is an Ambassador for The Reading Agency. Some of Dreda and Tony's books are currently in development as TV adaptations.

43201199R00173